Hokum

Book 2 in the Adventures of Avery Noble

HOKUM

Book 2 in the Adventures of Avery Noble

C.R. Endacott

iUniverse, Inc.
New York   Bloomington

Hokum

Book 2 in the Adventures of Avery Noble

Copyright © by C.R. Endacott

iUniverse books may be ordered through booksellers or by contacting:

iUniverse
1663 Liberty Drive
Bloomington, IN 47403
www.iuniverse.com
1-800-Authors (1-800-288-4677)

Because of the dynamic nature of the Internet, any Web addresses or links contained in this book may have changed since publication and may no longer be valid. This is a work of fiction. All of the characters, names, incidents, organizations, and dialogue in this novel are either the products of the author's imagination or are used fictitiously.

ISBN: 978-1-4502-0194-0 (pbk)
ISBN: 978-1-4502-0195-7 (ebk)

Printed in the United States of America
iUniverse rev. date: 12/29/09

Dedicated to my wife Sharon.

I cherish your love and I am the lucky one!

CHAPTER ONE

I hear a sudden cry of pain!
-James Stephens, The Snare [1882-1950]

Mercy Decked was old. At the age of fifty and one, he still farmed the thirty acres that his father had left him. The fertile land provided well for his wife, Aria and himself. They had long since decided not to have children. He had spent the earlier years of his life exploring the world of Afflatus; it was only after his father passed away, that he returned to take up his sacred deed of working the land.

The farm was located five miles from the town of Bragg, a community of little over a thousand people. The noble, Baron Gander Creed, owned most of the lands surrounding the town, including a water mill that threshed the wheat into flour. Gander was, as far as nobles were concerned, fair and charged a fair wage for the use of his mill. The town had a small market where the farmers would bring their produce and sell to vendors, who in turn would travel to the distant towns and cities to sell the harvests.

Most of the farmers in Bragg would work hard for the year, and at harvest, during the Harvest Festival, relax, sit

1

back and enjoy a cold ale or bottle of wine. Wineries were a booming industry in Bragg. Many farmers had forsaken their traditional crops, such as wheat and corn, for the grapes and berries, which they would ferment into wines that were sold over the entire world.

Mercy decided to stay with the traditional staples of the region, corn and wheat. He would often grumble about the politics involved with farming; he did not appreciate when Quagmire was Queen, having to send fifty percent of his harvest to her. He loved to farm. The smell of the manure fertilizing the soil was a magic that sifted into his soul, affirming in him the hard work and toil of working the land.

A warm breeze brushed past his face, cooling the beads of sweat that crested his brow; taking a deep breath he let the heat of the sun warm his lungs and he took out a grainy rag from his overall's pocket; wiping his face he glanced up to the sky and did not see a cloud. Turning back to his work he listened to the rhythmic sound of his hoe beating the soil; like an ancient drum sounding before war.

The breeze died back down and he could once again feel the blistering heat of the sun against his back. His straw hat covered the top of his baldhead and kept the burning sun from searing the back of his neck.

Even at the age of fifty and one, he looked good. His arms were muscular and tanned, his legs short and stocky. His body was fit and in perfect health, he couldn't even remember the last time he had been ill. During the plague of Measles twenty years ago, when many others had got sick, he remained steadfast and well.

One thing he hated was the heat. A farmer's best friend and worst enemy was the sun. "Blithering heat!" he cursed softly to himself. If it didn't rain soon the fields would be completely dry and his crop would die, leaving him with no harvest to speak of.

His wife often accused him of speaking to himself. Farmers were solitary sorts and he had learned to hum, and sing to himself to help pass the time. He smirked; it was true what they said; there is a little bit of crazy in them farmers!

Planting his hoe into the ground he scratched the surface to loosen the soil. He was content to manually turn the soil allowing air to reach the seed that was taking root in the land.

"Yearly sow, I plant the hoe and sing of days gone by," he sang. "To feed my wife and miss the strife that come from eating rye! A farmer's land is an extension of his hand, and the work is never by. Yet here I stand upon the land until the day I die! Until the day I die!"

He kept on humming several bars of the old farmer's tune. He let the silence of the world rush over him and soon his humming also ceased, leaving him alone in the vast world. He couldn't hear the meadowlarks singing, or the twitching of the grasshoppers; no breeze rushed through the field and it felt like the world was holding its breath. He held his.

"Hello!" he called out. His voice was like a foghorn in the stillness of the day, cutting through the silence.

There was no reply, but a soft breeze suddenly caught up and he shivered as the cool wind brushed against his uncovered arms; glancing down he saw goose bumps creating small mountains under the hair located there.

In the field adjacent to him the stalks of wheat grew as tall as a man and he could not see further than the plot of land he was standing in. An uneasy feeling settled into his stomach that reminded him of the day he married. He had been anxious and concerned about the future. That same feeling now sat with him. Something was not right.

"Aria?" he called out. "Is that you?" Often Aria would leave their small hovel and bring him a pitcher of water or freshly squeezed lemonade and bread roll; but he could usually tell it was she by the swish of her skirts and hum of her voice. She always sang.

There was no reply.

He shrugged off the feeling as nothing more than age and he started hoeing again, humming to himself to relieve the tension. A soft growl to his left interrupted him. Turning his head his eyes widened in fear.

"What the—"

Aria hummed to herself as she rolled a cinnamon bun into a white cloth. Wiping her sticky hands on her apron, she then picked up a freshly poured pitcher of water, it had been cooling in the shade all afternoon, and she headed out the front entrance of the hovel.

Her tanned dressed swished softly as she hurried through the front gate and small garden that Mercy had ploughed for her to plant carrots, lettuce and potatoes. The sun was hot in the sky, so hot that she felt herself perspire the moment she left the coolness of the hovel.

As she walked her breath came in short gasps, she was not used to too much physical exertion. After she and Mercy had finished their travels, around the age of thirty five, she had become the good housewife, even though they didn't have children to look after; after all, Mercy was enough to care for; at times it seemed like the man couldn't do anything for himself. She remembered how one time she had gone to visit her sister in the nearby town of Gashton, and when she came home, the bed was unmade and the dishes had piled up. When she asked Mercy about it, he said that he didn't know how to make a bed.

Shaking her head to herself she continued into the fields. The fields were Mercy's inheritance from his father and Aria thought herself lucky to have married a man with his own land. Her father had been a peasant working in Baron Gander Creed's fields. Even though they were treated well, they always wanted to save up enough money to buy their own farm. She had married into property. And since they did not have any children, one of her brothers was set to inherit it when they were gone. The rest of her family still worked for the Baron.

Her feet sunk into the soft soil and as she looked ahead, she could not see Mercy anywhere. She recalled that he told her that morning that he would be working in the northeast corner of their thirty acres. Trying to keep her feet in the furrow, she bustled as fast as she could.

The land seemed really quiet. She didn't hear the normal sounds of birds chattering idly by or field mice creating paths through the furrows to burrows deep underground. Usually she could hear her husband either singing or humming. But he was nowhere to be heard or seen.

Reaching the sector she assumed he would be in, she called out. "Mercy! Are you here?"

There was no reply. Something had to be wrong. Had his heart failed him? No, that wouldn't make sense because he was as sturdy as a horse. Had Anlan, the neighboring farmer arrived and taken him somewhere? That had to be it.

"Mercy!" she called again. "You better answer me, or you won't eat for a week."

She walked a few feet further, to their property line and let the wheat growing there, brush lightly against her fingers. The smell of soil and oat was mixed with something else, something stronger. It reminded her of when Mercy and she had stumbled upon a rotting cow in the fields. The vultures had torn it apart and even the rats and other scroungers were done with it. The only difference this time was it smelled fresher.

"Mercy," her voice was sounding more fearful, as her gaze darted around the field. "Mercy, quit playing around!"

Her gaze came to rest on some wheat that had been mowed over. It looked like someone had recently run through the human high grain. She approached the stalks and looked around. She gasped sharply; lying on the ground was Mercy's hoe.

Without hesitation she started following the mowed down path. She barely noticed as a second path intersected with the one that she was on. In the distance she could hear the sound of vultures screaming victory, as they found carrion lying on the ground.

"Mercy! Mercy!" she hollered as she continued to run. Abruptly she came to a stop; lying on the ground was Mercy's straw hat. It was ripped and she saw a red smear of blood along the rim. "Mercy," her voice softened in horror.

Suddenly she heard it, a mournful howl. A wolf! Yet wolves didn't usually travel this far south. They stayed up near the Taboo Forest.

Fear crept into her heart. She was a long way from her hovel, or from any people. Another howl started up, closer and she knew it wasn't a wolf's. A wolf would howl at the moon, and it would sound long and hollow. This cry was vicious and cruel. She could hear the taint of blood coming from the creature's lips.

She turned to start running. A growl and snort sounded to her right. It was right next to her. Turning her wild gaze she saw a black creature running on two legs, with jaws like a wolf's and claws like a badger's. It leapt, grabbing her around the chest!

Jargon Fodder stood on a pile of rock. Wiping the sleeve of his jacket across his forehead he glanced up to the sky; not a cloud. The sun beat down on him like a blacksmith's hammer on the anvil and he felt like he was in a furnace for melting steel. The rock he stood on was granite and as a member of the stone guild, the task of forming granite blocks for the king's castle, was given to him.

King Divine's Castle Ruins had been such, ever since Quagmire, King Divine's sister, had overthrown the monarchy and placed herself as ruler. She had destroyed the castle, but left it as a symbol of the old rule's demise. King Merrit had decided to rebuild the Castle and establish it as the capital.

Usually Jargon would have a dozen other men working with him, carving the granite blocks into squares, but today he was just adding some finishing touches. He was the craftsman, which meant he was responsible for making each block completely symmetrical. If they weren't they would not stack in perfect unison.

Coughing, he tried to clear his throat of the dust and grime that always floated around his chiseling. Needing a drink of water he glanced around for his flask. It sat on an already completed brick, a dozen yards a way.

Running his dirty fingers through his long black hair, he felt the braid that ran down his back, it too was now drenched in sweat. At the age of twenty-one and fit, he did not find his work overly laborious. With the change of a monarch, yet again, work was hard to find. Most people would only hire those that professed loyalty to the Divine family, even during the reign of Quagmire.

Jargon felt that he couldn't afford to be so lucky. He had willingly taken jobs that the Queen hired out; money was money, after all. People had to be careful during the change of a monarch; he had decided that long ago. He made it his philosophy to stay as neutral as possible. If the new monarch would hire him, so be it. Work was work.

Someday he hoped to find a beautiful girl to marry, maybe then he would settle down, have a few kids and teach his sons his trade. Till then, he decided, he would keep working, and keep spending his money at the local taverns in Bogmarsh.

He dropped his tools and belt on the piece of granite he was working on and strolled over to his water flask. The heat was unbearable; summer had felt long and dry. He looked forward to the day when the rains of winter would come; maybe they would even get some snow. Afflatus had not seen snow since before Quagmire's time. Her swamp had done something to the weather, changing the whole cycle of things.

Reaching his flask he took a long drink. A warm breeze blew through the hair on his arms, but it didn't feel chilly. He stopped mid gulp, as the breeze suddenly and mysteriously died. It was like the world had just stopped breathing. Slowly he lowered his flask. The grass around the quarry was still.

Once upon a time, it had been rumored that lions had wandered the plains of Afflatus. But that seemed far away and a distant time. There hadn't been anything worth being afraid of since the Muskags, Quagmire's minions, had roamed the world.

He glanced back to his belt and tools; they were a dozen yards away. His hammer was heavy and blunt and would do damage to a skull, if it were used as a weapon and his chisel, though used on stone had a sharpened edge, which would pierce any skin, especially if his hammer was slamming the chisel through it.

The stillness was suddenly interrupted by the sound of claws scraping the rock behind him. He turned quickly to catch sight of whatever it was. Nothing was there but the piercing blue sky. Was it invisible? He was positive that he had heard something. Despite the heat he felt chills start up and down his spine. Something was hunting him; closing in like a lion on its prey.

As quickly as it started, the feeling disappeared.

"Jargon!"

Startled, he turned. Arden, the stone hauler was walking towards him with a dozen other men. In their tow they had four sleds, used for hauling the rock. The four wheels were as large as a man, and three men were assigned to each sled.

"Hey!" Jargon called. He glanced back around him to where he had heard the sound, but whatever had been there before was now gone. "Glad you guys are here!" he said sounding relieved.

Arden and the others reached Jargon and stopped. There were several stones ready for hauling. "You look like you've seen a ghost," the dirty blond leader said.

Jargon laughed nervously and pulled on his braid for assurance. "Yah, I don't know what it was, but there was something here. I don't think it was friendly."

"Probably yer wife," Gummer said, another of the haulers. He was closer to fifty years old, but had been working in the stone industry so long; his fingers had filed away by the coarseness of the granite.

"Ha," Jargon faked a laugh. "I'm serious!"

Arden shrugged off the concern. His only concern was getting the stone from the quarry to the Divine Ruins. "This all the stone you got?" he asked. "We can haul more than four at a time you know."

"Hey, this job ain't for the faint of heart."

Arden laughed, "Sure not. I don't think I could handle working out here all alone, days on end. Most of the grunt work being done, the rest is up to you."

The haulers loaded the four finished stones onto the sleds. It would be an easy haul this time. They would not return until the next day. Jargon found that he could complete about four stones a shift, with slow and steady work. On good days he was known to complete six.

Arden waited until after the men had finished loading the stone. He approached Jargon and gave the stone mason a shake. "You going to be okay?" he asked. "I swear, if the heat is getting to you, you need to take a break, it'd be no good if the stone mason got sick and couldn't work. We'd have to find a new one!"

Jargon cleared his throat and hefted his chisel. "I don't know, it was weird, but I think it'll be fine."

"Right, we'll see you at camp tonight then," Arden said grabbing hold of Jargon's shoulder. "Don't work yourself to death, now! I could leave a guy or two if you want."

"Nah, they'd just get in the way."

"Suit yourself."

Jargon watched as the haulers disappeared in the distance. He again felt very alone and isolated. He usually didn't let the solitude phase him, but something was different. He couldn't shake the feeling that unfriendly eyes were watching him. In an effort to calm himself he hummed several ditties he had learned as a small child. As a young boy he had been afraid of the boogeyman and his mother would often soothe him with songs of love. It seemed cheesy, but it gave him assurance and security.

The sun was falling in the sky and he could see the orange and red glow of dusk stretching across the heavens. It was his favorite time of day, the sun was sinking and the coolness of night would soon be upon them.

Giving the last stone he was working on, a couple of taps, he slid the chisel into its place at his belt. Brushing his hands together to get rid of the dust he stood up. Then he saw them. Still in the field, a short distance from the quarry, three black shapes watched. They stood like men, but were covered with black hair from head to toe. Their muzzles looked like a wolf's and large, dagger like claws clenched and unclenched at their sides.

Jargon took hold of his chisel and hammer. There were three of them, but he would be damned not to put up a fight. Yet, he knew that if he did not flee, he was going to die. He had never seen beasts like these before. Even during the time of Quagmire when demons such as Muskags and Squalls roamed the land. He had even heard about werewolves, but they only attacked at night and when there was a full moon. It was dusk and these creatures were about and they stood much larger than a werewolf; but Jargon figured they'd be just a vicious.

Stumbling off the quarry, in a panic, he bolted for the Divine Ruins and the camp. At least there, there was safety in numbers.

The beasts, alerted to his sudden movement gave echoing howls. Their cries sounded like a wolf on the prowl. They were hunting and the lust for blood could be heard in their cries.

Jargon could hear the sound of the demon wolves panting just behind him and along side him. Nevertheless, he charged on like an army entering the valley of the shadow of death.

The demons were gaining on him and he could smell the wet dog stench in the air and the fleshy breath from prey they had previously devoured. His lungs felt like they were going to explode. Finally, he saw the shape of the Divine Ruins ahead of him. Spurred on by the thought of safety he started to out distance his pursuers. They gave a cry of disgust, but he knew they did not give up the chase.

He charged past the outer wall, which they had started to replace, though there were still gaping holes in many places. The stones he had been working on were being used to fix the breeches in the wall.

"Beasts! Demons!" he hollered as he entered the workers camp, just inside the main gate. Men had set up tents and most lounged beside fires that had been lit. A large cooking fire was roasting a pig in the centre.

Fifty heads turned in his direction as he stopped at the outer fringe of the camp. He gulped for air. "They're coming!" he cried. He pointed behind them. "Demons; evil!"

A beast jumped into the firelight. With the setting sun to its back, it looked to be leaping out of hell itself. The creature was as tall as a man, but more muscular. Coarse black fur covered its body; saliva dripped from its gaping jaws. The eyes were black as coal and its nose twitched in anticipation.

Grabbing Jargon around the waist the demon ripped. Looking down, Jargon saw his intestines fall to the dirty ground. He faded into unconsciousness as the demon pulled him out of the ring of fire, into the darkness, which was rapidly approaching.

Earo brushed a blond hair out of his eyes. Glancing over he noticed Bigwig Breeches, the newest member of the King's Forces, scuffling through the tall grass next to him.

The gnome had wanted to be involved so badly, that King Merrit finally decided to appoint Bigwig to a knew position created just for him; the King's Erroneous Tracker. His job was to make sure that all the trackers did not make mistakes in the field and he would accomplish this by making mistakes purposefully.

Earo sighed. Unfortunately it was his turn to travel with the gnome. Bigwig walked with his head high, but his chin barely came higher than the grass, since he was only three feet tall.

Bigwig cleared his throat. "I think that we should go this way," he said. He pointed with his knobby arms.

Earo frowned, "You don't even know what we are tracking. How can you know we should go that way?"

"I can sense it. By the way, what are we looking for? I am sure that whatever it is, I am the most qualified gnome for the job."

"I hate to see what an unqualified gnome would do," coughed Earo into his hand.

"What was that?"

"Nothing."

Bigwig continued unabated. "As I was saying—all the evidence that I have found so far points to the creature going this way," again he pointed, but in the opposite direction he had the first time.

"And what evidence is that?"

"Well, er, I saw a broken blade of grass."

"Where?"

"Right here," he pointed at a dead grass stalk that he had stepped on.

"You did that just now!"

"I did not!" Bigwig looked hurt. He crossed his hairy arms over his dirty uniform.

"When was the last time you cleaned your uniform? As a member of the King's Forces, you are expected to keep yourself and your clothes in immaculate condition."

"I washed it last month," Bigwig defended. "That should last me at least until next summer. I should think. What sane person, or gnome, would want to have something soaked in soap and water regularly; it only makes you itchy and smell like soap."

"That smell you are referring to is called clean."

"Well, whatever it is, I don't like it."

Earo shook his head lightly. "Come on," he said. "We might as well get this over with."

"What are we looking for?"

"There has been a creature of some kind, described as a werewolf attacking the men at the excavation site. The workers restoring the ruins are afraid.

"Ohh, a werewolf. I knew a werewolf once. His name was—well, I don't remember his name—but he was a nice guy except at nighttime. No moons for him, he just always turned into a wolf at night. I had to make sure he was never invited over for late dinner; you know, for fear of becoming dinner."

"Can't you just be quiet for a while?"

"I'm sure I could. By the way, I wonder what a gnome would look like after being turned into a werewolf. I should try to get bitten by a werewolf and then maybe I would turn into one and then I would know what a gnomewolf would look like."

"I don't think it would bite you," stated Earo.

"Why?"

"You would taste disgusting!"

Bigwig was hurt. But he fell silent as he contemplated what a gnomewolf would look like.

The excavation site was quiet. Most of the workers had left for the evening. Convincing people to work at the site was difficult, and consequently work on the ruins had almost completely halted. People were too afraid.

A small workers' hovel had been set up just outside the courtyard to the ancient castle and several men sat around a fire with a pig roasting on a spit. A King's guard waved at Earo and Bigwig as the two entered the compound. The rest of the workers had agreed to pull out the next day.

Earo headed straight towards Barret, the chief engineer. The man was in his late forties and had helped the Resistance defeat Queen Quagmire only a year earlier. He had a bushy beard and black hair that was pulled back in a braid down the center of his back.

"Barret," Earo reached out his hand.

Barret grasped and Earo held in a squeak. The man's grip was hard and made his hand appear small. "Earo, glad you made it. We lost five more workers today. Not to mention the half a dozen cattle and swine." The man's voice was a deep baritone.

"Merrit is concerned that the project will be suspended until this problem can be dealt with."

Barret nodded. "We haven't even been able to get a good look at the beast. We are pretty sure it is a werewolf, but that's strange because they should only come out at night." He pointed at a scrawny man filing a machete. "Jankins isn't sleeping any more. He is sure that he's next. Doren and Cal," he pointed at two other faces by the fire, "were sure the creature snuck right into the camp the other night. They managed to startle it; they said the beast only looked like a shadow, but it was too big to be a regular wolf."

The two men looked up at the sound of their names and acknowledged Earo with grunts. Earo waved back once. "I didn't see any sign of the werewolf on my way in, but Bigwig and I will be heading out towards the Taboo Forest. Most werewolves would come from that direction."

At the thought of the gnome Earo glanced around searching for the illusive critter and saw that Bigwig had skulked through the camp toward the fire where the pork was roasting. His small dagger was in his hand and he had just grabbed a hold of the pig's flank and was sawing through the flesh.

"Bigwig!" he shouted.

The gnome turned quickly, burning his fingers on the hot meat. "What? I wasn't doing anything!"

"You were going to steal their dinner," Earo muttered. His face stiffened in anger.

"Steal! Me! Never!" He blew onto his fingers to cool them. "I was only making sure the meat was cooked all the way through. After all, we wouldn't want the King's men to get sick or worse, worms. I heard that you can get worms from eating raw pig and those worms get big, you can only get rid of them by—"

"Get over here," Earo interrupted and pointed to his side, his tone menacing.

"Fine." Bigwig walked over, his shoulders were hunched and his head hung, his bottom lip pouted a little.

"I am so sorry about that," Earo said to Barret. "He is a handful at the best of times."

Barret chuckled. "No worries mate."

"We should be back later this evening."

"Be careful," The gruff man replied.

Earo grabbed Bigwig's arm and escorted him from the compound. Bigwig was humming to himself and admiring the late afternoon sun oblivious to Earo's hand squeezing him tightly. They headed towards the Taboo Forest and Earo didn't let go until they were well into the plains.

The Taboo Forest got its name because of the nasty creatures that lived there. It was rumored that ogres, werewolves, imps and even some remaining Muskags, called the dark place home. The trees that crowded against each other were black spruce and willows. Whenever someone entered the forest a heavy presence would descend and rest upon the very soul of that person.

As they moved closer to the trees that rimmed the Taboo Forest, Earo suddenly felt a strange sensation that they were being watched.

Nonchalantly, Earo glanced around, his gaze searching every shadow and bush. His gaze came to rest on a clump of roots from a fallen tree. That was the most logical place for a spy.

Slowing down he placed a restraining hand on Bigwig's shoulder.

"What's up?" the gnome quizzed, loudly.

"Shh!"

Scanning the edge of the forest, he waited. What was watching them, he wondered? It couldn't be the werewolf, it would have attacked the instant it saw them as prey.

A shadow suddenly darted from under the roots of the fallen tree. He couldn't make out what creature it was; but it moved quickly.

"Come on!" he said grabbing a hold of Bigwig's shoulder.

"What are we chasing?"

"I don't know!"

CHAPTER TWO

All jargon of the schools

-Matthew Prior, I am That I am, An Ode [1688]

Avery Noble attended Jeerson Junior High School. The name of the school was synonymous with her experience there. The others would jeer her at every opportunity. The school looked more like a prison than a facility for learning. The structure was made entirely of brick and concrete and bars covered the windows to keep out vandals. In reality, the opposite proved true, the bars kept the vandals in.

Strolling down the central hallway toward her locker, Avery admired the pristine floors; they were the nicest and newest feature of the school and any students caught trespassing with outdoor shoes on were practically expelled.

Her grade eight year had started with high hopes. Almost immediately she realized that being in the middle of middle school was the worst place to be. The grade nines looked down on them and the grade sevens were too intimidated by their own shadows to care what the grade eights were doing.

The worst part for Avery was that Holly Fitts was in her homeroom class. Holly was a tall, beautiful girl, and all the boys had a crush on her. Her blond hair was long and she would swing it out of her eyes as she walked down the halls. Her eyes were crystal ice blue, which made her completely exotic, and Avery had even heard Jared once mention that the girl looked intoxicating. She had snarled at the comment and asked him how he even knew such a big word and to suck the drool off his face.

Holly had it out for Avery.

Avery accidently stumbled as she entered her homeroom. She had grown several inches suddenly, after going through puberty; probably the last girl in her grade to do so; and it had made her a little clumsy.

Unfortunately Holly saw her. "Taking a trip!" she mocked. Whenever the girl spoke, it was like she was being nice. Her voice sounded sweet and innocent; but really she was mocking and suddenly everyone, already in the classroom, looked up and saw Avery's red face.

"How was Bermuda?" Holly asked, flipping her blond hair, catching the boy sitting behind her in the face; he beamed like it was a compliment.

"Huh?"

"Bermuda, you know the place with the mysterious triangle. You must have been to Bermuda, you've lost your brain!" the girl giggled, as did every boy in the classroom.

Avery smirked and squinted her green eyes. "Oh Holly, is that ketchup on your chin?"

"What?"

"Ketchup. There's a big red spot on your chin." Avery leaned in close to the girl. "Never mind! It's only a zit!"

"A zit!" Holly covered her chin with her hand. "Wait! I don't feel anything."

Avery sat down at her chair and dropped her backpack under it.

"I hate you!" Holly said. She glared.

Pushing her brown hair out of her eyes, Avery ignored the remark. She knew that a dozen boys would be glaring at her too. But what did that matter; the boys in her school were by far the dumbest breed ever to have existed.

She waited for her only friends in the entire school to enter. At the start of the year she had felt lucky to be in the same homeroom as Jared Swagger, Ruth Butterluv and Ferris Tobblame. Immediately, however, she realized that Miss Creant, their homeroom teacher, was out for their blood.

Miss Creant had been the vice principal when Mr. Prig had been principal. However, since the Prig had disappeared, she was now the Acting Principal and she felt that Avery and her friends were somehow responsible for Mr. Prig's disappearance.

Miss Creant was also the music teacher.

Avery waved at Jared as he entered. He didn't have a backpack, or any books with him and Avery was intrigued. Following him were Ruth and Ferris, obviously deep in conversation, those two had been spending a lot of time together and Avery wouldn't be surprised if a romance was starting to bloom. The two glanced up and smiled at Avery.

All the students rushed to their chairs as the final bell rang. Miss Creant entered the music room. She was a tall skinny woman and her skin looked like soft tanned leather that barely covered her bones. She didn't look tough, but no one messed with her.

She pushed her glasses up the ridge of her nose and stared down at her students. Her gaze came to rest on Avery and her upper lip raised. It could have been a snarl, but teachers were supposed to be unbiased and fair.

Resisting the urge to plug her nose, Avery smiled up sweetly to her teacher, trying not to gag. Miss Creant wore old lady perfume and far too much of it. The putrid stench drifted through the room and it felt like her eyes were going to start watering.

"Avery," the old woman started. Her voice sounded more like a man's.

Avery lifted her head again and looked the teacher in the eye. She had learned not to do anything that might seem disrespectful when it came to the grouch. "Yes?"

"It seems that several saxophone reeds have gone missing. You wouldn't know anything about that, would you?" her tone was accusatory.

"I can't say that I do, Miss Creant," she replied. She did not change her tone or pitch. It was imperative to sound polite when speaking to the grouch. Avery learned that almost immediately.

"I only asked because things seem to go missing whenever you are around, like principals."

Avery maintained a neutral face, and it took all she could, not to retort. Miss Creant was certain that she had something to do with Mr. Prig's disappearance, which she did, but it sounded so silly. Students abducting a principal! Really!

"There is an assembly last block today," Miss Creant continued like she had never accused Avery of theft. "Any student caught skipping the assembly will have detention for the rest of the week." She glared down at Avery, daring her to skip.

Avery smiled; it wouldn't be a problem. Her last block was study hall, and that was located next to the gym. She would make it with time to spare.

"That's it for homeroom; go to your first block classes. Dismissed!"

Avery caught up with Jared as they were filing out of the music room. "Where's all your stuff?" she asked giving him a soft hip-check.

Jared was several inches taller than her, with blond hair and brown eyes. He was a year older because he had repeated fifth grade.

"Couldn't find it," he replied. His voice had deepened over the summer and no longer cracked when he spoke.

"What do you mean?"

"I was shifted to a new foster home over the weekend. All my stuff is still in boxes," he replied stiffly.

Jared was a foster kid. Social Services took him from his real parents at the age of seven and since had lived with a foster family. Every year he moved to a new family.

"I'm sorry," she replied. "I know you liked the last ones."

"Whatever," he shrugged. "Can I borrow a pencil?"

"Sure," she dug into her pack and found a pencil. She also opened her binder and pulled out several sheets of paper and handed both to the boy. They had become good friends since their experiences in Afflatus. And, she knew that he was really trying to do better in school. But he had slacked off for so many years that it was now challenging for him.

"Thanks," he said taking the supplies. "See you at lunch?"

"Meet you in the Caff!" she nodded. They split ways with a wink.

It felt like time had slowed down. Every five minutes Avery would glance up at the clock, waiting, watching, for both the large and small hand to be pointing straight up; a signal that lunch had arrived.

She couldn't even concentrate on her mathematics, geometry her favorite unit. She loved to measure angles, and create equilateral triangles. Few of her fellow students had mastered the skill of using a compass to make triangles with exact equal sides.

The buzzer rang, a dying bumblebee. Closing her books she bolted for her locker. Grabbing her bag lunch she headed towards the cafeteria. The Caff, as it was affectionately known, used to be two large classrooms, but the wall had been taken out. A few tables had been scattered haphazardly around the room and students would sit on the back bookshelf, on the tables, the backs of chairs and even the floor, to find room.

It was crowded today, like usual. The familiar smell of peanut butter sandwiches and grape juice greeted her nostrils as she entered and she wrinkled her nose. Mixed in was the flavor of noodles and pizza.

Students were everywhere. All the cliques had their zone of habitation. The nerds would often sit by the entrance, ready to bolt should a jock or other bully approach them. The jocks and popular girls would take the centre tables, a desperate attempt to be the perpetual centre of attention. The Christians often sat by the windows, on the old bookshelves. They wanted to appear cool, but were often ignored by the others. Besides, they always seemed engaged in one conversation or another—they were as bad gossips as the gossips. The valley girls were the gossip girls. They would sit at their table, a look of superiority on their faces and occasionally would lean in and whisper, the others would turn and look around the room and sounds of: "don't look!" would be heard.

The rest of the students were part of the nomads. They were the ones that just existed and made up the largest group at the school. Avery and her friends were part of that group. Within the nomads there were groups as well. They seldom mixed with anyone other than their friends and tried to make it through with as little pain and strife as possible.

Upon entering, Avery immediately saw Holly. She was sitting on a table with her hands supporting her. She had her chest pushed out as far as she could make it go and she was surrounded by a half dozen jocks. Avery wanted to sneer because of Holly's obvious attempt to draw attention to her bust, but really she was envious because the blond girl was so much more developed.

"Oh Paul," the blond girl said, waving her hand flirtatiously at one of the jocks. "You are so funny!" her voiced cooed.

Paul was in grade nine and was the tallest boy in the school. He had curly blond hair and blue eyes. He was also the biggest flirt in the school. All the girls thought he was dreamy, but Avery didn't think he was that good looking. He was gangly and sometimes a little too loud. She figured just another desperate attempt to be the centre of attention. The more she thought about it, Holly and Paul would make a great couple.

Paul dribbled his basketball and the bounces echoed in the small room. "Watch this Holly," he said. He gave the ball a violent shove and it bounced up to the ceiling, hitting one of the lights; which flickered.

"Holy!" said Calvin, another one of the goon squad; he burst out laughing. "You almost busted it man!"

"Whatever!" stated Paul.

Holly smiled at Paul's attempts and asked, "Any of you guys jump high enough to touch the ceiling?"

"Piece of cake," replied Paul. He jumped and fell just an inch short.

"Hmm," said Holly pretending to be utterly unimpressed.

"Not fair!" Paul defended himself. "I can do it if I take a run at it."

Backing up he bumped into Avery. She just about told him to watch it when he shoved her aside. "Get out of the way freak!" he stated. Ignoring Avery's stern glare he returned his attention to Holly and took a couple steps before jumping and his fingers slid along the ceiling. The fiber panel jostled loose and fell to the ground.

The crowd laughed boisterously.

Avery saw Jared at a far table. He was already sitting with Ferris and Ruth. Making a beeline for her friends, she sidestepped the rowdy group and sat down.

"Bunch of losers!" Ferris said biting into his tuna sandwich. Avery plugged her nose at the smell.

"I don't know why everyone wants to be like them?" added Ruth. She was eating leftover Chinese food.

"You all right?" Jared asked Avery.

"Huh?"

"I saw that jerk shove you. You want me to talk to him?"

"Nah," she said. "There is no point. Like you said; he's just a jerk!"

Calvin heard the remark. "Hey Paul, this girl said you're a jerk!" he yelled.

Paul glanced at Avery and then to Jared. Holly egged him on. "You going to let her get away with that?"

Paul stalked over with his hands in his pockets. He put on his toughest face and sneered at Avery. "Dare to say that to my face," he threatened.

Avery lowered her gaze for a moment.

"I didn't think so," he said. "Little Cretin!"

Avery stared up again. She looked the jock in the eye. "You are a jerk!" she said deliberately. She stood up and walked around the table. "Now, what were you going to do about it?"

"Hit her!" Holly crowed from the back of the crowd that had gathered. "Come on, teach her a lesson!"

Paul glanced around for support. His friends were watching apprehensively for what he was going to do. "I don't hit girls!" he said after a moment. "Besides, I'd just make you cry." There was a tremor in his voice.

"Come on you coward," Avery threatened. "You too scared to hit me. You scared that I might actually hurt you!" Avery was shorter than Paul, but at the moment appeared to be ten feet tall.

Paul pulled back his fist and threw a punch at Avery's nose. She ducked and sent a return fist into Paul's stomach. He bent over and took in a deep breath of air. "You shouldn't have done that!"

Calvin stepped forward and grabbed a hold of Avery's arm. She tried to swing at the other boy, but Paul had regained his breath and punched Avery in the jaw. She heard a soft crack. Paul shook his fist; it had hurt him more than he had thought it would.

Calvin was trying to wrestle Avery to the ground. Kicking her right leg, she caught Paul right in the soft spot between his legs and he dropped to the ground, moaning.

Calvin swore at her. He positioned his leg behind her and threw her to the floor. As she fell her head hit the table and she suddenly felt dizzy. Calvin jumped on her and was about to start punching her in the face when a tough hand grabbed him from behind.

Jared wrenched the jock off of Avery. "You got the balls to hurt a girl. You want to take a chance with me?" Jared muttered. Plowing his fist into Calvin's eye the boy fell to the ground. "That shiner will help you remember we are not to be picked on."

More the jocks had gathered around the circle. Jared held up his fists. "Anyone else want to take a round?"

"Most of the other students backed away. The fight was over. The remaining jocks wanted nothing to do with Jared. They could probably take him if they ganged up on him, but Jared was strong and would do a lot of damage to them in the process, so they backed up.

"You are so dead!" Paul muttered.

Calvin having taken the worst from Jared scurried away without a comment.

Paul shuffled back to the table where Holly was sitting. Her face had a dark frown creasing it. Her lips were terse.

"Humph," she said. "You let a girl get the better of you! Wuss!"

"She kicked me where the sun don't shine. That was unfair!"

"Whatever!" Holly said jumping off the table. As she headed to the door, "You are such a loser!"

Many of the other students left standing there started chanting. "Loser! Loser!"

They stopped; Miss Creant entered the room.

"Avery and Jared! Go to the office immediately!" she bellowed. "This will be suspension for sure!"

The two students sulked out of the Caff with everyone watching them; a few stared at Avery in relative awe.

Ferris and Ruth tried to stay out of the encounter. Since Ferris had lost his notebook in the Divide River in Afflatus, he hadn't started a new one. In fact, he only really cared about spending time with Ruth, Avery and Jared. What other students did in the school was no longer any concern for him. Of course, because he had had the nickname Rat for so long, it still stuck and even his friends often called him Rat; but now it seemed more an endearing term rather than vulgar.

Ruth ran her hand over the tight braids in her hair. She had changed the fro style to one more controlled. Rat said that it looked good on her. She had lost weight over the summer and had since developed into a young woman. She wore a nicer white t-shirt and tighter blue jeans.

Ruth and Ferris tried to wave bye to their two friends that were sent to the office.

"That doesn't seem right!" Ferris said. "I mean they didn't even start the fight."

"I know, hey!" Ruth added indignantly.

"Miss Creant is such a, such a, such a miscreant!"

Ruth nodded her head in agreement as the two stood from their chairs and started out of the Caff. The bell was going to ring soon for first block after lunch.

They settled in the science lab. The lab had white walls surrounded by cabinets that housed chemicals, microscopes, and other miscellaneous materials for the various science projects. There were no desks in the classroom, instead there were separate counters that each had a sink and an on/off switch for gas to light Bunsen burners.

Settling at their counter Ferris started to take his books out of his pack. His hand was shaking slightly as his arm lightly brushed Ruth's foot. She didn't even notice the touch, however, as he placed his books on the counters his face was red and he accidently knocked the edge of his binder knocking the binder back to the floor.

"Crap!" he said. He glanced over at Ruth.

"You okay?" she asked politely.

"Yeah, sure. Feeling a little klutzy." He picked up his books again and sat ridged in his chair. He stared forward at the black board.

"You don't look well," Ruth leaned forward and looked closely at her friend.

Ferris shifted uncomfortably. "Um..." he started and then swallowed hard.

"Yes?"

Rat took a deep breath. "Okay, I think I'm ready," he said to himself.

"Ready for what?"

Rat breathed out and the air whistled through his lips. "I was wondering, and it is okay if you don't want to, but I was thinking, that maybe it would be fun, kinda, if you want to, you know?"

Ruth smiled slyly. "Ferris, are you asking me out on a date?"

"Uh, I suppose that is what I am doing. What do you think? I mean, I totally understand if you just want us to stay friends and all because really we are good friends, at least I think we are good friends and I wouldn't want our friendship to suffer a downturn, but at the same time I think you're really pretty and would like to take you out on a date."

Ruth blushed slightly and glanced around the classroom. Several other students were watching the exchange. "Ferris, I would love to," she said blushing even more.

A resounding cheer echoed through the room, with cries; "Good show Rat" and "way to go!"

Rat stood and took a low bow.

Jared and Avery sat on a hard wooden bench side-by-side. Miss Creant was writing down their infraction for fighting.

"So, I knew that you two were trouble makers. Ever since Mr. Prig disappeared, I knew that you both had something to do with it."

"Miss Creant," Avery started. "It is ridiculous to think that we students had anything to do with Mr. Prig. I don't know why you think we are somehow responsible."

Miss Creant placed her blue pen on the desk. "I think you had something to do with it because he told me so."

"Huh? You spoke to Mr. Prig?" Jared asked bewildered. He knew that they had forgotten Mr. Prig in Afflatus. And if the man had somehow found a way back, that could really mean trouble for them.

"No, he left a note!" she replied sternly. She opened the top desk drawer and pulled out a piece of paper. Clearing her throat she read loudly. "Avery Noble has had several altercations with Jared Swagger—twice she has given him a bloody nose. I know that these two students are up to no good. If the two of them ever become friends it will only be through mischief and a combined goal to do something far worse."

She lowered the note. "And so you see, I believe that you two did something to Mr. Prig and that has solidified your friendship. Someday I will find out what happened to him and you will both suffer severe consequences, hopefully a life sentence in prison!" she chuckled loudly.

"This is ridiculous. We didn't hurt Mr. Prig in anyway!" Avery defended. It was technically true. Sure it had been her *vaporatium* powder that transported Mr. Prig to Afflatus, but once there she had no control over gnomes snatching the man.

"Nevertheless, I am giving both of you in-school suspensions tomorrow. I will call your parents and you are to come to school and work the whole day in the office. Understood?"

"Good luck!" stated Jared. "Call my parents and they won't even care. In fact, if you can find my parents to give them a call, tell them that I said hi. I haven't spoken to them in over two years."

"Your guardians then, smart aleck!"

"I don't have parents," stated Avery. "You can call my mom, but she works so much nowadays it will be tough getting in touch with her. Anyway, I will probably be home first and can just delete the message."

"You are disrespectful, the lot of you, and it will not be tolerated, and I dare you to speak to me like that again. Go ahead!" They could tell that the woman was beginning to steam around the collar. They remained silent. "I thought not!" Miss Creant smirked.

CHAPTER THREE

Strength lies not in defense but in attack.

-Adolf Hitler, Mein Kampf (My Battle) [1933]

Quickly Earo placed his hand over Bigwig's mouth.

"Hmmmph!" the gnome said.

"Shh," hushed Earo. He squatted down and removed his hand. The creature stopped.

They had been trailing the black shadow for over an hour and had traveled deeper and deeper into the Taboo Forest. Earo had never been so far in before. The vegetation had thickened. Roots from tall trees decorated the floor of the dark forest. A few ferns grew from rotting logs that had fallen to the ground. A thick mulch layer covered the rest of the forest floor, only a few mosses and fungus grew.

He hadn't been able to get a good view of the creature they trailed. It didn't appear to be a large beast because of its agility.

"What is it doing?" Bigwig asked quietly trying to get a look around the muscular form of Earo.

The blond haired man's gaze darted through the ferns and tree stems. "I cannot tell."

Holding his breath he waited. The creature moved again. It moved like it knew predators were tailing it.

It darted past a dead tree and disappeared over a small hill. Earo and Bigwig instantly chased. They crested the hill and stopped abruptly.

"What in gnome's name is that?" Bigwig asked astonished.

On just the other side of the hill there was a black wall. It was like the forest just ended. It stretched from the ground to the clouds above. It was like they had reached the end of the world, but Earo knew that wasn't true. Also, the creature they had been following had disappeared.

"I don't know," Earo confessed. Cautiously he moved forward.

Bigwig ducked behind one of Earo's legs and held onto the warrior's trousers. He peeked out like a child hiding behind his mother's skirts.

Reaching the black wall, Earo reached out to touch it. His hand went right through. It felt like air but he could not see through it. It was a darkness that his vision could not penetrate.

Bigwig stuck his head out from behind Earo. He watched with fascination as Earo's hand disappeared into the darkness. Suddenly, intrigued, he walked up to the darkness and put his hand through the wall. It too seemed to disappear. But he could feel nothing.

"Hey, my hand still feels like it is moving!" his face suddenly turned pale white and he pulled his hand out suddenly. "I felt something!" he declared staring at his hand that had magically reappeared.

"What?" asked Earo.

Bigwig's eyes widened in wonder. "I don't know."

Earo took a few steps away from the gnome. The darkness went as far to the left and right that he could see. Something, it appeared, was slowly eating away the land of Afflatus.

Bigwig, unaware of Earo's thoughts was struck with another idea and he stuck his head into the blackness. From Earo's perspective it looked like Bigwig's head disappeared. Bigwig kept his head in the darkness and moved from the left to the right and it looked like a headless gnome.

"Earo!" Earo heard Bigwig shout. "What do I look like?" He pulled his head out of the darkness. "Well, did I look like the Headless Horseman?"

"Yes," sighed Earo. "Without the horse or I guess your butt could have been the horse!"

Bigwig beamed at the compliment. He started dancing (more like hopping up and down), "You do it!" the gnome commanded. "I want to see!"

"No way!" the warrior said.

"Come on, just once. Just for me?"

"Absolutely not!"

Bigwig folded his arms and pouted.

"Can you see anything from the other side?" asked Earo still running his fingers through the darkness. Looking along the black wall he couldn't see how the black cloud existed, nor what had created it.

"I'll tell you only if you stick your head in," bargained Bigwig.

"If I stuck my head in I wouldn't need an answer to my question."

Bigwig thought that over for a minute.

"Just tell me what you saw!" commanded Earo.

"Fine! It looked like it was nighttime. Everything inside was gray and shadowed. I couldn't see very far in front of me. It was like looking through a glass with dark liquid in it."

Earo convinced that he would not suddenly be sucked into a black hole decided to take a look himself. "Bigwig, I want you to stay here. If I am not back in two minutes, I want you to run back to King Merrit and tell him about this."

Bigwig nodded his head.

"What did I just tell you to do?" asked Earo; suddenly he wasn't so sure he should be leaving such a task to the gnome.

"Sorry, what?"

"What do you do if I don't return in two minutes?"

"Me...well...I wouldn't hold it against you. I mean I don't think you would intentionally ditch me or anything."

"No!" Earo sighed again. "Go to King Merrit!"

"Right now?" asked Bigwig.

"Never mind! Just wait here. Do not move! I repeat: Do not move!"

"I won't move. Where would I go? Jeesh!"

As Earo stepped through the blackness he hoped that the gnome would move and get lost and never be seen again. Though, he only hoped it on the surface, really he liked the annoying creature.

Inside the dark wall was just as Bigwig had described it. It was like looking at the world just at dusk and through a glass or through water. Everything shimmered as a dark shadow.

Reaching down he picked up a fern. The once green plant was brown and dead; it looked like all the life had been sucked out of it, but was still able to maintain its shape. A moment after he touched it, it crumbled to dust in his fingers.

BOOM! BOOM! BOOM!

Earo looked up quickly. The sound of army drums could be heard beating from somewhere further in the darkness.

Ducking behind a tree he waited, his gaze searching the darkness for a hint as to the whereabouts of the noise.

BOOM! BOOM! BOOM!

Slowly an army came into focus. It was the oddest army that Earo had ever seen. Marching in columns were gnomes. Thousands upon thousands of gnomes stood with dazed looks on their faces. They all wore loose fitting, black suits that covered their arms and legs. None of them wore any shoes and Earo could see their bare feet sticking out of the kimono suits. They all had a club across their back and a white belt holding the kimono in place.

There were two major divisions. The Rock gnomes made up the left unit, and the smaller gnomes looked awkward in their black kimonos. They were used to wearing little more than rags. Earo suddenly remembered helping Avery and her friends escape the rock gnomes little over a year ago. He looked around for their queen, the one that wanted to marry Jared, but he couldn't see her.

The Forest gnomes made up the bulk of the army. Their army was divided into three divisions and Earo could see that each division had five units a hundred strong. Quickly doing the math, that meant that a whole lot of gnomes were about to attack someone or something.

His gaze came to rest on the leader of the army. It was the man that he had been searching for. Ever since the fall of Queen Quagmire, many of her minions had disappeared, Governor Swale being one of them. Swale had been the ruler of Bogmarsh during the reign of Quagmire. He had allowed his Muskags to cook humans in what they called the Cookhouse and at times he was even known to join them.

Earo glared at the man that had caused so much grief to so many people. If Swale was here, Muskags must also be around. He was confident that a large contingent of Muskags had escaped with Swale from Bogmarsh, since most of the Revolution had taken place near Quagmire's palace further south.

Swale looked different though. Earo watched as the tanned skinned man rode a black horse at the head of the army. His robes were black, like the darkness around them, but his hair had turned white, like all the black life that had once been there had been sucked out. As well, the Governor held his left hand close to his chest. Earo tried to get a better look, without being seen, and eventually he found that Swale's hand was blackened, like he had stuck it in a fire and it looked crippled and disfigured. What had the man done?

Hunched over, walking next to Swale's horse was a demon that Earo had never seen before. The creature walked like a man; more like it shuffled. But he could see the strength in the forearms and legs. Its mouth had jaws with daggers for teeth and a snout like a dogs. Its lips would curl back, baring teeth and gums, as saliva dripped off its long tongue like slime out of a snail. Black fur covered the arms and legs of the beast; oddly however, Earo noticed that the creature had no hair on the very crown of its head.

The army came to a halt and Swale motioned with his hand to a small gnome that led the short army. It must be the gnome general. They probably had a weird name for the position, something like, Gnomeral or Gengnomeral, or something.

The gnome cleared his throat, and then spoke in a high-pitched voice with a tone of urgency. "My fellow gnomes! You gnome me! My name is Fusty Pungent and I am the Lord of the Gnomes." The gnome raised his arms and the gnome standing next to him got a whiff of the Lord of the Gnomes arm pit, he waved a hand in front of his nose like he was clearing a pungent stench.

"We are going into battle! The Giant Snail has commanded that we attack the humans!" The creature at Swale's side growled at the 'Giant Snail' comment.

"The Giant Snail has told us that the humans have for too long hunted in our forest, treated us like second class citizens and it is time for us to take back what is rightfully ours."

"It's Governor Swale, you buffoon of an idiot!" Swale swore at the little creature.

"That's what I said," Fusty Pungent defended himself.

"You did not you putrid little worm!"

"I'm not a worm. I'm Fusty."

"More like Musty!"

"No, that's my sister," the gnome replied, offended.

The creature next to Swale started to sniff the air. Earo ducked further behind the tree hoping that the demon had not caught a whiff of him. There was an odd moment of silence and finally Earo dared to peek around the tree again. Governor Swale was looking directly at his hiding place.

"Earo? Is that you?" he called. His voice sounded just as strong as always.

Earo debated briefly what to do. Drawing his sword he stepped around the trunk of the tree and faced his enemy.

"The King wants to have a word with you!" Earo stated. "You are a wanted criminal."

"Ah yes, the little twerp that ruined everything. I'm afraid to say that I want to have a word with him too."

"Why don't I just arrest you and bring you in, in shackles?"

Swale started to laugh. "I don't think so. So much has changed since Quagmire. You see—I am the one with the power now. When that wench of a girl destroyed the Queen, she sent the cursed spirit into the forest, and this darkness that surrounds us and offers me protection, is that curse. But I found something better. I found the source of Quagmire's power; she only barely tapped into what I am now capable of doing."

"Save the speech," Earo muttered. "I should kill you right now!"

Swale laughed again. "Ah, but that is the kicker. I cannot be killed. And I have magic that would kill you where you stand."

"You are nothing more than an evil man."

"You have no idea how evil I really am."

Earo approached closer and he took a moment to glance at the demon still next to Swale's horse. Swale glanced in the same direction. "You like my creation?" he asked. "So much more efficient than the Muskags. Those swamp things were good soldiers; but this, my creation, is a warrior. It is unstoppable. When I send it on a mission, it will complete it. It kills without mercy," he paused and then started laughing. "Actually it killed Mercy and his wife! I call it Menas! And soon, when I have more power, I will make more of my creatures and in time I will have an army of warriors that drink the blood of their dead."

"Not if I kill you first!" Earo rounded on the Governor.

Immediately the Menas stepped in front of its master and razor claws blocked the sword strike Earo had intended for Swale.

"Now my pet," Swale said softly, almost lovingly. "Let's give the hero Earo an opportunity to experience my new found power."

Earo kept his sword trained on the Governor as Swale dismounted his horse. Still holding the reins he walked towards Earo.

"What game are you playing at?" Earo asked hesitantly. He searched the tanned skinned man for any weapons, but could see none.

"Game? There is no game. I am giving you a chance to strike down your enemy!"

"Very well, your funeral!" Earo swung with all his might. His blade sailed through the air, whistling. As the blade struck the neck of Swale, Earo suddenly felt it give and deaden. It was like he was trying to cut through water and his sword sliced through the Governor's neck, but it mended right behind the blade and the whole time Swale did not stop laughing.

Earo stepped back. It had been a clean sweep through the Governor's neck, but he had inflicted no injury. "What kind of demon are you?"

"The kind that is going to kill your king! Now leave before I send my Menas after you. I'm giving you an opportunity to escape; go ahead tell your king about me. What will he be able to do? Nothing. Tell him I come and I will wipe his Divine blood off the face of the world."

Earo glanced at the army one last time before he turned and hurried out of the darkness and into the light, where Bigwig was still waiting; somewhat impatiently.

Avery tugged on her black backpack. A gray toque covered the top of her brown hair. She wore a blue winter jacket that was made of water resistant material causing her pack to constantly slide down her shoulder. She wore the pack like most eighth graders, one strap over the shoulder.

Jared walked next to her and she could see his breath in the afternoon air. The weather had turned cold, much colder than Vancouver was used to. Winter usually consisted of rain and temperatures just above zero. This year it was different. The weather had turned cold early October and it felt like it was going to snow.

Jared's dirty blond hair curled at the ends under his baseball cap and he wore a pair of cotton gloves.

"It is totally not fair!" he said. He didn't carry any backpack. He was still expected to return to the new foster family. However, it was their day for fencing practice.

When they returned from Afflatus the last year, Jared had convinced his social worker that fencing would be an excellent after school activity. His social worker, Carlyn Sweener, agreed and immediately enrolled him in the activity.

Avery was having a much more difficult time staying in fencing. Her mother had almost withdrawn her several times that year because it was too expensive.

Since Avery's father had died in the fire, times had been tight.

After investigation into the fire, the marshal found out that her father had been dealing methamphetamine from their house and making it in the basement. Some flammable liquid had spilt on the floor and when her father lit a cigarette, the house went up because of the fumes.

At first Avery's mother thought her husband's life insurance would help them out. However, a clause in the insurance stated that it did not cover such accidents at home and so they were left with nothing.

They had moved to an apartment closer to Jeerson Junior High School. But Avery's mother now worked more than ever. Avery would go home and have to make her own dinner. Her mom would arrive at home sometime around eleven at night, and Avery would only see her if she stayed up. By the time Avery got up in the morning her mom would be hurrying out the door. She worked two jobs. The mornings she cleaned hotel rooms and in the afternoon would do laundry at a local dry-cleaning. It allowed them to live.

Avery glanced over at Jared. She completely understood his frustration. It was completely unfair the way they had been treated. Miss Creant was out to get them. Jared breathed out a long cloud of white mist from his mouth. It was cold.

They walked down First Avenue. The roads were busy with cars and people. The cables from the electric buses rang in the coolness. Somewhere in the distance Avery could hear the sound of the Sky Train scream by. Ahead was an Esso gas station; as the temperature dropped the price of gas went up.

They reached the lot of the Esso station and suddenly a car screeched to a halt in front of them. It was a red Ford Tempo, an '87 model. There were four young men in the car. The driver rolled down his window.

The driver had dirty blond hair and piercing gray eyes. He had a cigarette hanging out of his mouth. He wore gloves that were cut off at the fingers, exposing his fingernails so he could flick his smoke. He wore a Jean jacket and a baseball cap turned at a slight angle.

"Jared!" the driver said.

Jared averted his eyes.

"Do you know this guy?" asked Avery standing slightly behind her friend.

"Yes."

The driver opened the door and stepped onto the lot. Reaching out he grabbed a hold of Jared. "Of course this boy knows me. Don't you little bro!" he lightly cuffed Jared on the side of the head.

Jared turned to Avery. "This is my step brother, CJ."

Avery looked CJ over and could see the resemblance.

"Same father," smiled CJ, "and the name is Hawker. At least that is what my boys call me."

"CJ is a few years older than me. He left home long before I was ever taken from it. He and my mother didn't get along, you see." Jared said to Avery.

"Giving your girlfriend our family history, huh! Anyway, I heard that they moved you again?"

"Who told you?" Jared ignored the remark about Avery being his girlfriend.

"I keep track of you, little bro. I like to know what my family is up to."

"Yeah, they moved me. This family is new to the fostering thing. They wanted to help an older child. I guess they liked me. I even heard that they may pursue adoption, but I don't think I want that."

Avery stared with an open mouth. She had no idea how complicated Jared's life was. If she had known a year earlier, she may have given him more slack.

"Are they rich?" Hawker asked.

Jared shrugged his shoulders. "I don't know. She's a teacher and he works for some firm downtown. They own a nice house, I guess."

"Did they give you any money?"

They had finally reached the purpose of CJ's visit.

"Nope."

"Come on little bro, I know they had to give you something for lunch. How much?"

"They didn't give me anything. What do you need money from me for anyway? Haven't drug sales been going well?"

"Shut up!" Hawker glanced around. "Get me something from that house that I can pawn. I need cash and I need it quick, a computer or gaming system, something. I owe this guy a couple hundred dollars and he wants it soon."

"I'm not going to steal for you," Jared stated bluntly. "You shouldn't want to mess this up for me!" He was getting more agitated by his brother. Avery could see the clench in Jared's jaw and the furrowing of his eyebrows.

Hawker leaned in close and brushed the front of Jared's coat. "If you don't help me out, I'm going to mess you up."

"I gotta go," Jared said finally. "I won't steal for you."

CJ frowned. "I'll deal with you later, when your girlfriend isn't around. You think about that."

He stepped back into the red Tempo and with a rev of the engine and hip-hop music blaring, peeled out of the lot, back onto the Avenue.

"Pleasant fellow," commented Avery.

"He is the only family that still talks to me. I only really see him when he needs money. He usually gets me to steal something from a foster family, which gets me kicked out."

"You steal for him?" she was shocked.

"Sure. I have many times. Most times the family doesn't even realize that I have done anything. When they find out, if I play it right, I get to stay. However, if more stuff goes missing, I am to blame and usually sent to a group home and then a new foster family."

"You're not going to do it this time, are you?"

"I have to."

"No, you don't. He is just using you. You are the one that suffers."

Jared's face turned red. "You have no idea what you are talking about," he said loudly. "He is family. The only family I got."

Avery fell silent. "I'm sorry. But stealing is wrong."

"It's too bad. I really liked this one." Jared was also quieter. "They might have wanted to keep me."

They continued walking in silence. Avery shoved her pack up on her shoulder again. They only had fifteen more minutes to make it to the run down church that doubled as the sparring gym.

Avery cleared her throat. "Funny what your brother said, huh? About me being your girlfriend."

Jared's face deepened to a soft auburn color. "Ah, yeah, silly hey! I mean, who would think that you and I were boyfriend and girlfriend."

Avery's face fell, but she turned away so that Jared would not notice. "Right," she replied. "Like, we are friends, so I am your girl friend."

"Right, pals."

They walked in silence the rest of the way to the fencing gym. The building was an old Lutheran Church. Avery was never sure when the church had abandoned the building. But someone had the idea to turn it into a fencing school, a karate club and a judo club. On different nights, different clubs had the church booked. The sanctuary had been replaced with a hard wood floor.

On fencing nights, mats were set up, making the amateur piste. At the entrance to the piste stood a large white board. On it were listed all the bouts that were going to take place that evening.

Classes were split into two sections. In the first section, coaches presented individualized lessons for level. Students were expected to master, jabs, parry, and strike.

Avery had advanced to senior intermediate. Jared, having only started that year was still mastering beginner; but he was learning fast. His coach would often comment that Jared seemed natural with the saber.

Avery had lost sight of Jared after exiting the change room. So she went to look at the white board. She wanted to see whom she would have to fight. Next to her name she saw, Hannah Strawland. Hannah was pretty, blond hair and perfect teeth.

Hannah was a couple of years younger than Avery, but she was a fighter and had mastered her divisions easily. Avery knew that she would be able to win, being a higher level, but it was best never to enter a contest too confident. She had learned that from fighting Jared in Afflatus.

Scanning the board her gaze found Jared's name. He was slotted to spar with Olly Impian.

Olly was robust and strong, not very tall, but athletic. He had black curly hair and a square chin. He was in grade eleven, and was the best fighter in the club. He had been part of the fencing school since its conception, and had mastered all the levels. He was also the son of Coach Impian; who was just an older version of Olly.

Jared was going to have the fight of his life.

CHAPTER FOUR

a little help from my friends
-John Lennon and Paul McCartney, With
a Little Help from My Friends [1967]

The town of Bogmarsh had officially changed its name to Kingston. After the fall of Queen Quagmire, the people of the town revolted against Governor Swale and since the Eternal Bog dried up with the disappearance of Quagmire's magic, the people felt that the town should no longer be called Bogmarsh. However, try as they might to change the name, everyone still referred to the place as Bogmarsh, even King Merrit.

The town itself had transformed as well. During the reign of Quagmire, the place was dingy, and putrid. There was no color except for the occasional green moss or mold. The streets had been dark with mold and mildew, and all the buildings were tattered and crumbling.

It had changed a lot. King Merrit had decided to make Bogmarsh his temporary capital, at least until the ruined castle could be reconstructed. He had taken over the Governor's House and the Bevypolis army took over the barracks the

Muskags once occupied. The first order of business had been to destroy the Cookhouse. The people of Bogmarsh cheered loudly the day it turned to dust. The streets were cleaned up and houses rebuilt. Merrit had made it the second order of business to open the treasury and fund the rebuilding of all the major towns in Afflatus. He called it Little-Loans because he would lend owners enough farthings to replace and rebuild, and people would have to repay the loan, but without paying interest.

The incident that gnawed at Merrit and the people of Bogmarsh was that Governor Swale had managed to escape with a contingent of Muskags.

The Governor's House, temporarily called the King's House, was also much changed. During the rule of Swale, the building had been decorated with gargoyles and statues of demons and other evil. Those had yet been replaced, but most of the evil figurines were now smashed or covered with tarps.

The small meeting room, that had once been Swale's office, had been turned into a temporary throne room. Merrit agreed to take all visitors there and all decisions were announced from the balcony leading off of it.

The room had a large oval shaped table situated near the center on a tanned colored rug. A dozen chairs, made of deep mahogany wood, with intricately carved armrests and padded seats, surrounded the table. At the head of the table was the throne. It looked the same as the other chairs, but with several added cushions.

Merrit sat on the chair, his hands folded neatly in front of him. His black, wavy hair hung just past his ears, and framed his face much like a lion's mane. He looked like a boy that had spent a good portion of his life in the sun. Being only sixteen years old, he often appeared unconfident and insecure. These feelings were magnified within himself because he had spent over five years under a curse from Quagmire. He would often wake in the middle of the night wracked with guilt for the harm he had caused Afflatus as the Dragon Incubus.

Seated to the King's right, was the Jester. The Jester still wore his colorful garb and pointed hat. Even though Afflatus was in a time of peace, he refused to change into more modern and newer clothing.

The Jester, also a powerful wizard, had been the leader of the resistance, until he went insane. He had fused his soul with Merrit's, while Merrit was under the curse and the result was he went insane too.

The curse was now broken, but it left residual affects. The Jester occasionally still spoke in riddles.

Also around the table were nobles that had remained mostly loyal to the Divine family. Some of them had lost their lands to Quagmire. Skirkem Cache had a castle in the southern part of Afflatus. His lands were the closest to where Quagmire's swamp palace had been located.

Skirkem had distinctive Asian features, and he was strong, and handsome. A black braid hung down past his hips and he wore a black robe, loose, with baggy black pants. He carried a samurai sword somewhere on his person, but it was hidden in the folds of his robes.

A small black goatee shifted as he spoke. "It is the most intriguing thing," he said. "Quagmire's palace is still there. But vines have grown up over it and it is completely covered. There is no way in or out of the swampy structure.

"Speaking of intriguing," said Gandar Creed. He was a blond haired man. His fingers were thick and he had a bushy blond beard with streaks of red in it. He smelled like a cow farm. Even though he was noble, he liked to work the fields with his workers. It was because of this that he had one of the most productive farms in the southwestern part of Afflatus.

His voice was deep. "One of the independent landowners near Bragg and his wife went missing. The man, his name was Mercy, had to be near fifty years old, but he consistently worked his farm. The poor man had no descendants, so I was given his acres. Suppose I should give them to her brothers."

"What do you mean; went missing?" asked Merrit. "We have had reports of people going missing from all over Afflatus. Were any remains found?"

"No, just a hat and a pitcher of water."

"I am sure that Swale has something to do with it," Merrit muttered. "The work on the ruins has all but ceased. Some kind of creature is attacking the workers. One was taken just inside the courtyard. I don't think I will ever get the palace rebuilt; it looks worse now than it ever did."

Merrit turned to Jenna Safeguard, the last person seated at the table. She was second cousin to Jamima Safeguard, the woman who had given Avery the *vaporatium* powder in the Palpable Earth. Jenna had volunteered her services, at least until a more suitable candidate could be found, to be head of the spy agency. Someone had to keep an eye on the Kingdoms to the South.

"Have we any leads as to his whereabouts?" he asked Jenna. "Governor Swale, I mean."

She didn't possess any magical ability, like her cousin had. Rather she was quite ordinary. Her whole family had been magical in one-way or another, but she was left out and it was a source of discontentment.

"The Bevypolis is still tracking down small pockets of Muskags," she reported. "We haven't heard anything about Swale. He has gone underground. Most of the Muskags we find now are located in or near the Taboo Forest. I assume that a King from the distant south must be hiding Swale. Those other kingdoms swore treaties with Quagmire. They may not have liked her, but they are terrified of magic."

"So we are really no closer to securing our kingdom?" Cache uttered. He was a warrior. His eyes shifted uneasily. "We are at our weakest right now. You need to make alliances with other nobles, maybe with our southern neighbors. That is our only hope."

"It doesn't help that half our nation has disappeared in the Mystical Desert. I just don't understand how entire towns and cities could just vanish."

Jenna nodded her head. "The Mystical Desert started encroaching on Afflatus shortly after Quagmire started her rule. But even she was concerned about it. It has to be a magic more powerful than hers was."

Gandar interrupted. "You need to send troops to all corners of the land. People in Bragg are not feeling safe anymore. We need protection. Instead of hunting down the Muskags, use the warriors to protect the villages." He was gruff.

"I cannot spare the warriors," Merrit stated. "We are trying to rebuild the army; but it is difficult. Most people are more concerned with rebuilding their own homes. And I do not want to stop hunting for Swale. His is the biggest threat we have right now, especially if he has Muskags with him. He may not have been more powerful than Quagmire, but he is still a fearsome adversary."

"As I said," Cache broke in, "form an alliance with the South and ask for assistance protecting the land."

"I will not have a foreign army on Afflatus soil," Merrit shook his head.

"I agree," said Jenna. "At the moment we are going to have to do our best protecting our lands."

Gandar grumbled. Cache half sneered.

The door to the meeting room opened and Earo Haansu entered, interrupting the discussion; Bigwig Breeches trailed him shortly. The gnome instantly hopped up onto the table and sat cross-legged at the end.

"Mornin' your highness," said Bigwig. The gnome dug into his dirty uniform pocket and pulled out a piece of jerky and started gnawing on it. He was making smacking noises with his mouth and Baron Cache leaned forward.

A look of nausea flooded his face. "Are you, ah, enjoying that?" he asked the gnome.

Bigwig nodded. "Mouse jerky is tasty. They are buggers to catch, but once caught easy to turn into jerky."

Cache nodded his head and turned away with a pale face.

Merrit greeted Earo with a nod. Turning to face the others at the table he said: "I sent General Earo to the North to investigate the attacks on the ruins and workers."

Earo sat down at the table. He gave a contented sigh as he sank into the cushion. "I have news."

"You bet we have news!" interrupted Bigwig. "I made my head disappear! It was there one minute and gone the next!"

"What's he talking about?" asked Merrit. He directed the question to Earo; it was never good to try and get a straight answer out of Bigwig. It was actually one of the few times that he saw Bigwig without his shadow, Lumpy, trailing after him. However, Lumpy was often teaching Torrent how to be a gnome—rather ironic and humorous. She had been accepted into their tribe.

Gandar gave a snide look towards the gnome. The farmers in Afflatus hated gnomes. Since the farming corridor was located near the Southwest, it was near the gnome forest, and consequently gnomes would often tread through the fields creating burrows and trails through the crops. As well, many gnomes stole; purely innocently, they thought no one owned it.

Bigwig's eyes widened and his mouth dropped. "Making my head disappear was nothing compared to Earo. He made his whole body disappear. Talk about intensely cool!" He was so excited he stood up on the table. He was speaking with large gestures and some saliva from his mouse jerky flew through the air and landed in Gandar's beard.

"Get that disgusting creature away from me!" He wiped the spit from his beard and grimaced.

Merrit circled the table and motioned Bigwig to have a seat on one of the chairs.

"Earo," Merrit began again. "What is he talking about?"

Earo frowned. "A darkness has covered the Taboo Forest, it is a magical wall to hide evil. Inside I met with Governor Swale. I am afraid that Afflatus has a new enemy. Swale has powerful magic—I sliced my sword through his neck and it didn't harm him at all. He also is delving deep into forbidden magic. He has tried to create his own creatures. He has made a demon, he calls it Menas."

Merrit turned to the Jester. "That must mean something is happening in the Taboo Forest." The Jester nodded.

"There is more," interrupted Earo. "While I was inside the darkness I saw an army, and it was led by the Menas."

"An army?" Cache asked.

Earo turned to the baron. "An army of gnomes."

Gandar scoffed. "That's got to be a ragtag group of warriors; any one they attack would defeat them, probably without raising a weapon."

Earo shook his head. "They were organized. The head gnome, Fusty Pungent, said that the great snail, er, Governor

Swale, told them to attack the humans. The Menas kept a tight rein, but some magic must be controlling the gnomes because rock gnomes and forest gnomes were lined up together."

Jenna's face darkened. Any time there was danger to the kingdom of Afflatus she appeared to take it personally. "How dangerous do you think this army is?"

Shrugging, Earo replied, "They could do some damage; but no matter what, they are still gnomes."

Bigwig wiped his nose. "You should be wary of an army of gnomes." He said it so bluntly it took the others off guard.

"Why?" Merrit asked.

"You don't know the history of the gnomenal wars?" Bigwig was shocked. "They are like the greatest wars of history. You see the gnomes used to live in the forest..."

Gandar interrupted, "And let me guess, you did something, something and then the gnomes lived in the forest again."

Bigwig turned to the bulky man, his eyes widened. "How did you know the story? I thought only gnomes knew it." He squinted at the man. "Are you sure you aren't a gnome?"

Gandar grunted in disgust.

"You still did not answer my question," stated Merrit to the gnome. "Why should I fear a gnome army?"

"Because there are so many of them. There are hundreds of thousands of gnomes, the rock gnomes, the forest gnomes, the plain gnomes, and the homeless gnomes, when they unite; there are thousands upon thousands. They could cover the city of Bogmarsh in a moment, like locusts."

"I get it," stated Merrit. He turned to the Jester. "What should we do?"

The Jester had been strangely quiet. His head bobbed several times like he was sleeping, but his eyes were open with a vacant look. He slowly turned his gaze to Merrit. "I fear the gnomes we need not hark, I am more afraid of the dark. Deception works under cover and out of sight, that is where Depravity finds its might." He didn't rhyme all the time, but often the curse would trigger insane moments.

"What does that mean?" asked Cache. "Why do we keep the loopy guy around?"

"Because he is a great wizard," replied Merrit, "and I trust him."

"Some great wizard—can't even talk good."

Merrit grimaced. "Nevertheless, he said that the darkness is there to hide the activities of Depravity."

Jenna added, "Deception magic is about hiding the truth. If Depravity is planning some kind of attack or something worse, it would do it under cover where the Truth could not see it."

Merrit's gaze darted to the wall behind his throne. Hanging on the wall was a black sword. The sheath was black with a single green gem embedded just below the hilt. It was the Nightshade.

"So what we need is a Truth Seer," Merrit said his gaze returned to the others at the table.

Jenna looked to the wall where Merrit's gaze had been moments earlier. "You wouldn't be thinking about a particular young girl, by any chance?" she smiled slyly.

Merrit blushed. "She would be able to see through the darkness and find out what Deception magic was going on." He defended.

Cache snorted. "The little girl again. What good would she do?"

"If I recall she defeated the Lavaryn Squall and freed the King from the curse!" Bigwig jumped into the conversation. "She is a hero!"

Cache snorted again. "She only did what she did because of that Seeker Stone and the help along the way. She had no great magic." He beckoned to the Jester. "Besides, we have a wizard, isn't he good enough?"

Merrit watched the Jester. He didn't say anything.

Gandar cleared his throat, "We don't need to make a decision right now. It is getting late; I suggest we meet again tomorrow morning after sleeping on the idea. I think that we shouldn't do anything rash. We don't know enough yet."

"That is sound advice," agreed Jenna Safeguard.

Merrit nodded his head, but his gaze strayed to the Jester. The Jester looked up and nodded in the direction of Merrit's personal chamber. Merrit nodded his head again and dismissed the meeting.

Merrit's room was a large suite with a King sized bed with a down mattress. The room had a lavatory off to the left side and a large bay shaped window on the right. A small breakfast nook was set up in front of the window with an oval oak table and two oak armchairs.

The Jester and Merrit walked in silence to the King's private chamber. Once they were seated, they both looked out the window. Merrit had commanded his personal guard to keep all visitors out of the room.

The Jester flourished his baggy sleeve and a flash of color, green, red and yellow, flared. As if out of nowhere a small leather satchel appeared on the table in front of the young King.

"What is this?" he asked. "What did you want to talk about?"

The Jester smirked, his tone had returned to normal and he no longer looked vacant and distant. "As I said, I fear the dark, it will continue to draw nearer to us. The Truth Seer can fight the night. Without her help your kingdom will fall, so take the satchel and send a call." He winked at the intentional rhyme. He was aware that he often relapsed into the crazy rhyming speech.

Merrit looked at the satchel. The leather was worn. Reaching out he opened it and saw a fine white powder. He had heard about this powdered magic; it was called *vaporatium* powder.

"Should I go?" he asked.

The Jester shook his head and Merrit understood. It would be bad if he left now, the people of Afflatus might think he abandoned them. Wracking his brain he considered who would be the best for the assignment.

The Jester stood from his chair. "Send Andora. She has the ability to find Avery and her friends. She is the best alliance we have."

It dawned on Merrit; Andorra would be perfect. She used to live in the home when her uncle, Governor Swale had ruled Bogmarsh. Andorra was a couple years younger than Merrit, and he still kept in touch with her. She was now part of an organization looking after young children that had been orphaned because of Quagmire and the war against her. She was barely older than a child herself, but she had become a leader among those at the orphanage. Besides, she was always willing to help Merrit out whenever he asked. She was more loyal than all the nobles that had been in the meeting room.

Merrit reflected on the nobles as the Jester left the room. Baron Cache, Baron Gandar and Baroness Safeguard, claimed loyalty to him immediately upon his succession and coronation to the throne. However, he couldn't help but feel each of them was there for his or her own interests and didn't actually care about the kingdom, or the people of Afflatus.

Night had fallen, a cloak covering everything. A figure stood on the street, just in a shadow. The person wore a cloak with the hood up, a strand of long black hair danced in the breeze. The shadow came just past the person's eyes, but her lips were full and beautiful.

Another person approached from the East. A wind rushed down the street blowing the other's cloak behind him.

The first figure could see another shadow a dozen paces behind the one approaching her. But she knew there was no reason to fear.

The two met and the third shadow stayed just out of earshot. The second person handed a worn leather satchel to her with a piece of paper. Reading the note she nodded her head. She knew what she had to do.

Sliding through the darkness she disappeared down the street. The two other men watched her go.

CHAPTER FIVE

I want to seize fate by the throat

-Ludwig van Beethoven, Letter to Dr. Franz Wegeler [Nov. 16, 1801]

A soft drizzle soaked the street and everyone walking on it without an umbrella, not uncommon in the city of Vancouver. The smell of buses and cars driving by polluted the air. Businesses lined Granville Avenue, a clothing shop next to a restaurant and coffee shops everywhere.

Ferris and Ruth had selected a *Subway* shop located several blocks off the main bustle of the busy arteries of the city. The *Subway* had large glass windows with posters advertising the sub of the day. Inside, the walls were painted brilliant yellow with wallpaper advertising the subway of New York City.

Ferris and Ruth sat in a booth with subs sitting in front of them. The smell of baking bread reached their nostrils. There was a slight chill in the air, every time another customer would enter the restaurant and Ruth would give a soft shudder as the cool breeze rushed in through the door.

The meatball sub was Ferris' favorite and he had decided to go with the foot long. Being a growing young man, he felt hungry all the time. Next to his wrapper was a bottle of iced tea.

Ruth, deciding she didn't want to look like a pig on her first date had chosen a six-inch, vegetarian wrap. She wasn't a big *Subway* fan, but Ferris offered to pay—which she almost refused—but relented after he insisted. Besides, the *Subway* was a short bus ride to the cinema, where they would see a movie. It wasn't the classiest date she had ever imagined herself being on. But it was with Ferris and she liked him.

Ferris glanced at Ruth occasionally and smiled. Ruth smiled back. Since Rat had picked her up, he had barely said two words to her.

Ruth shifted in her seat and then looked at the wall.

"Is your sub good?" Ferris asked finally.

"Hmm?" she was startled and looked back. "Sorry, what?"

"Do you like your sub?"

"Oh, yes, it's fine. Thank you."

Rat bobbed his head.

Ruth sighed as she watched Ferris. He was wearing a hoody with blue jeans. His hair was slicked back and his eyes danced like stars twinkling in the darkness.

Ruth looked down at her own wardrobe. Maybe she should have gone with the sweater, instead of the t-shirt she was now wearing. She took a bite of her sandwich. It did taste good. Rat had suggested that she add some of the Italian dressing; it really brought out the flavor.

Rat sighed awkwardly. "How come this is so weird?" he asked.

"I don't know, hey?" she replied. Weird wasn't exactly how she wanted to define it. But it did seen odd that they weren't comfortable with each other. After all how many times had they eaten together at the school cafeteria? They hung out all the time.

"So, do you think the date was a bad idea?" Ferris asked. She tried to read his face—maybe he didn't actually like her. Was she not beautiful enough? She had lost some weight since last year, but her built was naturally stocky.

Half smiling she replied. "I think that we should just hang out. You know, like we do anyway. Why make it something all, you know, professional? It's just too much pressure."

"Okay," Rat sighed easily. "So this is a date, but we are just having fun."

"Right."

They felt the tension leave their shoulders and the room and suddenly Ruth felt like she could eat her sandwich without being judged. She took a few big bites and chewed loudly. Rat did the same.

"What movie are we going to see?" she asked between mouthfuls.

"I was thinking *Raging Robots.*"

"What movie is that?"

"Well, you see, there is a planet of robots in another part of the galaxy and the evil ones want to come and conquer earth, but the good robots also come to stop them and they can take the form of any electronic device and there is a great battle..." he fell off silently. "Oh, um, not your type of movie?"

"It sounds great," Ruth smiled, half-heartedly. "I think it will be fun just hanging out. But I might get scared."

Rat chuckled nervously. That knowledge presented him an idea. Girls that trembled in fear often sought comfort in the arms of a boyfriend! "What time do you have to be home?" he said trying to redirect.

Ruth replied, ignoring his semi-ominous chuckle. "My mom wants me home by ten. I guess I could always call if the movie is going to be later."

"My mom says that she can drop you off afterwards."

"That'd be great; I don't want to take the bus that late at night."

"It's settled then."

They finished their sandwiches and cleaned up their wrappers, tossing everything except the iced tea bottles into the garbage. A blue dish tub was sitting on top of the garbage can and they tossed the empty bottles in to be recycled.

Outside they caught number three bus, which would take them to the *Famous Players Movie Cinema*.

Stepping off the bus the rain hit them instantly and Rat pulled out his umbrella. Opening it up he offered to share with Ruth and she obliged. She had to stand really close to Rat and she felt her hand lightly brush his. She wondered what it would be like to hold Ferris' hand. Since she had never had a boyfriend before, this was completely new territory.

Ferris had also flinched slightly, very conscious of the skin-to-skin contact. He had been planning all afternoon how he was going to get his arm around her during the movie. He could make the move by pretending to yawn and then just, do it, place his arms around her shoulders. He hoped that she wouldn't pull away. He imagined again the two of them cuddled in the movie seats watching a movie together.

They sky was growing darker as they entered the cinema. The clouds were opening up, about to let more than rain through.

Rat paid for the two tickets while Ruth grabbed the popcorn and soda pop. The theater was crowded, people scurrying in every direction. A dozen other movies were playing and even though start times were staggered, it seemed everyone in the city had decided to make it movie night.

Once everything was paid for, they met up again at the entrance to the theater, number twelve. They found the sign, *Raging Robots* and entered.

The room was massive with fifty rows of seats that stretched close to the ceiling. The screen was also massive. Already a hundred people were seated in their seats, all chatting ably about their own business.

Ferris explained that he liked to sit a bit higher up because his neck felt strained otherwise.

Walking up the steps they found two seats off the right side. The only exit was back down the stairs they had climbed.

After twenty minutes of previews for other movies the intro credits started running. There was adrenaline-pumping music as the starring actors' names flashed on screen, interspersed with action sequences of robots flying to earth.

The intro scene was just starting and an intense discussion was taking place between the good robots; they needed to find some mystical cube before the evil robots.

Ferris glanced over at Ruth. She was looking hot. He had to make his move soon or else he would lose all nerve. He yawned and just about put his arm around her, but then didn't and relaxed his arm on the chair rest.

Ruth watched as Rat did his fake yawn. She smiled. This was it. He was going to put his arm around her. She slightly leaned forward to give him better access, but then he rested his arm again on the armrest. Why didn't he do it? She wondered.

Rat worked up his nerve again. Yawning he lifted his arm.

The scene was suddenly interrupted by the sound of a scream and a black shadow fell from the ceiling to the floor just in front of the big screen. Following the scream was a solid sounding, *umph!*

"What the heck?" everyone heard a person at the front of the theater state.

"Shh!"

"Someone just fell from the ceiling."

"Are you okay?" another voice stated.

"It's a girl!"

"I'm fine."

"How can you be fine after a fall like that?"

"Never mind."

Rat placed his arm back on the armrest and strained his neck trying to make out what was going on at the front of the theater.

"Ferris?" a female voice hollered from the front.

Rat was confused.

"Who is that?" asked Ruth, also straining her neck to see.

"Shut up, we're trying to watch a movie," another customer said.

"Ferris, where are you?" the female voice crowed again, interrupting the whole theater.

"I recognize that voice," Rat said after a moment.

"Ferris, where is Avery?"

Ruth was confused.

Rat turned to face Ruth. "I think that is Andora."

"From Afflatus?"

"Yes."

"What is she doing here?"

Ferris shrugged. "Obviously she didn't show up to interrupt the movie."

Or our date thought Ruth. Or maybe she did!

Rat stood up and started walking down the aisle. He motioned for Ruth to follow him.

"Where are you going?" she asked following him.

"Well, I can't have her keep yelling for me."

Ruth followed reluctantly. People stared at them as they descended the stairs. Andora saw them before they could make her out and she rushed towards them. She was wearing a black cloak with the hood pulled up. Standing just in front of a couple moviegoers she gave Rat a big hug.

"What are you doing here?" Ferris asked. He tried to take her shoulders so that they could move out of the way. She didn't move.

One of the moviegoers piped up. "What are you wearing?" he asked Andora. "Is it Halloween and I missed it, *Harry Potter*."

Andora turned to the man with a frown on her face. My name is not Harry, thank you very kindly. I am called Andora." She turned to Rat. "I just got here from Afflatus!" she started.

"You just got here from the looney pen!" the moviegoer retorted.

Rat quickly ushered Andora out the main exit. Ruth followed; her date was officially over, she realized.

"What are you doing here?" Rat asked again. "When we left Afflatus I thought that I would never see you again."

"We have to find Avery," Andora said suddenly. "Afflatus needs a Truth Seer again."

A couple holding hands walked past the trio and looked at them funny.

Ferris pulled Andora to a more secluded corner.

"Avery isn't here," he replied. "Ruth and I were just, well, were just watching a movie together."

Andora glanced at Ruth, noticing her for the first time. "Ruth, it is good to see you too," she said.

Ruth nodded her head in acknowledgement. She had only briefly met Andora on their first trip to Afflatus and it was right before they had gone home.

Ferris was staring at Andora with a distinctive puppy-dog look in his eyes. Ruth was sure he was even panting and trying to keep from slobbering on himself.

"We've got to find Avery," she said again. "I'll fill you in on what's happening as we go. Where is she?"

Ferris shrugged.

Ruth interjected, "Her and Jared are just finishing fencing practice. If we want to catch them we will have to catch a bus to the Old Church."

"Let's go!"

Avery was standing next to Jared at the bus stop just outside the Old Church. Jared's head hung with dejection. His fight with Olly had not gone well. The Impian boy had five touches before Jared had even worked up a sweat. The coach told Olly to take it easy after that and Jared felt humiliated in front of everyone else.

"I know it doesn't help, but you can't let it bother you," Avery said. She rubbed Jared's coat sleeve. He didn't look up. "Olly is like the best."

"You're right, that didn't help. I should have been able to find the balance. But I couldn't focus on anything. It was all I could do just to keep facing him. He was a much harder opponent than the Muskags ever had been."

The door to the Old Church opened and Olly exited. He was walking with several other boys from the gym.

Olly's dark hair and slanted eyes smiled wickedly at Jared. Jared felt like flipping the other boy *the bird*. But refrained.

Olly started walking down the street. The other boys glanced at Jared with the same smug look on their faces. He knew that they were talking about him as they disappeared around the corner.

"I just want to beat him so bad!" Jared clenched his fists and then kicked at a McDonald's cup at his feet.

"Let it go," Avery replied. "I know how good of a sword fighter you are."

Shrugging his shoulders, Jared looked at the ground again. "I just want to disappear."

Down the street Avery could see a bus coming towards their stop. She would have to wait another two buses before hers arrived. Jared used to live a short walk away, but since he moved to a new foster family he had to catch a bus as well.

The bus stopped in front of them and the sound of the buses air breaks, burst through the air. Five people exited the bus before Avery heard the sound of screaming and yelling: "Wait! Hold it!"

The bus doors opened again and three young people ran off the bus. Ferris was leading the charge with another girl and then Ruth close behind.

Avery glanced from Ruth to the other girl. She knew that Rat and Ruth had been on a date and was confused why another girl was with them. Especially a girl dressed like *Harry Potter*.

She took a hold of Ruth's jacket and whispered to her. The other girl was staring at Avery with an open mouth. "What is going on?"

Ruth nodded in the direction of the girl. "That is Andora. She is here from Afflatus!"

"Afflatus?"

Andora approached and took a hold of Avery's hand. "It is such a pleasure to meet you; I mean, now that you are awake. I only got to see you just before the Jester sent you and the others back to the Palpable earth. You know, before."

"Yes," Avery said hesitantly. "I remember Ruth and Ferris telling me about you. But why are you hear?" She was afraid she already knew the answer.

Andora's large brown eyes narrowed. "I was sent by King Merrit. He told me that it is important that you return to Afflatus. We need a Truth Seer."

"A what?"

"A Truth Seer. You are the Truth Seer. There is something threatening the kingdom. We need you."

Avery frowned. "You need me?" She was skeptical.

Andora held out a piece of paper. "This is the note that the King gave me. It explains everything.

Avery took the parchment. It was made from homemade paper. Her gaze barely scanned the parchment. It didn't sound like her kind of thing. Did she really want to put herself in mortal danger again? Life here in her real world was just beginning to have a semblance of normal again.

Avery handed the letter to Jared. Immediately she saw Jared's eyes light up. He was probably thinking that it was a good chance to escape and to go on another adventure.

"I don't know," she said finally.

Ferris cut in, standing next to Andora. "Come on Avery. It seems that they need us again."

"Us?" she asked. "I don't recall hearing anything about bringing anyone else along."

"Well, of course I would bring Ferris," said Andora without thinking.

"What about Ruth and Jared?" added Avery.

Jared beamed. "I'm going for sure. I mean, there I was a warrior and I didn't have to deal with pathetic teachers and stupid brothers or Olly Impians."

"And all you have to worry about are dragons and demons and other nasty beasts trying to kill you."

Avery looked down the street. Her bus was fast approaching the stop. She would have to make up her mind quickly.

"What do you say?" Andora was sincere.

The bus pulled up and the air breaks let out a sigh of pressure. The door opened.

"I don't think so," Avery said finally. "I am not putting my life in danger again. There is too much going on here for me. I won't do it." She waved to Jared and then stepped onto the bus leaving the others dumbfounded on the sidewalk.

She watched them through the window as the bus drove away. Had she made the right decision? Of course, she decided. She did not want to almost die again!

CHAPTER SIX

Discipline is the soul of an army

-George Washington, Letter of Instructions to the Captains of the Virginia Regiments [July 29, 1759]

The garden behind the King's Mansion in Bogmarsh was developing beautifully. Gardeners had transplanted shrubs and created a maze taller than six feet and encompassing an acre of area. At the very center of the maze stood a three sided altar and benches surrounded it. The altar had been brought from the ruins. A pond had been dug around it and filled with small gold fish. A stone path led through the pond to the pedestal and altar in the center.

Merrit sat on one of the benches facing the altar. The plaque in the middle was like a magic eight ball. It would flash different riddles to the person that needed to hear it. It had been silent since Quagmire had been defeated.

The air was fresh and the sound of water trickling into the pond, along with several coos of city pigeons, were the only sounds he heard. The young King liked to come here, to the peace and quiet, away from the stresses that he already found often overwhelming.

In the Kingdom of Afflatus there were a dozen nobles that had once made up the Crown Council. Of course when Quagmire had taken over, she all but disbanded their authority. The ones that signed alliances with her did so to preserve their holdings and wealth and Merrit could hardly hold them accountable for that. Now that Quagmire was gone, the nobles were jockeying for position in his favor. The more they fought among themselves, the more he realized they didn't really care who was in charge, as long as they could get something out of it.

Skirkem Cache, Gandar Creed, and Jenna Safeguard, had been the first to arrive and so he kept them more in his council. They had also been the ones that lost the most during the reign of Safeguard. They mostly stayed out of the affairs of Afflatus during the dark times.

With the reemergence of Merrit, Cache, and Creed made sure he knew they were loyal subjects and Jenna Safeguard had lost all her lands. Actually, her sister, Jamima Safeguard had lost the lands. The Safeguards had always been loyal to King Divine and his family, and so as soon as Merrit had the throne, Jenna, the only remaining Safeguard in Afflatus, joined with him.

A voice interrupted Merrit's thoughts. "Your Majesty," it was Baron Cache. His Asian figure skulked through the maze and approached the king. "I am glad to have found you. There is a messenger waiting for you in the hall."

Merrit shuffled on his bench so he was facing Cache. The man stood with an air of dignity and authority. When he spoke it was with assurance and command.

"Your Majesty?"

Merrit motioned for the man to sit down. He obliged. "I know that you weren't a hundred percent for me bringing Avery Noble back from the Palpable earth. Why?"

Cache hesitated momentarily. His stern gaze met Merrit's and he said, "You are a new King, and a young King. You were very young when your father was overthrown. You have no experience leading the country and you were under a curse for five years. I must say that there is a significant lack of confidence in you at the moment. If you appear weak to anyone, including other nobles, such as Gandar or Safeguard, you could find your throne taken from you." Merrit was aware that Cache left his own name out of the comment. The man also didn't seem to be sharing because he was concerned for Merrit.

"So it was purely out of concern for me and my perception of power that I should not call on the Truth Seer."

"If you seem too dependent on outside forces, it makes you seem weak. Appearing weak is your greatest weakness. Even though you are weak right now, give the perception of power. You have me as an ally. Use that to your advantage. If you would let me sit at your right hand, everyone would know that you have my backing and support, both physically and intellectually."

Merrit nodded his head. But would people then also think that he was a puppet to Baron Cache? Would people take his orders as serious when Cache was not around? In a sense with Cache at his right, the man could make many decisions without the knowledge or authority of the King. Merrit made an instant mental note to keep Cache on a tight leash.

"Well, I thought you should know that I sent Andora to fetch Avery Noble. She will be arriving soon, I hope." Merrit confessed.

Cache's face hardened and he looked like one of the stone gargoyles that Merrit had had covered up. He growled, "You should not have made such a decision without the backing and support of the Crown Council." He trailed off before continuing, "Nevertheless, I will support my King's decision," he added quickly with a moderate cool tone.

Standing from the bench, Cache did the same. "Now, who is the messenger that is here?" Merrit asked.

"A rather peculiar one," Cache admitted. "He claims to be a spokesgnome. He refused to say any more and that he would only give the message to you himself. The dirty little beast looked to be in some kind of trance or something."

"Odd. Let's go see what the gnome wants."

It took the two, half an hour to escape the maze. Even though Merrit knew all the trails, the size alone made the walk longer. When they exited the back garden and entered the King's Mansion; the place was in an uproar.

Jenna rushed to meet him. She looked first at Baron Cache. "I'm so glad you found him. We are potentially in a state of alert."

Merrit took her aside and kept walking. "What is going on?"

She shrugged her shoulders. "There are rumors of an army approaching from the North!"

"Army? What kind of army?"

"We aren't sure at the moment. The reports are fragmented; a few farmers that don't really know what is going on."

Smiling Merrit said, "Well, it could be the gnome army. Cache told me that a spokesgnome is here."

Nodding Jenna pointed at the kitchen table. A very distinguished looking gnome sat on one of the chairs; but his chin barely crested the edge of the table and he looked like a child sitting, waiting for dinner. The gnome was wearing military garb. A breastplate with a helmet and a small sword hung from his belt. In his hand was a parchment.

Bigwig was sitting on the table in front of the gnome. His finger was waving in front of the other gnome's eyes. "Excuse me! Hey! Excuse meeeee! Can't you hear me?"

The other gnome ignored Bigwig. He kept repeating. "My name is Fusty Pungent and I must see the King." Then he would brush at Bigwig's finger like it was an annoying fly.

"How rude? I think I know you. Aren't you the gnome that stole my tribe from me?"

Fusty, the gnome, looked suddenly shocked. "You're Bigwig. I barely recognized you. By the way, you have been banished."

"Wha, huh? How can you banish me? I am Overlord of the gnomes."

"Precisely. Overlord. I am the lord now."

"The lard maybe. Looks like you have put on a few pounds."

"You are banished because you have included a gigantic in your new tribe."

"But the gigantic is my friend."

"You know the gnomenal laws. No tribe may be formed with a creature taller than four feet."

"That is just a silly law," defended Bigwig. "If it were true then you could include a bug in your tribe."

"If the gigantic was a bug, then you would not be banished. But because the gigantic is a gigantic, you are banished."

Bigwig stood in a huff on top of the table and squatted in front of Fusty. "I think...I will...You are...How...Errr!" and he kicked the gnome right in the mouth. It was rather funny because Fusty's head flew backwards and his metal helmet fell to the floor with a bang. The loud bang scared the gnome so badly he jumped out of his chair and fumbled to pull his sword free, looking for the enemy.

"That's enough, Bigwig," said Merrit approaching and sitting down in a chair across from where Fusty had been seated.

The gnome returned to his chair and stared at the King with as stern of glare he could manage. Because he could not glare very well it looked like a dog's face seeking attention and Merrit was tempted to reach out and pet the gnomes face. He refrained.

"What are you here for?" Merrit asked the gnome. "You claim to be a spokesgnome. What is that?"

"I speak for all the gnomes," the gnome said.

"Not me," added Bigwig quickly.

Fusty amended his proclamation. "I speak for all the gnomes, except him." He pointed at Bigwig.

"And not Lumpy."

Fusty growled. "I speak for all the gnomes, except him and Lumpy Knickknack."

"And not Torrent either," Bigwig interjected a third time.

"She's not a gnome."

"She's in my tribe."

"But she is illegal and a gigantic, she doesn't get a vote."

"Enough!" ordered Merrit.

"Ahem," Baron Cache cleared his throat interrupting. "Your majesty, I would like to talk with Jenna Safeguard and Gandar Creed about the decision that you made without our advice. I think they should know the actions you have taken. It might help us deal with the repercussions."

"Fine," said Merrit. His jaw was clenched, it was a pain having to deal with nobles and these ones were so preoccupied with power, it was a shame that they were the ones he trusted the most. He waited while Cache escorted Jenna Safeguard and Gandar Creed out of the room. He turned his attention back to Fusty. "What do you want?" he demanded.

The stinky gnome raised his nose. "We want your surrender. I am to return and give my commander your answer. But trust me when I say, fighting us will be like a wave that you cannot fight."

"Huh?"

"I mean, waving us will be like a fight you cannot wave—no wait, I had it right the first time!"

Merrit leaned back in his chair. "So what happens when you go back to your commander and tell him my answer?"

Fusty sounded regal. "You will either be attacked and destroyed or you will open the gates and let our army in."

"What happens if I don't let you go back to your commander and he never hears your answer?"

The gnome was startled. He hadn't thought of that. "You can't do that!" he said in a high-pitched panic. "I am a spokesgnome and I have free passage."

"Nope. You are my prisoner. You have come here declaring war on me and you want me to let you go? How silly would it be for me to just let you go?"

"Very silly indeed," Fusty admitted sadly. He held out his arms like he was about to be led away in shackles.

Gandar storming past the room interrupted them. He glared at Merrit as he left. Merrit could only assume the man was upset by what Cache had told him. Maybe sending for Avery Noble so soon was not a good idea.

He turned his attention back to the gnome. "How about this? I will send you back to your commander, but only you tell him you have surrendered."

"I surrendered?" he was confused.

"Yes, you will not be allowed to fight the people in Afflatus. You will return home and not set foot here again."

Fusty mulled it over. "What if he doesn't agree to the terms?"

"Then you have to return here and be my prisoner."

Fusty was very troubled because he knew that the general would not accept the terms of surrender, but he didn't want to be a prisoner again. He was already feeling too trapped as it was.

"I guess I have to agree," he said more sadly than before. "If my general does not agree, I will return and be your prisoner," he sighed heavily.

Merrit smirked.

With that settled Merrit took the gnome by the hand and escorted him out of the King's Mansion. The streets were strangely silent as Merrit and his personal guard made for the front gates.

They quickly found where all the people in town had headed: to the city walls. The walls were lined with men, women and children standing tiptoe to get a view of something outside the city.

At the front gates Merrit found Earo standing with his sword drawn. "Your majesty," he said with a short bow. "There is an army of gnomes camped just outside our gates."

Merrit was dumbfounded. "I have to see this; open the gate."

The guard holding a large wooden plank in place lifted it and the gate swung partially open. Pushing Fusty through the crack, Merrit then took a look. As far as his eyes could see were gnomes, armed and ready for combat.

"There has got to be a hundred thousand of them," Merrit stated to Earo. "Where did that many gnomes come from?"

"Who knows," shrugged Earo, "but they do breed like rabbits; or so I've heard."

"Are the walls supported with troops?" asked Merrit. "I would like to enlist every able-bodied man or woman with the courage to fight to suit up and prepare for attack. They are just gnomes, but a hundred thousand of anything will be a tremendous battle."

"Yes sir," Earo saluted. He ordered his second in command to do as the King commanded. The Major trotted off hollering out the orders.

Motioning to Earo to follow, Merrit headed back towards the King's Mansion. "We need to develop some kind of strategy here."

"We need help that is for sure," added Earo.

The sun set and darkness covered the land. Behind the gnome army was a wall of blackness deeper and darker than the night that covered the world.

Because of the deep shadows no guards on the walls of Bogmarsh noticed a rope slither down the brick. A shadow started climbing down the rope to the ground just outside the city walls. The figure slunk into the night with little trace of its passing.

The gnome army was not even aware as the figure made its way through their ranks.

The figure reached the wall of darkness, an evil blanket. The figure stepped through with only a slight hesitation.

Inside the black wall he found a tent had been set up. Making way through the shaded grass, the figure came to the entrance and listened.

Fusty Pungent was speaking. "My lord, I regret to say that the boy King has refused to surrender and has said he will only accept our surrender."

"We will not surrender," a deep voice uttered. A growl echoed the voice's command.

Fusty Pungent sounded upset. "I was afraid of that," he said sadly.

"What are you talking about?" the portentous voice stated.

"I said that I would return and be his prisoner if you didn't accept the terms of surrender. I knew that you wouldn't accept them, but that was the only way I was getting out of that city."

"Ridiculous," the general replied.

"I'll be going now," said Fusty.

"Where?" the general asked.

"Back to the boy King and give myself up."

"You will not," the general said.

"But I promised him," Fusty replied.

"Then break your promise. You are free now! In war there are no bonds of trust. He is the enemy and who cares what he wants. Do you understand?"

Fusty had obviously not considered breaking his promise. "I will do as the Great Snail commands," he said.

"Swale, my name is Swale, you pungent little creature. Mix up my name again and I'll turn you into an imp!"

Fusty ran out of the tent, past the figure hiding just at the entrance. The figure got a glimpse of the gnomes face as he left; he looked like he was actually considering being turned into an imp, just for the experience.

"Get in here," General Swale ordered.

The figure slunk into the tent. The canvas room was lit by a single candle and General Swale, once Governor Swale, sat behind a small wooden desk. He had maps of the city Bogmarsh opened.

The General didn't even look up at the hooded figure. "What news?"

The figure whispered. "The King has sent for the Truth Magic. The girl will arrive soon."

Swale did look up at this. He could not see under the cloak's veil, but he knew who the person was. "You are certain?"

"Yes."

"Groth" Swale ordered. A dark shape shifted at the back of the tent and the hooded figure was startled. The wolf-like man stood, hunched over with claws clenching in and out. Fangs seared through snarled lips. If the Menas had ever been human, it looked to have lost any resemblance.

The Menas snarled in response to its master's summons.

"Take a platoon of gnomes to the ruins. Several children are arriving. Kill them the moment they appear in Afflatus."

"I will," Groth replied. His voice sounded more like a grunt than speech.

"Oh and you may eat them as well."

The Menas' lips smacked together and suddenly he bolted from the tent.

The hooded figure waited in silence. After a moment General Swale looked up. "You still here?"

"Yes, I thought you might have more orders."

"Get back to Bogmarsh and keep spying on that young King. We will have the city long before he ever suspects a traitor in his midst."

CHAPTER SEVEN

Home is home, be it never so homely

-English Proverb, [c.1300]

Avery sat at a small circular wooden table in the two-bedroom apartment she and her mother called home. Her mother, Mandy Noble, had found the place after extensive searching. Since Avery wanted to stay at Jeerson Junior High, it was imperative that Mandy find a home nearby.

The walls in the kitchen/dining room were yellow, not painted, just evidence of many years of tenants, some smokers. The floor was linoleum and had gouges in it from tables and chairs being shuffled across it; not to mention several burns from dropped cigarettes.

Avery's mother was not home yet. Glancing up at the small black clock on the wall, Avery saw that it was nearing ten o'clock at night. Avery had eaten a bowl of *Kraft Dinner* and she left the dirty dishes in the sink. Often she would do the cleaning, since her mother worked two jobs and seldom ate at the apartment.

A math textbook sat opened on the table, but Avery was not looking at it. The math was still basically review from grade seven. They were multiplying four and five digit numbers— but Avery had mastered multiplication in grade five.

Tonight however, she couldn't get her mind to focus. She was still remembering meeting with Andora and reading the letter from King Merrit. How could she possibly go back to Afflatus? She was almost killed there. She had had to fight a demon, and a dragon, and even though she lived through it, there were times that she awoke in the middle of the night after having a terror dream about the Squall. The poison that had penetrated her so deeply had taken a part of her. Even though Jwen had taken all the poison out of her system, the memory of the beast's horror stuck with her.

Her mother would be home soon. But that thought didn't reassure Avery. Her mother was so worried about paying the bills; she barely even acknowledged that Avery existed.

Mandy's second job ended at nine thirty, but she wouldn't be home until ten at the earliest. She would come home, have a bite to eat and then go to bed, just to get up at five in the morning to go to her first job again.

Avery often tried to understand why her mother did that. Sure, money was tough, but to Avery it seemed like her mother was trying to distance herself from her daughter. Would she even care if Avery tried to talk with her? What could Avery say without her mother thinking she needed to be committed to an insane asylum? She needed to talk to someone.

Picking up the phone she dialed Jared's number. However, she immediately hung up, that was the old number. He hadn't given her the new number of his foster family. The only other person she could call was Ruth.

Dialing the number she waited. Ruth had her own line into her room. "Hello?" Ruth asked.

"Hey, its me," said Avery in a soft voice. She took the cordless phone to her room, in case her mother came home sooner.

"How are you doing?" asked Ruth. There was concern in her voice. "You took off so fast, we didn't know what to think."

"I know. I'm sorry. I was just really confused. I don't know if I want to go back to Afflatus?"

Ruth sighed. "The boys are gun-ho about going back. Jared thinks it will help him escape his problems here at home. Doesn't he remember that time is different there than here; eventually he will return to our world and have to deal with his problems all over again."

"What about Ferris?"

Ruth let out a soft growl under her breath. "He is just goo-goo over Andora. She could ask him to go to the moon or mars and he would go."

"By the way, how did your date go?"

"Oh, it was great until Andora showed up. I even thought that Ferris was going to put his arm around me. He did that cheesy yawn thing and was about to do it when Andora practically fell into our laps."

"That sucks!"

"I know. As soon as Andora showed up, it was like I didn't even exist. I completely understand; I can't compete with her. She is so beautiful and I am just not good enough."

"You are very beautiful," Avery reassured. "Ferris is just being stupid."

"I mean, I lost weight and everything and things were going great until she showed up."

"So are you going to go back to Afflatus?"

Ruth was silent, thinking. "I don't know. As you pointed out, King Merrit only asked for you. If you don't go, what is the point of us going? He needs a Truth Seer."

'What does that even mean? Jwen told me that I perform Truth magic. But last time I was only able to do anything because of the Seeker Stone. This time the stone is gone. I would be on my own and despite what Jwen said, I can't do anything. I can't make fire shoot out of my fingers, or make enemies evaporate into thin air. I can't do anything. What is the point of being able to perform magic if there are things you can't do?"

"She said that Truth Magic is the most powerful available to humans," added Ruth. "So there must be more to it."

"You have more magic in Afflatus than me," said Avery, her tone mellow. "I saw you heal a wound. That is cool. Yet, I can't do that."

Ruth didn't reply. She didn't know what to say.

"I'm sorry," Avery said after a moment. "I didn't want to make you feel bad. I just don't know what I can do." She paused suddenly struck with a thought. "By the way, where is Andora staying tonight?"

Ruth gave another soft growl. "At Ferris' house," she sneered.

"How is Ferris going to explain that one?"

"I don't know and I don't care," stated Ruth. She was trying to sound indifferent, but Avery could tell her friend was upset. She was probably imagining Ferris cuddled up to Andora on the sofa watching a movie together or something.

"Try not to let it bother you," Avery tried to reassure. She heard the apartment door open; her mother was home. "Look, my mom just got home. I should go. I'll see you tomorrow?"

"Yeah, bye."

"Bye," she said and then hung up the phone.

Exiting her room she saw her mom leaning against the kitchen counter. She was an older looking version of Avery. She had mousey brown hair and green eyes, but the light that had once been so bright in her eyes had faded; she was just tired all the time. She wore a nurse's uniform, even though she wasn't a nurse, just a lowly janitor.

Her mother was rubbing her eyes and staring at the sink full of dirty dishes. Hearing Avery she turned to face her daughter.

"Why didn't you clean up? You know how tired I am when I get home. I can't deal with this too."

The rebuke stung. How often did she clean the house, cook dinner, and do the dishes? Avery wanted to yell at her mother. "What kind of mother are you?" she said instead, allowing the disrespect and anger sound in her voice. "How many nights am I here alone?"

"Don't talk to me like that!" Mandy stated. "I work so that we can afford to live in this part of town. I work so that you can eat. I work so that you can keep going to those precious fencing lessons. That class takes a lot out of my budget."

"Budget?" Avery snorted. "You don't budget."

"I'm too tired for this Avery," her mother's voice changed. It was like she had given up and Avery suddenly felt bad for the way she treated her; but she couldn't back down. Her mother made her angry most of the time.

"I'm sorry that I am not the mother you want to have. I am trying my best."

Avery softened her stance. Not sure what to say she offered to make both of them a cup of tea.

A few minutes later they were both sitting in the living room. Her mother turned on the television set and was staring blankly at a news broadcast as she sipped her tea. It was a mint flavored tea and the smell wafted into the room, filling their senses with calm.

"Mom," Avery started. "Can I ask you a question?"

"I'm sure you can and you may ask me a question," Avery groaned inwardly, her mother still corrected her grammar constantly.

"If you were the only person able to do something; no one else could do it; would you use your ability, even if it meant you could lose your life."

"That is a really odd question. I don't think I understand."

Avery thought about it for a moment. "What if you were able to do some kind of magic and no one else in the world could do your magic and someone was in trouble and your magic could help them, but it could mean risking your own life; would you do it?"

"That would really depend on who the person I was saving. I would do it for you, but not for any stranger on the street."

"So, other people aren't our concern. We should care only about those that we care about?"

Her mother thought about it for a moment. "Life is crazy and I am just trying to live through it."

Avery was unconvinced. "So if you saw a person being mugged and you could do something about it, you would choose not to because it might put you in harm's way?"

"That is a bit different," her mother replied. "Of course if I was able to do something to stop an injustice, I would. But I wouldn't put myself in danger. I would call 911 or something." Her mother waited. "What do these questions have to do with anything? Did something happen that placed you in danger?"

"No," Avery replied hurriedly. She was thinking about her own answer. If she saw a person in trouble, would she try to help, even at the risk of her own person? Immediately she knew the answer. "Thanks for the chat mom," she said standing and heading toward the kitchen to drop off her empty mug. "I'll do the dishes tomorrow. Good night."

"Good night," her mother said, perplexed by the odd conversation. "Sleep well."

The next morning when Avery awoke, her mother had already left for work. She made herself a quick breakfast of cereal and milk, did the dishes and headed to school.

The air was brisk as she walked the dozen blocks to Jeerson Junior High. The smell of exhaust permeated the air and a mist fell from the sky, like rain, but not. This kind of weather was common in Vancouver. A melancholy settled over her as she walked. She knew what she was going to do and suddenly she wondered if it was the right decision. The night before she toyed with her decision, second-guessing herself numerous times.

Entering the school she headed straight for her homeroom. Several students were already present, including Ruth. She sat on a chair by herself; Ferris had obviously not arrived yet, since as of late the two of them had been inseparable. However, with the arrival of Andora, things were definitely strained.

"Hey," Avery said, sitting down.

"Hey," Ruth replied. The dark skinned girl looked tired, like she hadn't slept much the night before. She took out a small blush powder and mirror and dabbed some cover up on her cheeks.

Avery rubbed her friends shoulder. "You okay?"

"I can't help but feel hurt, and then upset and angry. How come boys have the ability to make you feel so good, but then in the next moment so horrible?" She snapped the blush and mirror container shut and stuck it back into her pocket.

"I don't know," Avery replied truthfully. "I think its because they have smaller brains. They can't pick up on little things, you know, like how a girl is feeling."

"Boys are stupid!" Ruth agreed.

Holly Fitts, entering the room, interrupted them. Her entrance was always boisterous. "Hello all!" she said with a sweep of her hand. Instantly several of the boys made their way over to where she was standing. "Boys, I need someone to grab my book bag, I left it just out there in the hall." She pointed.

One boy, a shorter blond hair kid, acne covering his face piped up, "I'll get it for you Holly," he said.

"Eww! No!" she smirked. The blond haired boy, Evan, turned away a hurt look on his face.

Jeffery Thompson strode up, "Don't worry Holly," he stated boldly. "I'll save your pack from the hall." He left. When he walked he was bull legged, like he had been riding a horse, and his shoulders were about as thick as a horse. He was the schools local redneck. His uncle owned a ranch on the outskirts of the city, and he had learned to ride bulls.

Avery turned to Ruth, "See, puny brains!"

Ruth laughed.

Ferris and Andora entered the classroom. Ruth saw them first. "Why did he bring her to school?" she asked to herself, out loud.

"I don't know," Avery said.

Andora and Ferris came and sat down next to Avery. Ruth again felt like an outsider.

Andora didn't say anything to Avery. She was waiting for Rat to make the first move. They didn't get the chance because Miss Creant entered the room. Her stale perfume preceded her. Avery suddenly felt like sneezing, but held it in, making a funny snort sound, which caused every one to turn and look. She turned red and lowered her gaze.

Miss Creant took one look at Andora. "Who are you?" she asked. Her tone resounded with bitterness, like she had drunk black motor oil instead of coffee that morning.

Ferris stood. "This is ahh," he stuttered.

"Ahh," Miss Creant interrupted. "Funny name."

"Andora," Ferris spit out.

"There are no visitors at school. Unless your parents have called ahead to warn the teachers that they will have another student to deal with."

Ferris continued. "She is, ah, my cousin, visiting from Mississippi."

"Really," Miss Creant feigned interest. "Which part of Mississippi?"

"The middle part," Ferris said, sitting down a little red faced.

Miss Creant waved off the comment and sat down to take attendance. Andora leaned over to Ferris. "Hey Cuz!" she said. "I didn't know we were related."

"It was the only thing I could think of to get her off my case. She is a mean, mean lady."

Andora shrugged. Turning to Avery she asked, "Have you thought more about why I am here? I know you said that you didn't want to return to Afflatus, but I believe that you are the only one that can help us. The others are more than welcome to come too, but King Merrit asked specifically for you."

Avery was about to reply when Jared entered the room. He gave a sidelong look at Avery. Something was amiss with him today, she could tell instantly. As he came closer she caught a musky scent in the air. It clung to his clothes and hair; it smelled like smoke.

Jared was very uncomfortable as he sat down. His eyes darted to and fro, like a rabbit searching for a way to escape.

Miss Creant had seen Jared enter. "I am so glad that you were able to join us," she stated sardonically. "Late slip?"

"I forgot," Jared muttered. His voice sounded slurred. Avery recognized it immediately; she had heard her father speak with the same tone a hundred times before he died. Jared was either drunk or high.

Shaking her head at her friend Avery turned back to Andora. "Meet us under the grand stands at recess break. I have something I want to tell everyone."

"No announcements now get to your first class—dismissed! Avery and Jared, in school suspension!" Miss Creant said, and immediately all the students started to scatter.

Recess break started at ten thirty and it could not come soon enough. Shortly after the bell the five young people made a beeline for the grand stands. They were located in the field behind the school, where the jocks played football and baseball. There was enough space for people to gather under the seats. There was a lot of garbage, empty pop cans, chocolate bar wrappers and chip bags.

Avery was the last to make it out of the school, due to the suspension. She did not glance around, as maybe she should have; unaware that someone was following her. Holly

Fitts had noticed all of them making for the stands. Intrigued into what they were doing, she followed Avery. When she saw them meeting under the stands she quietly climbed onto the seats to listen in to their conversation.

Avery was speaking. "I have decided that I will go to Afflatus again. I am terrified that this time I won't make it back. I almost died the first time, and this time I don't have the Seeker Stone so I don't know what I will be able to do. Jwen is also gone; but if King Merrit wants help, I will go."

"That is super!" screamed Andora.

Holly furrowed her eyebrows. What were they talking about?

Avery spoke again. "Do you have the *vaporatium* powder?"

"Yes," Andora replied.

"Are we all ready?"

"Ready as we will ever be," Jared replied.

Holly wanted to know, ready for what.

Andora threw the *vaporatium* powder into the air. Holly gave a soft sneeze as some of it lighted on her. Suddenly everything went black and it felt like she was standing in a swimming pool of water.

Avery felt the same sensation of being loaded up, like a webpage. She could hear Jared in the darkness; he wasn't laughing this time; this time he was retching his guts up.

Ferris was giggling and Ruth and Andora were screaming. Suddenly Avery heard a scream that she recognized, but didn't want to. Why was it that her enemies always came to Afflatus with her? She thought. The scream belonged to Holly Fitts. She was coming to Afflatus too!

CHAPTER EIGHT

Shaking the dust of ages, will transcribe My chronicles

-Alexander Pushkin, Boris Godunov [1825]

Someone was screaming.

The world was starting to gain focus and Avery could feel the familiar sensation of tall grass brushing against her legs.

A girl was still screaming.

The world focused more and she could see the shape of the old ruins beginning to take shape. She could see the misshapen tower, and rubble lying around. The sky was blue and a few puffy clouds dotted the horizon. It was warmer than back home and a breeze brushed her hair and a stray brown strand danced just in front of her eyes.

Taking a deep breath she breathed in the air of Afflatus. It was so clean, and fresh. The smell of the grass reminded her of a freshly mowed lawn.

The screaming continued relentlessly.

Turning around she saw the source of the high-pitched wail. Holly Fitts was standing with her blond hair blowing behind her. Her eyes were closed and her fists were clenched at her sides. Her mouth was opened as wide as it could go with a continual, ear shattering, screech.

"Shut up!" Jared yelled finally.

Holly gave two more half-hearted spurts and then closed her mouth and slowly opened her eyes, first one and then the other. She saw Ferris, Ruth, Andora, Jared and Avery glaring at her. She started to look everywhere, her eyes wide and wild.

Avery ignored her and turned her attention back to the ruins. They were different. Scaffolding surrounded parts of the walls, and a small camp was set up just outside the courtyard. But there was no one around. It looked like Merrit had been trying to fix up the ruins.

"Where are we? What did you do to me?" Holly suddenly started saying. "Send me back home right now!" she ordered.

Jared sneered at her. "Can't," he said bluntly. "You are in Afflatus now. None of your little boyfriends to stick up for you!"

"Aff—what?"

"Afflatus," Ruth piped in. "You are in another world."

"Whatever, I am," she said with a valley-girl flare. "I'm going home now."

Without another word she started walking away from the others, towards the plain.

"How do you know that is the right direction?" quizzed Jared sarcastically. She ignored him and continued walking. "Fine go ahead and get lost; you'll never find your way home!"

Avery tried to reason with her. "We need to stick together!" she called. Suddenly her vision caught site of some creatures hiking towards them. "Look!" she said pointing, "Gnomes!"

"Yes, but what is that black thing that is leading them?" asked Ruth. She recalled the fear she had the first time in Afflatus, of cannibals.

They watched silently as the gnomes suddenly surrounded Holly. There was another high-pitched wail, when one of the gnomes brought a club up in a threatening manner. Holly pushed the club aside, stuck up her nose and tried to walk past, but the black creature blocked her.

This new creature was something that Avery did not recognize. It looked like a man dressed up in wolf's skin, with the jaws and head of a wolf. This one had a particular bald portion on the top of its head.

Holly screamed anew as six gnomes jumped on Holly. When they were finished Holly was completely trussed up. The gnomes were not the best at tying knots and so Holly was completely wrapped with ropes and unable to move.

The black creature now motioned at the rest of the students standing with gapping mouths.

"Ah, guys," Ferris started. "I don't think they are friendly."

"But the gnomes were friendly before," defended Avery.

Ruth tapped Avery's shoulder. "Not the ones that knocked me on the head and kidnapped Mr. Prig." Mr. Prig was their principal before their first trip to Afflatus. He had mistakenly been brought too, and they had left him in the mystical land.

"They are getting closer," said Jared. He turned to Andora. "What is that black creature?"

"I don't know," she replied. "But I agree with Ruth and Ferris. Those creatures could mean trouble for us."

"Where can we go?" asked Ruth.

Avery's vision scanned the plains. There was little in the way of cover. Before when they were fleeing the Agitates they went to the forest. Glancing in that direction she was in for another shock. A large black wall was separating the plains from the forest—that direction seemed impassable. Their only option was to flee into the ruins and hope to make a stand. After all, gnomes shouldn't be too hard to defeat.

"To the ruins," she ordered. "We might find some weapons to defend ourselves."

"Good thinking," added Jared. "I call dibs on the black thing."

Still a good distance off were the platoon of gnomes. They had left several gnomes to watch the captured Holly. The others fanned out in an attempt to herd the students towards the ruins.

Without further hesitation, the students bolted.

Jared was the first one to enter the ruins. Avery was close behind. She saw that it was still much the same on the inside. The ceiling was still collapsed and rubble dotted the area. There were no weapons to be seen. Ruth ran up to the dais where the thrones had once been, intent on being as far from battle action as possible. Ferris was not too far behind her.

Just as he reached the foot of the dais, Ferris tripped. Sprawling head over heals he landed with a thud at Ruth's feet. She glared down at him.

"Help me up," he asked. Holding out his hand.

Ruth braced herself by hanging on a torch holder and pulled Ferris to his feet. At the same moment she heard a clicking sound. Behind her the wall suddenly shifted.

Shocked, Ruth looked into the darkened doorway that had magically appeared. "Avery," she called out, "here is an exit."

The others rushed over.

"Too bad we didn't know this was here the first time," sighed Jared. He remembered having to run with two gnomes attached to his legs.

"I'll say," agreed Ferris. "After all, I was the one captured by the stupid Agitates."

Behind them they heard a growl and they all turned simultaneously. The platoon of gnomes and the black creature had entered the castle and were fast approaching.

"We are going to have to make a run for it," said Avery. "The only option I see is this dark hall—let's go!"

They darted into the dark corridor. Avery wondered how they would close the door behind them, but the dilemma resolved itself. Jared was the last one through the door, and he stepped on a cobblestone that clicked and suddenly the door dropped shut behind them, leaving them in complete darkness.

There was the faint sound of water running, and the scuffling of feet. But they could not see anything—it was darker than the darkest of nights back home.

"Can anyone see anything?" Ruth asked.

"What a stupid question!" mocked Jared. He was feeling uptight and some of his anger issues surfaced.

"We need to do something," said Andora. She had been strangely silent, but the tone of her voice now echoed fear.

"We need light," stated Avery. She felt along the sides of the walls and her fingers closed over a wooden-like substance with a papery texture near the top. "Hey, I think I found a torch. Anyone got a match?" She had meant to be sarcastic but suddenly a red flame pierced through the darkness and she could see shadows dancing around Jared's face as he held a light a few inches from his chin.

"This help?" he asked.

"Of course," she replied. "Where did you get a lighter?"

"It's none of your business," he replied his tone brisk. "If you need to know, my brother gave it to me."

"CJ?"

"Yes."

Avery was concerned. "You aren't using drugs or anything are you?" she asked, her tone was sharp. She remembered her father's addiction to booze and drugs and that was the last thing she would wish on even her worst enemy.

"None of your business. You don't even know what it's like."

"What? Using drugs? I sure do. I know that it makes you into someone that you aren't."

"Leave me alone!" Jared said loudly. He grabbed the torch out of Avery's hands and lit the top portion, instantly light flooded into the corridor.

They could see stonewalls heading downward into ever darkening gloom. The floor was cobblestone and they could see the faces of everyone there.

Ruth was feeling along the wall they had just come through, but could not find any evidence that a door was there. "We can't leave Holly captive to those creatures," she said quietly.

"Whatever, it's not like she was ever nice to us," said Jared. His face was still livid with rage. What right did Avery have to judge him? It was his life and he would do what he wanted to do!

"But that will be the second person we brought to Afflatus, mistakenly, and had them captured by gnomes."

"There is nothing we can do about it now," replied Avery. "If we go out there now, we will surely be captured too!"

"They are just gnomes," said Ferris. "I mean, how much trouble could they really be?"

"Well, now that you mention it," sighed Andora. "Gnomes can be a lot of trouble indeed."

The corridor headed in a steady downward direction. They stopped numerous times to take stock of the situation. Ferris remarked that they had to be a mile below the surface of the land at one point, which shocked Avery. Nothing of their surroundings changed as they walked, except that it was slowly getting warmer.

They had been walking for about half an hour when they saw a golden glow ahead in the tunnel. Heat was pouring out of the glow and it felt like they were walking into a sauna.

The closer they got to the light, the brighter it appeared. It was like a sun in the center of the world. Because they had been in the dark corridor for so long, the light was overwhelming and they had to shield their eyes.

Finally they reached the light and stepped into it. They entered a room that had walls of gold. On all corners of the room were shelves with various objects. Staffs and wands, stuffed rats, potted plants, statues of every manner of creature and marbles and rocks of many different sizes and shapes. At the very back of the room was a large fireplace, gold brick surrounding the hearth and a roaring fire cast out abundant heat. The ceiling was a dome and the gold bricks were what lighted the room, they were like light bulbs casting a radiant light.

Situated in the center of the room were four wooden tables. On the tables were parchments. Magically, feather pens floated over the dozen parchments, writing. They wrote without ceasing, floating over the paper. It was like invisible hands were writing a story.

Ferris intrigued by this magic made his way over to one parchment and started reading. His eyes grew large as he read.

"Guys," he said, "you got to come and see this!" he sounded excited.

They gathered around and Avery started reading at the top of the page:

Five young people entered the Record Keeper's Chamber. They stared at the various objects around the room. The one named Ferris approached the parchment and exclaimed, "Guys, you got to come and see this! The other young people gathered around....

Avery stopped reading. She was astonished.

Ferris pointed to the bottom of the page and just before he said it, the pen wrote: *The boy named Ferris said, "This pen writes it down before it happens!"* said Ferris.

Andora stood at Ferris' shoulder. "What an amazing observation Ferris," she said sweetly and the pen wrote it down.

Ruth felt jealousy creep up in her. She needed to say something to—at least try to get Ferris to acknowledge her again.

The pen wrote, just as Ruth said: "Ferris, you are really smart!" *said the girl named Ruth trying to win attention from the boy called the Rat.*

Ferris watched in fascination at the comment the pen made and then he looked up at Ruth. Ruth suddenly realizing what the pen must have written strode quickly over to Rat.

The pen wrote: *the girl named Ruth slapped the boy named Rat across the face.*

Rat looked up just as Ruth's hand careened across his cheek. The sting sent him staggering back and he decided that he didn't want to read anymore.

Avery was examining some of the other parchments, and they were recording many different stories. There was a method to the madness. The pens would stick with one story for a while before moving on to another—they wrote of people and places that Avery had never heard of before.

She had stopped paying attention to the others around her and was startled when a shadow moved from a wooden door to her left, which she hadn't noticed before.

A man exited. He was old, with wrinkled skin and white hair. He wore a goatee that came to a sharp point just below his chin and his eyes were sunken deep into his face. He had very large, very pointed ears; they reminded her of Yodda's ears from *Star Wars.*

He hobbled on a staff; his back was hunched over and he barely acknowledged the children in his chamber.

"Hello?" she asked approaching the man.

His deep, knowing eyes glanced at her. He did not smile.

"Who are you?" she asked.

"I am the Record Keeper," he said. His voice sounded like a whisper of the wind. "It is my station to record everything that happens in the world so that when the Creator returns to reclaim the creation, the Creator will know how to judge the faithful and the deceived."

"But these scrolls tell the future," Ferris interrupted coming over. Andora and Ruth were close behind.

The Keeper whispered again. "The future is a dangerous thing to know indeed. How can you change that which will definitely happen?" He turned to Ferris. "Knowing the slap was coming did not benefit you in any way—the knowledge did not keep the slap from taking place."

Ferris leaned in close. "How did you know about the slap?" he quizzed.

"I know many things."

Andora was a little less sure of the man. "Are you for good or evil?" she asked. "Do you support King Merrit or those that oppose him?"

The Keeper did not answer. He pointed at a fifth wooden table near the fireplace, a large, leather bound book lay opened, upon it. "It is my task to record the deeds of the world and file them into the Book of Life and Death."

"So you are neutral then? Not on any side?" asked Ruth.

"Now, now child, is it really possible to be completely neutral?"

No one had been paying attention to Jared. He had started exploring the room after Ferris had first found the enchantment of the parchment. Jared had found more interesting things. He started examining the objects placed haphazardly on the selves. There were small plaques explaining what each was. He picked up a marble, the plaque under it read: Coral Stone of Fear. He quickly put it down. His fingers brushed over many other objects until his gaze came to rest on a gnarled oak staff. The plaque stated: Staff of Terminus. Picking it up he walked over to where the others were standing.

Holding the staff out he showed it to the old man. "What is this staff for?" he asked.

Long fingers caressed the staff with loving care. "This is the Staff of Terminus. It has the magical ability to send you to any place that you have already been before."

"How does it work?"

"Beware because there are some that can use the magic found in staffs and wands, for others it is only a staff. Only if you have the magic, can it work."

"Why should we beware then? If you can't use it, you can't use it," Jared shrugged his shoulders.

The Keeper chuckled; it was soft, also like the whisper of the wind. "Magic doesn't just exist you know—it has to come from a source. All magic comes from the Creator. He made it all. However, those that practice Deception Magic have taken what was once good and turned into something unrecognizable.

"Magic that is good cannot be used with evil intentions. However, good magic can be hidden in Deception and used for evil."

Jared frowned and his face flushed slightly.

Avery was curious; she still didn't understand what magic was and how it worked. She was told she had Truth Magic; but what did that really mean?

"I hear your question," the Keeper whispered. "When the Creator made the worlds, they were created good. There was only good magic. Everything existed in a perfect balance of love and peace. However, the Creator does not make subjects, he wanted creation to be fluid, changing, adaptive and in order for it to be as such the Creator gave Choice. The root of all magic is Choice. The very soul of your person is Choice."

"That doesn't really make sense," Ferris said. "Sometimes we make good choices and other times bad. It still doesn't explain how magic works.

"Magic has always been dependent upon the user. The Creator has blessed some with abilities stronger than others. When your Choice is to use Deception Magic, it gives the illusion of power, but in reality to use the Truth Magic is far more powerful, it depends on faith and believing it is truth."

"But why is there Deception Magic anyway?" quizzed Ferris. "I mean, if there was no evil, than we would never do the wrong thing?"

The old man chuckled softly. "In the beginning, when the Creator made the worlds, heaven and earth, it was good— but the problem is, he gave all creatures the ability to choose and it is because of that, the first people made the mistake of breaking oath and were lead astray by a celestial being that desired to replace the Creator."

The man hobbled over to one of the parchments. The pen was reaching the bottom of the page. Pulling another piece of paper from a stack of blanks on the corner of the table he replaced the parchment and then hobbled over to the leather bound book. After flipping though several pages he placed the parchment into the bind. A light flashed and when it had dissipated the page was sealed in the book.

"Once a page is in the book, it is there forever, only the Creator can take pages out. Only the Creator has the magic powerful enough to remove those things we have done and the Creator will only do so after judgment.

"You see, I keep record of all Choice made. Sometimes Choice infringes on the rights of others and it causes others pain. The Creator wants everyone free to use Choice, and that is why there is pain in the world. Until the Creator comes to judge all Choice—there will be those that suffer because of some Choice people make."

"So what is Truth Magic?" asked Avery. "I keep being told it is the most powerful form of magic that humans can possess; but I cannot do anything without help, like the Seeker Stone."

"That is the greatest Truth of all!" the old man whispered softly. "That magic is the ability to not be led astray by Deception. What more power could you ask for?"

Avery felt the sweat dripping down her face. It was still confusing and she was getting very warm. It was time to leave. The room was too hot. Turning back to the old man she asked. "Is there a way for us to get out of here? We need to get to Bogmarsh and find King Merrit."

A gnarled finger pointed to the door he had entered from. "Exit through there and you will escape the Menas that is chasing you."

"The Menas?"

"The black wolf. It was man once, but Deception Magic has turned it into something much more terrifying. Beware of the Menas! Beware of the Deception Magic that covers the land. Find the Jester and he will direct your way."

"Again we have to find the Jester," stated Ruth. "Seems like we are always looking for that guy."

"Come on," Avery motioned the others.

They headed out the door and immediately the temperature cooled. There was another corridor leading back up, but this one was lit with small gems in the ceiling that cast a reddish glow around them. They had only walked for ten minutes when they came to a base of stairs. Since the only direction was up, that's the way they went.

Before long they came to a wooden door with a golden engraved handle. Pushing with all their might they opened the door and stepped onto the plains. The door stood in the middle of the plains, there was nothing around it, it was just a door, and as they closed it, it disappeared altogether, and they were alone on the plains. Far to the south they could make out the husky shape of the ruins.

"We still have a long way to go, before we get to Bogmarsh," Avery stated.

"Not if we use this," replied Jared triumphantly. He was holding the Staff of Terminus.

Avery was shocked and suddenly very afraid. "You stole the staff!" she yelled.

CHAPTER NINE

Truth, crushed to earth, shall rise again

-William Cullen Bryant,

The Battlefield, st. 9 [1839]

"I can't believe you took the staff! What were you thinking?" Avery said again.

"He obviously wasn't," Rat remarked with a sneer.

Jared glared at the two that seemed to be ganging up on him. But he didn't say anything.

Andora saddled up close to Jared and admired the staff. "I think that it was a brilliant idea," she said.

Ferris quickly came and stood next to Andora. "I guess we could find it useful, hey?" he changed his tune quickly, suddenly sounding much nicer.

"How does it work?" asked Ruth.

Avery stared at all of her companions. She couldn't believe what she was hearing. All of them seemed to support the idea of using a stolen magical item.

"I don't know," said Jared.

"We have to return it," Avery interjected. "It isn't right that you stole something that doesn't belong to you."

"I didn't steal it. It was just sitting there..." he trailed off.

"You don't take a chocolate bar from a store shelf, that is just sitting there," she replied huffy.

Andora was still looking closely at the staff. "I wonder if it takes everyone or just the person holding it?"

"It doesn't matter, we aren't using it," said Avery. She stormed over to where Jared was standing, holding the staff and grabbed it from his grip.

He wasn't prepared for the assault, "Hey!"

"We are taking it back to the Keeper, guy!"

"I suppose you know where that is?" Jared smirked.

Avery turned around and remembered that the door had disappeared. And since they didn't dare go back to the ruins incase the gnome warriors and the Menas (as it had been called) was till waiting for them. As she was holding it she felt a tickling sensation flowing through the wood into her a hand. Startled she held up the staff to look at it. Letters started to appear around the head of the gnarled staff, they were brazen orange and made the staff look like it was on fire.

The words said: Seekers find that which was lost, Courage treads on paths previously crossed. Love and Wisdom will oft make the right Choice, Terminus needs to hear your voice.

"Think about it," Jared said after Avery repeated what was written on the staff. "It would be so much nicer if we could get to Bogmarsh right now, rather than walk all the way there."

"But this is stolen!" Avery was adamant.

Ruth leaned in closer to her friend. "We could just use it and return it when we are finished," she offered. She also liked the idea of being magically transported to Bogmarsh.

Avery thought for a moment. She didn't like the idea of using the staff because they had taken it without permission, however, on the other hand it would make it much easier to travel around Afflatus, if they could go to places they had already been to.

"Okay," she said at last. "We will use the staff, but we have to return it before we leave Afflatus," she added, "I sure hope that the Keeper doesn't hold it against us."

"So how does it work?" Ferris asked. "The writing said something about the staff needing to hear your voice. Is that just your voice, or is that everyone's voice?"

Andora added, "What would happen if everyone said something different?"

"Good question," Rat congratulated resting his arm briefly on Andora's shoulder. He quickly moved it suddenly aware that he was touching her.

"I think that everyone should be touching the staff," said Ruth. "We don't want to leave anyone behind."

Nodding heads in ascent they all took a place around the staff and everyone took a hold of it. The letters still glowed brilliantly orange. "Okay, where do we want to go to?" asked Avery.

"Bogmarsh," Andora replied.

"So, we should all say, Bogmarsh together," suggested Avery. "I hope this works."

On the count of three all the young people said, "Bogmarsh." But nothing happened.

They were still all standing on the plain glancing from one confused face to another. "Well that obviously didn't work," stated Jared.

"All the writing must be a clue somehow," Avery said. "But it doesn't make sense."

"Maybe we just have to be more specific," stated Ferris. "I mean; Bogmarsh is a pretty big place. What place have we all been to in Bogmarsh?" he asked.

"I don't know," Avery said. "The first time we were there, you weren't with us. We spent time at Benik's tavern and the prison to rescue Dragonfreed."

Ferris smiled, "I was at both those places too. Though, when I was at the prison I was actually a prisoner, no thanks to you guys," he sputtered on the last comment.

"It wasn't our fault the Agitate took you and dropped you in the river," Jared defended. "If the gnome hadn't fed us Agitate eggs, everything would have been fine."

"But things worked out, didn't they," Avery jumped into the conversation. "I mean everyone played a role in defeating Queen Quagmire."

"So are we going to try this thing, or what?" asked Andora trying to bring everyone back to the task at hand.

"So should we go to the prison?" asked Avery.

"I'd rather not," said Ferris. "How about we go to Benik's tavern?"

"Good. But what was the name of it?" asked Jared.

"The Poop Deck," Andora said. "The king has been there many times and it has become quite the hubbub."

Again on the count of three all the young people said, "The Poop Deck." Again, nothing happened.

"We might have to walk after all," shrugged Ruth in disappointment.

"I thought for sure that would work," said Avery.

"We are still missing a step," Ferris added. "Wait, maybe we just have to address the staff. It might not know we are talking to it."

Jared scoffed, "That is ridiculous, a staff doesn't think and it doesn't hear. Magic is magic, it should know the difference."

"Actually you might be on to something," Avery said. "There are always rules to magic. In this case the staff has to know we are asking it to do something. Otherwise, if you were holding the staff and you said any place you had been to before then it would take you there. The staff needs to hear specific directions."

"Good idea, so we just have to say, 'Staff of Terminus, take us to The Poop Deck!' and it will do it!" agreed Jared.

The moment all of them said the magic words, they felt a sensation like they were being sucked up a straw. They could still look around, but the world looked roundish. They started to move and they could see everything moving past them in a blur. They flew past the ruins and saw the dark forms of the Menas and the gnomes still searching for the missing young people. The grass flew by under them like an ocean wave. Had anyone looked up they would not have seen them, the watcher would only feel a slight breeze on his or her face.

The young people soared over the Divide River and past the turnpike until they saw the walls of Bogmarsh approaching. A large army of gnomes could be seen encamped around the city. There appeared to be thousands upon thousands of them. Suddenly the staff lifted them up over the walls and they came to an abrupt stop in front of the tavern, The Poop Deck.

They landed as they had been standing on the plains. But their hair was muffed and matted like they had been in a windstorm. Jared's face was a shade of red, he had been wind burnt. They all immediately started to straighten their clothing, as shirts and pants had been twisted around their bodies during the flight.

"That was fun!" Jared cooed. "Let's do it again. Where else can we go? We could go to the northern mountains, the Bevypolis caves!" he said enthusiastically.

Ferris was bent over and holding his knees. He looked like he might be sick. "I don't think so," he said in reply to Jared. "I hate flying, and that was too close to flying for me!"

"Don't puke here!" Ruth stated. "That'll make me feel sick too!"

"Just a moment," he said. "That's all I need!"

Avery was admiring The Poop Deck. The tavern had a fresh coat of lime green paint, her favorite color. The trim was also newly painted a soft brown and the sign was brand new. In bold red letters under 'The Poop Deck' it read: The King's choice!

"Benik must be doing very well," said Avery.

Standing in front of the entrance were two soldiers. Avery didn't recognize either of them. They wore silver chain mail, and had spears crossed, blocking the entrance. Their helmets looked Roman and they wore tanned, leather slacks with thigh guards. On the chain mail was a picture of a dragon (it reminded her of Incubus) holding a black sword.

Avery turned to Andora, "Why did King Merrit choose the dragon as his emblem? It seems so evil."

Andora nodded her head. "It isn't used to show the heart of his kingdom, rather, he chose the dragon so that he would never forget what had happened to him, and so that the people would always remember what happens when evil takes control."

"The dragon is holding the Nightshade," stated Jared. The Nightshade was a black sword that Dragonfreed had used to stab the dragon. The cursed blood of the dragon had seeped into the metal sword, also making it a thing of evil. Jared remembered how Dragonfreed, the original owner of the blade had given it to him. Dragonfreed had sacrificed himself so that the others could heal Avery and free the land of Afflatus—he had been trying to earn his salvation even to his death. Jared hoped that the man had done enough.

Avery made a move for the front door but the soldier on the left halted her. "No one may enter, the king is present," he said.

"But we are here to see the king," Avery said. "I'm sure that if you tell King Merrit that we are here, he will let us in."

"I am not supposed to leave my post," he said sternly. "And I am under orders to let no one enter."

Jared growled, "Listen don't you know who we are? We saved your bacon last year! Let us through!"

The guard, not aware of the student's idiom replied. "Saved our bacon?" he was confused. "I don't remember having any bacon."

"What is bacon?" the other guard asked. "I didn't know that it needed saving!"

Jared was confounded.

Andora stepped forward. "You know me," she said. "I am a personal envoy of the king, you must let me through. They are with me!"

The guard eyed her. "I don't know. Just one moment."

The guard opened the door and peeked his head in. "Sir Benik!" he called. The students heard a familiar rumble of a voice inside. "There are some wee ones here to see the king. What should we do?"

"Wee ones!" Benik yelled.

A moment later the head of Benik came to the door. He was much larger than Avery remembered him. His hair had turned a gray color and his belly protruded so far in front of him she was surprised that he didn't fall over!

"Avery! Ruth! Jared!" he roared. "How are ye?" He opened his arms and took all of them in a giant bear hug. Ferris was standing a bit back. Benik let go of the others and glanced at Ferris. "Little Rat!" he said. "I remember ye too! Come give me an 'ug!" Ferris blushed slightly and relented. The big man's arms wrapped around him and Ferris was momentarily lost in the hairy arms.

Stepping back he said, "These are my friends. They are safe," he assured the soldiers. They pulled back the spears and the young people followed Benik into the tavern.

The inside of the tavern was drastically different. The chairs had all been replaced with padded booths and the tables had a beautiful finish and fancy designs engraved onto the legs. Small candles decorated the center of each table. The bar had stools lining it along with nice glassware hanging from racks just above the bartender's head. A woman in her twenties stood behind the counter, she was as tall as Benik, but far slimmer and more beautiful.

"This is my daughter, Joslyn, she runs the tavern for the most part now," he said. "Do ye like what she has done with the place?"

Joslyn nodded at the newcomers and then went back to wiping down the counter.

"It is beautiful," said Ruth staring all around.

"And we have special meetin' rooms upstairs," added Benik. "We have had very important visitors. The King often comes here when he is making special appointments. Needless to say, it has been very good for business."

There was a pause as he looked up a set of stairs leading to the second level. "The king is here now," he said in hushed voice.

Suddenly Avery started to feel it. There was tension in the air, a calm before the storm. "What is happening?" she asked.

Benik led them to a table, and motioned them to sit down, "The king will wait a moment," he said. They sat down and Benik joined them. "I am glad to see you again," he started, "but you have arrived at troubled times again. There is a gnome army, led by a Menas, parked just outside the walls of Bogmarsh. You must have seen them when you arrived."

Avery nodded her head.

"Why are the gnomes attacking Bogmarsh?" Ruth asked. "Bigwig isn't part of it, is he?"

"No," Benik replied and the children sighed in relief. "He is outside attempting to discuss a treaty with the gnome general, Fusty Pungent."

"Is he in any danger?" Jared asked. The gnomes were not his favorite of people, but he was still concerned about Bigwig.

Benik shook his head. "No, Torrent and Lumpy are with him and his majesty made Bigwig promise to stay behind the gates. Besides, Torrent is quite formidable when she wants to be. At least that helps keep the gnomes in tow, a little."

"We will do what we have to, to help," said Avery. "That is why we came."

"The king has a lot on his plate and the Jester has been the King's number one advisor." Benik paused again. "There are a few other nobles also in the war room," Benik began. "I would be careful what ye say around them."

"Why?" asked Ferris.

"Well, Merrit seems to trust them well enough. But they were never that supportive of the Bevypolis, during the reign of Quagmire. In fact, they silently went about their own business rather than oppose her. But his majesty says he needs the support of the nobles if he wants to maintain control of the kingdom. After the common people overthrow one dictator, they believe that they can do it again, and they may be pickier the second time around. Someone has to keep the masses in line."

"Why don't they just form a democracy?" asked Ruth. "That is how our country is governed."

"How is that any different than a monarchy," Benik asked. "Do ye still have the rich and the poor?"

"Yes."

"And do the rich still control most of what happens in the country?"

"Yes."

"And are there more rich people than common, or workers?"

"No."

"So basically, yer system of government is exactly the same as a monarchy. Ye just believe that ye have some control because ye decide who will lead ye. But no matter what system of government is in control, someone is having their ideals, their freedoms, and their rights infringed upon."

"But we choose based on what a leader can do for us."

"And that is a better way?" asked Benik. "When there is a benevolent king the people are happy and the nation flourishes and all people have a better life. Of course the reverse is also true. However, as we experienced with Quagmire, the people's needs still need to be met and when they are not, they revolt. If Quagmire had cared more about the people, and made sure all their basic needs were met; I bet it would have been more difficult to get people to rebel against her."

There was silence around the table. Finally Benik stood up. "Ye should go and see the king now. Just remember what I said; beware what ye say around the nobles. I think that they also may have ambitions—remember, people ultimately will only look out for their own interests. There is an inherent selfishness in human beings and these nobles are no different. They want something too; we only need to know what."

CHAPTER TEN

Soon spreads the dismal shade
-William Blake, The Human Abstract [1794]

The war room King Merrit established on the second floor of The Poop Deck, looked like a regular conference room. A large round table with oak wood chairs around it, dominated the room.

Avery entered first and when her eyes first fell on the young king she inhaled sharply. His black wavy hair framed his face nicely and when his stunning eyes rested their gaze on her she suddenly felt weak in the knees. The young king was the epitome of grace and beauty.

Jared watched with narrowed eyes and his right fist unconsciously clenched.

Sitting around the table were four other people, the Jester and three others that Avery did not recognize.

The moment King Merrit saw Avery he circled the table and took a hold of her hand. Getting down on one knee he said, "My lady, it is my honor to have you join us, here at our greatest hour."

Avery blushed and Jared stepped forward between Avery and the king, breaking the grasp.

He said, "No need to propose to her," muttering.

Merrit brushed off the snub and introduced all the others around the table. When he was finished he returned to the head of the table, where a large map of Bogmarsh and the surrounding area had been set up.

He pointed to the northern gate. "Most of the gnome army is parked in front of these gates. We have seen several Menas around; they seem to be in command. They haven't surrounded us yet, and that troubles me. So, we have concentrated our troops at this gate as well."

Ferris stepped next to the King and Baron Cache clucked loudly. No one should presume to stand next to the king. Merrit didn't even notice.

Ferris began, "Has any one figured out why the gnomes are revolting?"

Suddenly Jared started laughing and few others joined in.

"Because they don't bathe," Jared said, still chuckling.

It took the Jester a moment to catch the joke and suddenly he started laughing, so loudly that it filled the room and he kept repeating, "why the gnomes are revolting, revolting! Because they don't bathe, they are revolting!" Everyone laughed loudly, partly because the Jester's laugh was funny to listen to.

Finally Rat restated, "What I meant to say, is why are the gnomes attacking Bogmarsh?"

The Jester would let a few chuckles out at intervals, he said, "That isn't the primary concern. Our army here can deal with the gnomes as it stands. I am more concerned about a darkness that has covered the Taboo Forest. The darkness is hiding some evil goings-on. We need the Truth Seer to go on a quest. She is the only one that will be able to see through the darkness and make it disappear."

"How am I supposed to do that?" Avery asked. She hadn't really been able to use the magic since arriving in Afflatus. "I don't even know if I can do the magic anymore."

"You have just lost your way. But never fear, it will come when you need it to," the Jester said.

Ruth noticed for the first time that one of the nobles was staring at them with hard eyes. The King had introduced him as Creed, Gandar Creed. She felt a fear start to tingle in her stomach and quickly darted her gaze elsewhere in the room.

Merrit spoke again. "I have asked these young people here because they are the ones that freed me from Quagmire's curse. I trust them—"

"You should trust your subjects more," Gandar growled softly.

Merrit ignored the remark. "Nevertheless the Jester has told me about a magical object that the Seer can use to dissipate the darkness."

"It is the Seerer Mirror," the Jester finished. "It is a magical device that contains powerful magic, it shows the looker the truth about the Choice he or she makes or has made."

"How is that supposed to get rid of the darkness?" asked Ferris.

The Jester continued, his voice suddenly darker. "Darkness hides the truth. Deception magic is powerful and only through the bearer of the Deception seeing the truth about themselves, and then makes a Choice to go a different way, will the darkness subside."

"What if the person in control of the darkness does not make a different Choice?" asked Avery.

"Than the Truth magic will cut him or her to the quick so intensely, they will either live by making the right choice, or die because once the truth is known, it can not be hidden again."

"It still doesn't make sense," said Ruth.

The Jester rested his arm on her shoulder. "Everything comes clear in the end. Those that travel with the Seerer must also beware. Everyone must pass through the cleansing fire before the Truth about others can be seen. You cannot judge, until you have been judged."

"What does that mean?" Ruth was very confused. "So all of us have to go through some cleansing fire?"

"No," the Jester replied. "Only three of you will go on this journey. Torrent, Avery and Jared," the Jester said.

"Four," Merrit interrupted. "I am also going with them."

"Why Torrent?" Ferris asked, his voice sounded hurt. "And what about Ruth and me?"

"Torrent has been chosen because the Seerer Mirror is hidden in the Kingdom of Giants. The giants are not unfriendly to humans, but they will not allow humans into the kingdom unless a giant speaks for them."

Avery remembered from their first time in Afflatus that Torrent had been found by a fisherman from Haddock Village on Lake Sagacity. But the young giant didn't have a clue where she was from. "How will she know where to go?"

The Jester cleared his throat. "She will have to return to Haddock with you and ask her father—he can tell you on which mountain he found her."

"Why don't you just tell us where to go?" asked Jared. "You seem to know everything?"

The Jester laughed. "I am not God. I see visions and paths that are set out, but I do not know the future, nor am I omniscient. All I see is the way for you to go. The Creator is the only one that knows the future. I am aware of paths and when I look at each of you I know that you have decisions to make, your Choice, is what dictates what the outcome is going to be."

Jenna Safeguard had been sitting quietly listening to the conversation. When the King had said he was also going she had frowned. Now she felt was an opportunity to speak. She said, "I do not think that his majesty should go on this quest. He has a responsibility to the people."

"I agree," said Cache. His black hair was pulled back into a long braid and it whipped onto the table as he joined in. "It is dangerous for him to go."

The Jester paused and closed his eyes. When he opened them again he said, "The king must also make his Choice." He shifted his gaze to meet Merrit's. "Make sure that you go on this quest for the right reasons."

Merrit glanced at Avery, briefly, only Avery and Jared caught it and he said, "If this quest is to the land of the giants, I should go and meet them—call it a diplomatic mission."

The Jester nodded sadly. "Very well, the Choice is set."

Jenna cut in, "Who is going to lead the army here?"

"Earo," Merrit said without hesitation.

"But what about executive decisions? Who makes the decisions?" Gandar asked.

Merrit thought for a moment. "All decisions must be run through the Jester."

This statement was met with grumbling from the nobles, even Safeguard. Avery noticed that Gandar's hard stare turned on the Jester.

The Jester said, "It is a responsibility I do not wish to have. But I will retain the position until the King returns or dies."

"So what about us?" Ruth asked, pointing between her and Ferris. "What role do we play in all of this?"

The Jester chuckled, "As Ferris put it so efficiently—you are going to find out why the gnomes are revolting."

"Huh?" said Rat.

"It is imperative that you find out what has happened to Gnomedom. The gnomes are generally harmless folk and there must be some dark magic happening to them. As well, it will give you an opportunity to find the other person you brought to Afflatus the first time."

"Mr. Prig!" said Ferris. "Of course, we need to find him."

"You are forgetting about Holly," stated Ruth.

"Who?" asked the Jester.

"Holly," she continued, "she somehow was brought here too. But the ugly creature and a dozen gnomes took her prisoner."

Jared shook his head and sighed, "Why do the gnomes keep taking people we bring to this land accidently?"

Avery was silent for a moment before saying, "I don't like Holly at all, but we failed to find Mr. Prig, we can't leave her or Mr. Prig here, it just wouldn't be nice."

"Are you sure?" Jared was hesitant.

"About what?" Avery asked.

Jared continued, "I know that Miss Creant is not much better than him, but if he is returned we will have detention for the rest of our lives."

Ruth was horrified, "How can you say such a thing? He is still a person, with family and friends (though I'm not sure who would want to be friends with him) and that means we have to do the right thing."

"I'm going with them," Andora said quickly, moving next to Ferris.

Ruth's face fell, but she quickly smiled again so that no one noticed.

"Very well," the Jester replied. "Rescue the principal and the girl; however, I would hope that an adult would go with them, but Earo is unavailable now." The comment wasn't directed per se at Merrit.

"We can manage," Rat said. "We have been here before."

Ruth wasn't so sure, "Yes, but Earo or Dragonfreed were with us most of the time."

"And you have no one that can use weapons," added Jared. "At least Avery and I can use a sword."

The room fell silent as everyone stared at the table, as if it would enlighten them all. Baron Cache suddenly rose from his seat. "Fine!" he grunted. "I'll go and be the babysitter." His tone was abrasive. "I don't know why you trust children to do these great things. How can they handle any of it? You need warriors and wizards; these kids are nothing."

Ferris nearly choked. Suddenly the prospect of a journey with an adult, especially one that didn't like them, seemed unbearable. At least he would get to be with Andora. He smiled in her direction.

A loud knock on the door interrupted the conversation. Immediately following the knock the door opened and a tall, lanky blond hair man entered the room, he was breathing rather heavily. His eyes were wild and his forehead was perspiring, as if he had run a marathon.

"My lord," he said, panting. "I am glad I found you." He swallowed a gulp of air. "You have to come, immediately!"

"Where?" asked Merrit approaching the man with his hand held out.

"To the wall."

"What is happening at the wall?" he asked. He grabbed his maroon cloak sitting over the back of the chair and rushed to follow the man.

"Bigwig! The gnome! Stupid!" The man was sputtering.

Jared piped up, "We know the gnome Bigwig is stupid, what has he done?"

Merrit rested his hand on Jared's shoulder. "Come, friends, let's go and find out what our small boney friend is up too!" Merrit did not seem too concerned about whatever it was Bigwig was doing.

They left The Poop Deck and headed to the front gate. It took them only a moment to arrive. Immediately they saw Earo standing, speaking with a dark skinned man, his arms moved as he spoke, but they could not hear what was being said. He appeared upset.

Turning Earo saw the students and he quickly smiled before making a beeline for the King.

"Your majesty," Earo started. "I tried to stop the fool, but he disobeyed a direct order. I should have him hung from the nearest beam for such dishonor."

"What has he done?" asked Merrit. He took a hold of Earo's flailing arms and tried to calm him down.

"The gnome, at this very moment is outside the gate, facing the attacking army, trying to reason with them."

"He is what?" for the first time since they received the news Merrit's face changed to a look of horror.

"Yes!" replied Earo. "He said that he will try gnomeloonacy, which I have to guess is a version of diplomacy. But you can imagine what he is going to say. If we don't stop him he could give away half the kingdom with a single nod. Or worse, he could tick them off and start an attack. So far the gnome army has been content to just park out front our gates. But if they attack we don't have the man power to hold the wave back."

"Is he alone in this?" asked Merrit.

"No!" Earo was more horrified than before. "He took Lumpy and Torrent with him. With our luck the second little thief will try to lift something and tick off the army again. As for the giant, she is the only sane one out there. But she is an easy target. I wouldn't want her to get shot with a stray arrow because her gnome friends say or do the wrong thing."

"Open the gate," ordered Merrit.

"My lord," one of the guards replied; he raised one eyebrow in question.

"We have to talk the G³ back behind the walls," said Merrit.

"G³?" asked Avery.

"You know, G to the power of three—Gnome, Gnome and Giant! That is the name that we gave their silly tribe."

"I think it is cute," smiled Ruth.

The gate was partially swung open and Merrit started for the opening. "My lord," said Earo stepping in front of the king. "You cannot go out there unattended. They might attack."

Merrit hesitated, "We don't want to appear like a threat," he said. "Very well, Avery and Jared will accompany me. Someone give them swords."

Two sabers were handed to Avery and Jared; they sheathed them at their belts and followed Merrit through the gate.

As soon as they were clear of the town walls they could hear Bigwig talking. He was standing next to Torrent and

Lumpy. Torrent's shadow covered the two gnomes and her gaze shifted steadily. In her hand she held a stone club. She had grown up in the year passed. Her blond hair was tied in a braid down her back, it looked thicker than a rope, and she wore slacks, specially made from several cowhides.

Lumpy's gaze was narrow as he glared at the gnome army. It made him look rather funny. In his hand was a stuffed mouse.

Bigwig was wearing a soldier's uniform, but it was covered in dirt. As he spoke he paced to and fro with his arms resting on his hips.

Bigwig was saying, "My fellow gnomes. Beholdeth—"

Avery turned to Merrit, "Beholdeth?"

"He thinks old tongue makes him sound smarter," the king shrugged.

Bigwig continued uninterrupted, "I am one of you. I walk on the same grass, with the same feet and eat the same food. Whatsoever doth thou thinketh you art doing?" Avery stifled a chuckle.

"By what gnomenal idea doth thou attacketh this cityith?"

"Cityith?" whispered Avery, stunned.

Merrit took a hold of Avery's shoulder and pointed to the ranks of the gnome army. They did not appear to be paying any attention to G^3. Rather, they could see a Menas ushering troops to the line. They moved quickly upon the appearance of the king through the gate. Gnome archers were moving into position.

"They will be killed," stated Avery.

Merrit nodded his head and placed his hands next to his mouth, "Bigwig! Lumpy! Torrent!" he hollered.

Bigwig stopped mid-sentence.

"Get over here," ordered the king.

"You interrupted a very good speech. I think I was reaching them," stated Bigwig. Lumpy nodded his head enthusiastically.

The moment he saw Jared, Lumpy dropped his stuffed mouse and ran, arms out in front of him directly to Jared's feet and hugged the boy's leg.

"Get off of me!" Jared said kicking his leg. But Lumpy held on with all his might. His eyes were closed and it looked like he was hugging his favorite pet. He would even occasionally pet Jared's leg.

"We have to go," said Merrit pointing to the archers.

"But I haven't finished my speech yet," Bigwig sulked.

"I don't think they want to hear it. They are getting ready to fire upon us!" Avery said.

They could see the archers fixing arrows to strings.

"We got to go now!" ordered Merrit.

Torrent picked up Bigwig and started running for the main gate. Avery and Merrit followed close behind.

Jared was a little slower; Lumpy still clung to his leg. "Get off me little pest, you're going to get us both killed!" As he ran he tried to knock the gnome off, but Lumpy held on even though his head would hit Jared's knee with every step.

The sound of a hundred hummingbirds sounded behind them. Glancing back Jared saw the arrows soaring through the air. With a burst of pressure he launched himself through the gate. Two guards with shields stepped in front of the opening and he heard the sound of arrows bouncing off the shields and sticking in the wood of the gates.

Breathing a sigh of relief he stood up. Lumpy still hanging on to him like nothing else mattered.

CHAPTER ELEVEN

A journey of a thousand miles must begin with a single step

-Lao-tzu, The Way of Lao-tzu

They retired to the war room above The Poop Deck. Baron Cache took aside Ferris, Ruth and Andora; he wanted to get them ready for their journey into Gnomedom. The Baron was polite, but every time one of the children looked at them he got a sulky look on his face.

Merrit, Avery and Jared sat on one side of the table facing the Jester on the other. The other nobles returned to their mansions in the city.

The three young people waited for Bigwig, Lumpy and Torrent to show up. After rescuing the trio from certain death, they had been taken aside by Earo, who was giving Bigwig an earful about obeying orders; after all, the gnome was part of the King's forces.

Waiting in silence, Jared's eyes darted around the war room. His gaze rested on the Nightshade, the sword given to him by Dragonfreed, the first time he had been in Afflatus.

He was curious why the King had hung it on the wall. The blade unsheathed and dark as night. The unique aspect of the blade was it did not reflect anything, not light, nor image.

Merrit saw where Jared looked. "You can take it back," he said, breaking the silence. "I had it mounted so that I would always remember the curse that I had been under."

Jared stood and walked around the table. Reaching up he took a hold of the blade. It felt good in his hands. The blade whirred as he whipped it through the air. Taking the sheath from the wall as well he slid the sword home. Sighing contentedly he returned to his seat.

They heard Bigwig before they saw him.

He was saying. "I want to see them now!" he demanded in excited tones. "I haven't seen them forever!" he said.

Another voice replied, "I'm hardly sure it has been forever," a grumpy Earo replied. He sounded tired.

"But, but, but, where are they? Come on, we have to hurry now!"

"You'll see them soon enough."

The door opened and Earo entered with Bigwig, Lumpy and Torrent in tow. Bigwig, seeing Avery and the others pushed past the soldier and grabbed a hold of Avery's hand and started to dance around her, in circles.

"You came back—Oh, happy day!" he giggled.

Lumpy immediately returned to clutching Jared's leg. The boy tried to shake the gnome off once, but immediately gave up and sat down. Torrent had to duck in the room and sat in a chair in the far corner. She was too big for the chair and her knees almost came up to her chin. Resting her elbows on her thighs, she tried to look lady like—but only looked like an adult sitting in a child's chair.

The Jester cleared his throat. His head moved in a circular fashion (Jared said it made the joker look retarded) and he clapped his hands together. "We must decide, now that we're here, where to search for the Mirror. Safely tucked in a giant's cave—the Seerer Mirror will us it save. Torrent is the one to lead the way—If it not her the others will stray."

Torrent's head jerked up at the mention of her name. "I have to lead?" she was shocked. "I don't know where Giantland is."

The Jester replied; his speech often diverged between his crazy riddling and normal language. "You have to return to where your father found you in the mountains. From there you will find your way."

Bigwig jumped up. "An adventure! I love adventures! It will be just like last time, except Queen Quagmire won't be around, and the Dragon Incubus won't be chasing us," he glanced briefly at King Merrit, "Oops."

Jared and Merrit both equally got strained looks on their faces. Merrit remembered being the cursed beast and Jared remembered almost being killed by it. Merrit cleared his throat. "Ah, yeah. Um, Bigwig," he started.

"Yes," the bouncing gnome said, bounding over.

"I don't know if you will be joining us on this mission."

Bigwig instantly stopped bouncing. "Huh?"

Merrit glanced around the room and his gaze rested on Earo. Earo was shaking his hands and arms in a wild fashion to tell Merrit not to leave the gnome under his care.

Merrit continued, "Well you see, I have a very important task for you. It is imperative that you accomplish this mission."

"Imperative?" Bigwig's eyes misted up.

"Really important," Merrit clarified. "You see; you are the best gnome for the job."

"I'm just the gnome," a little of the bounce returned to his voice.

"Yes, I need a gnome to peel potatoes for the army and all the people in Bogmarsh. Without you the whole town could go hungry and starve to death." his voice dripped with sarcasm.

"Without me the people are going to starve?" his voice was in awe. "Well, I will do it. I will be the best potato peeler in the land. I will peel mounds of potatoes and slice 'em and dice 'em too. The people will not starve while Bigwig is on the job!" he puffed out his chest and saluted.

"I'm glad to hear it," sighed Merrit.

"Although," Bigwig continued, "What is an adventure without a gnome on it? I will leave my trusty first mate to travel with you. Lumpy, will be the gnometector."

Jared's face fell even further.

Bigwig continued unabated. "He is a good first mate."

Merrit swallowed, "Are you sure," his voice pleaded. "Can you go for a while without him; don't you think you will miss him too much!" he suddenly sounded hopeful that Bigwig might retract his offer.

Bigwig clasped Lumpy's shoulders, "I will dearly miss my best mate, er I mean, first mate. But you need him more than I."

Jared coughed in his hand, "More like extra baggage."

"Hmmm?" asked Bigwig.

"Nothing."

"Well, okay, if you insist," Merrit sighed again.

Avery tapped her fingers on the table. "So in order to find out where Giantland is, we need to find Torrent's adopted father. He is the only person that knows where Torrent was found and he can point us in the right direction."

Jared looked at the Terminus Staff at Avery's side. "Can we use that? It brought us here, maybe it can bring us there too."

The Jester shook his head and Avery answered. "The staff of Terminus can only take us to places that we have all been to before. Since only Torrent and none of us have ever been to the town of Haddock, we cannot travel using the staff." The Jester nodded in agreement.

Frowning, Merrit said, "That means that we are likely going to be followed by gnome soldiers and even more likely a Menas."

"If we leave in the middle of the night, we should be able to sneak away unawares," offered Avery.

Jared slid the Nightshade free from its sheath. "Running and hiding is for cowards. I say that we just fight our way out. Who cares if they try to follow us, we will deal with them as we will." He talked much bigger now that he felt he had more training with a sword.

Merrit frowned. "That could be very dangerous. If the gnome army thinks that I have left the city, it might spur them on and attack sooner—before we can return with the Seerer Mirror."

Jared shrugged and spoke what the Jester was thinking. "So maybe you should stay here and just Avery, Lumpy, Torrent and I go. The fewer people that are traveling—the better."

Merrit smiled over at Avery. "I wouldn't leave Avery to travel on her own. I would give anything to be her traveling companion." Avery blushed but did not reply.

Jared sneered, but quickly covered the look—no need to look like some jealous two-year-old. "Whatever," he said.

"So it is decided, we leave tonight," stated Merrit. "I will make sure that we have several packs ready with supplies, as well as weapons and clothing. In the meantime, Avery and Jared, if you want to change out of your world clothes, I can have some slacks, jerkins and boots ready for you. You can use the guest quarters in my palace in the city."

They were just about to dismiss and go their separate ways when the door opened and Ferris, Ruth, Andora and Duke Cache entered. They were all dressed in traveling clothes, with packs on their shoulders and green cloaks. Ferris and Ruth were equipped with daggers at their belts, and Andora and Duke Cache carried swords. The duke's sword was strapped across his back, under his pack; Andora wore her sword at her hip.

Ruth stepped over to Avery and gave her a hug. "We are leaving and I just had to say good-bye. Since both of us are heading into dangerous situations, I want to make sure you are going to be careful."

Avery hugged her friend back. "We will be careful, but you guys too." Avery leaned in close and whispered in Ruth's ear. "Don't forget to fight for what is yours. He may have forgotten for the moment. But I know in his heart, you are the one for him."

"Thanks," Ruth replied.

Ferris was busy shaking hands with Jared and Duke Cache was exchanging a few words with the King—last minute instructions. They were to find Gnomedom and find out why the gnomes had abandoned their peaceful habitation in the forest and joined forces to attack the humans.

They were going to be walking because it would be the safest way to sneak out of Bogmarsh. Since the gnome army had not surrounded the whole town, the four of them would leave by the back gate and hopefully be in the fringes of the forest before any scouting parties found them.

Cache was concerned that enemy patrols already controlled most of the forest edges, but Merrit said they should be able to find their way through.

With no more need for good-byes, last hugs were given out and the friends all parted company.

Ruth walked a couple steps behind Ferris, who was walking beside Andora. The dark skinned girl seemed content to befriend the once Rat. Cache walked ahead and did not look back to make sure that the others were following him or even keeping up.

It seemed to Ruth that Ferris had completely forgotten that he and she had been on a date together before this all happened. Would he ever like her again? Could she trust him even if he did? He might always go running off to the next cuter girl he came across.

The gate to the city loomed in front of them. They were going to exit the town and follow a short dirt road into the Western Forest. The Western Forest was the most southern part of the Taboo Forest and it was safer for travel.

They reached the gate and Cache stopped for the first time. He tightened the sash of his pack, glanced at the young people following and then darted through the opening. They all followed.

The sun sat low on the horizon and the red glow of its rays streamed across the treetops. They would be traveling directly into the sun for several minutes before it set enough behind the forest's hills. This would put them at a disadvantage because they could not see in front of them clearly.

Ruth had to shield her eyes with her hands as they headed west. All she could make out were the silhouettes of her traveling companions ahead of her.

They had walked for about twenty minutes when Cache called the first halt. Ahead of them Ruth could see where the road they walked on disappeared into the forest. The sun was sinking fast and the darkness was starting to press in around them.

Cache motioned for them to be silent and he whispered. "I fear that patrols are searching the woods. If they find us, I cannot defend everyone. The best thing to do is run deeper into the woods. Keep heading west. I will be able to find you."

"We aren't as helpless as all that," Ferris whispered back. "I can't use a sword like Avery and Jared, but I can fight."

"Sure," Cache's voice did not sound like he believed it. He turned to Andora, "I know that you are at least capable. Stick with them, should anything happen."

Andora nodded.

Cache pointed ahead and spoke to Andora, "We will move in twenty yard dashes. I will go first. I will stop about twenty yards ahead and then you three follow. Andora lead them another twenty yards ahead of me and then I will catch up. If you see anything suspicious as you are running stop immediately and duck and cover."

They all nodded.

Ruth watched as Cache darted ahead. He stayed low to the ground and his hand rested on the hilt of his sword. His black clothing and green cape made it difficult to see him. He almost disappeared when he stopped and motioned the others to catch up.

Andora led the way. She also ran close to the ground, her black hair flying behind her. She kept her hand on her sword's hilt. They caught up to Cache and kept moving another twenty yards into the forest. The air was getting warmer. The sun shining on the trees all day created a greenhouse effect, and the heat stayed trapped under the leaves. There were many ferns and fallen dead trees on the ground, and the smell of rotting vegetation was everywhere. Ruth decided it was residue from the swamp that had once covered the land. The swamp had disappeared, along with Quagmire.

They continued the duck and move technique until they were deep in the forest and Cache called halt.

"We should have made it past any patrol lines," he said hoarsely.

It was now thoroughly dark and they had to stay close to see each other.

"Do we stop for the night?" Ferris asked.

"Not yet," Cache replied glancing around. "I think we are past the area patrols might search, but there is no guarantee. This forest is dangerous, despite being the most southern part of the Taboo Forest. There are still Nasties that lurk in the night: werewolves, goblins and imps. They will not hesitate to take all of us."

"Where will we stop?" asked Ruth. She was breathing heavy and took a puff from her asthma inhaler, which she had remembered to bring this time.

"There is a hill about an hours hike in called Hillock Summit. There is enough of an opening there that we can set up a camp and be protected."

By the time they reached Hillock Summit, it was too dark to see more than a few meters in front of them. But Ruth could feel the coarse grass brushing against her legs and the opening in the trees allowed some of the starlight to reach them.

Cache immediately set about lighting a fire; while Ferris and Andora found some fallen logs in order to construct a makeshift lean-to.

Ruth pulled out some jerky, raw vegetables and bread and set them on a stone for the others to eat. She nibbled some of the bread, but her appetite was not what it used to be. She kept glancing over at Ferris and Andora. As they were building the lean-to, parts would fall over and then the two of them would laugh. At one point Ferris was attempting to tie a log to a higher point on a tree and Andora held a log he stood on. The log cracked and snapped in two and Ferris fell on top of Andora, then they started laughing.

Ruth looked back to the food, "Stupid boys," she said quietly to herself.

Once camp was set up and everyone had eaten, they sat around the campfire. Ferris sat close to Andora and he would occasionally glance at Cache.

Ruth thought the man was thoroughly intimidating. His long black hair was braided down his back and his moustache was long and hung past his chin in a traditional Chinese fashion. He and Genghis Khan could have been brothers, she thought.

"Why did you come on this quest?" she asked Cache suddenly.

He looked up with narrowed eyes. "I do the bidding of the King," he replied. He chewed a piece of jerky.

Andora nodded, "He is one of His Majesty's most loyal barons."

"But where were you when Merrit was under Quagmire's curse? Surely, if you were such a loyal subject, you would have been doing everything in your power to find the prince."

"Those were tough times," he responded. "I did everything I could just to keep my own lands from falling into Quagmire's hands. Sacrifices were made. But you are only a child, you don't understand anything about responsibility."

"I understand more than you know," she said quietly. She recalled her first trip to Afflatus. It had been traumatic for her fighting demons, Muskags and a dragon. Even though she had never entered into battle, she was a healer and it was her magic that had healed Jared. He would be dead without her.

Cache continued unabated. "This is a man's quest. The king should have sent me alone to find the source of evil."

"But what about Mr. Prig?" asked Ferris.

"I don't care about him. I only care about vanquishing this evil and..." he trailed off, and looked sharply at Ruth and Ferris, like he had said too much.

Ruth could see the edge of the forest that surrounded them. The light from the fire cast shadows that danced to and fro. They were only about a hundred paces from the rim of trees and they looked like a dark forbidding wall.

Just at the edge of the forest she thought she saw movement. Straining her eyes she glared into the darkness, wishing her eyes to see what they could not. Another shadow moved, were her eyes deceiving her, or was something trying to sneak up on them.

She turned around and saw more movement behind them. "Guys," she whispered. "I think something is out there in the darkness."

Cache turned his head. "I don't see anything."

A twig snapped in the darkness and suddenly everything went utterly quiet. A dark cloud crossed over the moon and Ruth could only see the faces opposite her through the twitching firelight.

"But I heard something," Cache responded. "Quickly, gather your things." They started grabbing packs. Ruth loaded up the food and tossed it into her pack and threw it across her shoulders. "Faster!" Cache urged.

A howl sounded to their left and another howl answered the first.

"They are going to try and surround us!"

Ruth could hear branches cracking all around them. "There must be a squad attacking us," she said horrified.

Cache ran for the trees and the three young people scurried after him, into the darkness. It was difficult to follow the dark man, and they could only keep up because they could hear the sound of his footsteps.

All around them cries started. A horn echoed behind them. The gnomes were closing in fast. "What are we going to do?" Andora huffed just to her left.

"Keep running," answered Ferris. "Grab hands so that we don't lose each other." They felt around the darkness and grasped hands. Ruth held tight to Andora and Ferris had Andora's other side. "Where is Cache?"

"Up ahead, can't you hear him?"

"I can't see him," Ruth replied.

"He has got to be there," Ferris replied.

Ruth could feel her asthma starting to act up. She would need a puff from her inhaler in a moment or she would not be able to breathe. "I have to stop," she wheezed to the others.

"We can't," Andora was adamant.

"She can't breathe," Ferris said. He slowed and they waited beside each other as Ruth took out her puffer.

She took two puffs and tucked it into her pocket. "It will take a few seconds to work," she said, still panting.

"We don't have a few seconds."

"And we have lost Cache," added Andora.

"Psst!" a whisper said to their left. "Follow me. I'll lead you out of harms way," said the voice.

"Who are you?" asked Ferris peering into the darkness.

All around them they could hear the horns of the gnomes, as they chased their prey.

"I say we trust her," said Andora suddenly.

Following the voice they headed into the trees. The figure that led them was about their height, but occasionally a moonbeam would cut through the trees resting on the figure's head. Her hair was blond and cropped close to her head, making her ears evident. They were larger than human ears, and were pointed.

"I think she is an elf," whispered Andora.

"A what?" Ferris was shocked.

"An elf."

The figure led them to a large oak tree in the forest. She rested her hand on the trunk and suddenly what looked like paper tearing, the tree pulled apart and they were standing looking into another land, a magical land. Ferris peered around the tear and could see nothing. The rip was leading them into another dimension.

"This is the land of the elves," the elf said. "You will find protection here."

They stepped through the rip in time onto a grassy field, in the distance they could see a large city, it looked like it was built on three tiers, in the middle of the plains.

As they stepped through, the tear closed behind them, cutting off the pursuers.

CHAPTER TWELVE

I do wander everywhere
--William Shakespeare, A Midsummer Night's Dream [Act 2, Scene 1, line 8]

Night had descended and three horses danced on the cobblestone streets. Avery, Jared and Lumpy, and Merrit sat on horses waiting for the gates to open. Avery was riding a chestnut brown horse with a white stripe down its nose. The stable boy had told her that the horse's name was Gôntlit. Jared and Lumpy rode a black horse with white around its ankles, like they were socks; she did not know his horse's name. Merrit's horse was solid black, and the king looked very handsome on his steed. His Majesty wore traveler's clothes, a brown tunic, leather slacks and a dark green cloak. His sword was strapped to his waist and a dagger was in his boots that rode to his knees.

Avery examined her own weapons. The armorer had given her a saber, which was sheathed at her waist, and in her hand she clutched the Staff of Terminus. Her cloak was also dark green and she had the hood up, shadowing her features. Since most women in Afflatus wore only skirts and loose fitting pants, she had selected from the men's piles and wore tight brown leather pants, her shirt was a tight fitting t-shirt which made her feel conscious about her developing chest and she continued to pull the cloak across her whole body.

Torrent was standing next to the King. She was too tall to ride a horse, but she had said she was content to run alongside anyhow.

Earo had decided that the best way to get them out of Bogmarsh was to create a distraction. He and several soldiers were going to attack the far side of the enemy encampment, which would give them access to the gate, and they would be well on their way to Haddock before the enemy was even aware they were gone.

The signal was to be a flaming arrow shot into the sky— that is what they were waiting for now.

Two guards stood by the gate ready to fling the beams open at the signal. Avery could feel a pressure in her stomach as she double-checked the reins of her horse and the belt around her waist holding the sword. She had only ridden a horse one other time, and that had been in Afflatus the year before.

The torched arrow careened through the air and the gates flew open. At first Avery's horse did not move. She kicked the animal in the side, which startled it, and then they were bolting through the gate. She followed close to Jared—he looked funny with a small gnome clinging to his waist. With every bump the gnome's backside would bounce out of the saddle and he would trail behind Jared like a cape until he could right himself into the saddle again.

The quad moved through the darkness. There was a bright moon and numerous stars so she had no trouble following the others. She glanced back briefly to the walls of Bogmarsh—

she saw a dozen shadows detach from the wall and start after them—leading them was a Menas.

"We have company!" she warned. "We are being followed!"

Merrit darted a backwards glance and then spurred his horse to a greater speed. "We make for the ruins of Cragg!" he shouted. "We are on horse so we should be able to out distance the enemy."

"What is Cragg?" asked Jared.

"An old settlement on the Seaweed Sea. Most of it is sunken under the salty lake, and the rest is overgrown with seaweed. We will be able to find a defensive position there."

"Sounds good to me."

It took a while but eventually Avery was able to find the motion of riding a horse. At times she would forget to move her body with the horse and that would throw off the rhythm, jolting her butt, which felt like an awful spanking.

They were going to ride several hours to Cragg. She was worried that the horses would not be able to handle the high rate of speed for too long—but Merrit was obviously more of a horse person, because after half an hour he slowed their pace to a trot.

Their horses were sweating profusely and hers was snorting occasionally. She remembered hearing at one time that it wasn't good to allow a horse to eat while riding, but she could not hold the reins tight enough and her horse would catch snacks as they trotted along.

She wasn't sure how long they had been riding when the smell of the ocean greeted her nostrils. She inhaled deeply, missing the salty stench. One of her favorite things to do in Vancouver was catch a bus to the University and go down to the beach and walk along the rocky shore. She closed her eyes and imagined herself listening to the waves crashing against fallen logs, which dotted the rock and sand.

Suddenly her horse stopped and she opened her eyes, brought back to the reality of Afflatus. Merrit was standing in front of a stone gate, which was covered in green slime.

"The city of Cragg was once a metropolis of trade," he started. Countries from all over Terik would bring goods here."

"Terik?" quizzed Avery.

"The world, my world," he explained.

"What happened to it?"

Merrit pointed to the north. "Lake Sagacity is up there, there is a small channel that connects the two. One day the channel dried up and no more fresh water entered this part of the lake—it started to get saltier and then the seaweed started growing. As you can see it covered everything up the banks of the lake. It became inhabitable and people drifted away. That was the downfall of Afflatus. My kingdom has been small ever since."

"I wonder why the channel dried up?"

Merrit shrugged. "There are rumors that a battle between the Mermaids and Mermen raged and that during those battles, the channel stopped flowing—one of them must have plugged it up."

"There are real mermaids?" asked Avery. "Are they beautiful?"

Merit was horrified. "They are creatures that you should never desire to meet. They are not beautiful. They are animals that snare fishermen. All fishermen release one catch a year to the sea as tribute to the merpeople. If they did not, the Sirens would drown them all."

"I always thought they were lovely," Avery lowered her gaze.

"Maybe they are in your world."

"We don't have mermaids in our world," she said.

"Then count your blessings," Merrit continued. "Anyway, the city of Cragg just disappeared under the salt sea, and what you see here is covered in seaweed."

"Is it safe for us to hide here?"

"Of course."

Avery got off her horse and a tingling feeling started up her legs as the blood rushed back into them. Taking the reins of her horse she started to lead the animals into the seaweed city. Gôntlit at first jerked his head at the entrance, but followed nevertheless.

They found a small room with an open ceiling; the seaweed wasn't as pervasive in the room. Several chunks of wood sat nearby and soon Merrit had a fire going. Besides the smell of salt it was cozy. Avery found she could lie on her back and stare into the heavens—there were so many stars in Afflatus.

They didn't eat anything but instead lay down to sleep. They felt safe inside the seaweed city; even Merrit seem unconcerned that enemies would attack them. Avery only briefly thought that they should set a guard, but soon overcome by the smell of the salty lake, the thought drifted from her mind.

Lumpy was walking around the room examining various nooks and crannies. He came to a place where some wet seaweed was soaking the wall. He reached out and took a sample. He chewed carefully and suddenly his eyes opened wide and he started coughing. He reached up and grabbed a hold of his neck. His face was turning red.

Avery ran over to the gnome. He was choking. "What did you do?" she asked. The gnome was now rapidly running out of air. She hollered over to Merrit and he ran over. "He's going to die—do something!" she said.

"What did he do?"

"He ate some of the seaweed, I think," she said.

"Stupid gnome," Merrit cursed. "Quick, grab my water bag!"

Jared hurried over with the water bag. Merrit turned the gnome over on his back and opened the knobby creatures mouth and proceeded to pour water down his throat. Avery thought that this would drown poor Lumpy, but almost immediately the gnome stopped choking and his eyes and face returned to normal.

A moment later Merrit stopped pouring. Forming a fist he hit the gnome hard in the chest. A small bit of green seaweed spit out and suddenly Lumpy was choking again. Merrit pressed the gnome's chest several more times until water poured out of the crevices of Lumpy's mouth. Once all the water was out, Lumpy's breathing returned to normal.

Merrit sat back, "Stupid gnomes."

"What was that all about?" asked Jared. His eyes were wide open in shock.

"This seaweed has special properties. When ingested, it somehow allows a human to breathe water. The problem is if you aren't in water, you drown. It is deadly when eaten as a live weed—many people have used the dried seaweed to swim under water for a long time. However, it has to be dried. The live green stuff will attach itself to human lungs and start to grow there. Once it is firmly grown in your lungs, it will never get out. The dried stuff stops working after a couple of hours."

It took awhile for everyone to calm down again. But eventually they were all lying back on the floor. Avery cuddled with Lumpy to try and calm the small gnome down and he snuggled right back in.

Jared was having the nicest dream; suddenly a horse letting out a high-pitched whinny wakened him.

Opening his eyes he glanced around. He saw the three horses standing where they had tied them. But no one else was in sight. Glancing around he saw that the room had transformed. Seaweed now covered everything. He glanced to where Avery had been sleeping; all he could see was a mound of slimy green seaweed.

"Avery!" he yelled. "Lumpy! Merrit!" But there was no reply. His hand went instinctively to his side where the Nightshade was sheathed.

A horse gave out a loud whinny again and he darted to where the horses stood. He watched in horror as green seaweed was making its way up the legs of Avery's horse. The chestnut brown was stomping its feet trying to shake off the slimy tentacle.

Drawing his sword Jared sliced through the green slime and he heard the sound of three screams. Avery, Lumpy and Merrit were suddenly screaming as if in pain.

"Where are you guys?" he shouted. He saw another mound of seaweed where Merrit had been sleeping. It was starting to shake and suddenly the three gave a cry again.

Where was Torrent?

Then he saw her. She was standing next to the wall covered in seaweed. The green slime had covered most of her body— her eyes were wide in terror, but green tentacles were inside her mouth keeping her from speaking.

Jared rushed over with the Nightshade and sliced through the green tentacles near her feet and yanked the seaweed from her mouth.

She yelled, "Look out!"

Jared turned and dodged just in time as a large club of coral smashed down where he had been standing. Jared's mouth gapped open. Holding the coral club was a green monster. It stood taller than an NBA player and was wider than and NFL player. Green tentacles dripped off the demon's skin like hair. It had no neck and its eyes were sunken black rocks of coal. It didn't seem to have any teeth, but on the bottom side of the tentacles, Jared noticed suction cups and he surmised that the demon ate like a leech. That meant that the others were also covered by the seaweed, and were being drained of their blood as he waited. But why hadn't he been attacked? He wondered.

"Get the others free!" Jared ordered Torrent. "I'll take care of this!"

He just had time to dodge another swing of the coral club. Slicing through the air Jared advanced on the creature. It waited for him to approach and then a tentacle snapped out like a whip and the suction cups encircled the blade of the Nightshade. The beast gave a yell of pain and then suddenly let go.

"So you don't like my sword!"

Jared danced forward with timed jabs. He blocked each stroke of the coral club until he was standing a hair's breath away from the demon. The seaweed jaws started to open, but Jared sliced upward and danced away. His cut parted the demon down the middle, but like glue the two parts closed in together, fixing the gash.

"How am I supposed to kill this thing?"

Torrent was ripping bits of seaweed off of Avery, Lumpy, and Merrit. They were dazed and looked in pain.

Jared again dodged and danced with the creature. But each time he got close enough to strike, the creature would just heal itself. He inched in close, blocking the strikes from the demon's club. Again, the green jaws started to open wide. This time Jared waited. The beast's jaws didn't have any teeth, but he noticed at the back of the creature's throat a small light.

He stopped fighting and admired the light. It was so brilliant and intoxicating. His sword arm dropped and he reached forward with his other hand to touch the hypnotizing incandescent.

"Jared! Snap out of it!"

Jared shook his head in shock. The demon's jaws were starting to encircle Jared's upper body and he could smell dead fish.

"Jared!" Avery yelled at him.

Her voice was like the sun cutting through the darkness. He raised his sword arm again, slicing through green seaweed. The creature tried to heal itself, but Jared kept slicing until the Nightshade's blade was next to the incandescent light. With a flick of his wrist the blade cleanly sliced through the muscle that held the light in place. It went out and dropped through the gapping mess Jared's sword had made.

There was no howl of pain as the creature fell apart. The seaweed in the room instantly dried up and died. It only took a moment and then they were all standing in the room, just as it had looked before, save for a small ball, that had been the creature's hypnotizing light.

Jared reached down and picked it up. If felt warm, like a light bulb does after it has been on for a while.

"What the fruit cake was that?" asked Jared.

Merrit was stunned and did not reply right away. "I don't know," he said finally. "Maybe it was what the mermaids and mermen were fighting and the only way they could beat it was by blocking the channel."

"Good guess."

Avery had moved to the entrance of their building. "Guys," she said softly. "I think we had better move."

They heard a howl from the Menas. They had been found.

CHAPTER THIRTEEN

A man cannot be too careful in the choice of his enemies.

-Oscar Wilde, The Picture of Dorian Gray [1891]

The beaches of Sagacity Lake were all rock and large waves crashed upon them with rhythmic consistency. Avery noticed that the distant shore was small and it would take a good day of sailing to make it across the lake. There were no islands, except one, cresting the water—the lone island was like an oasis in the middle of a desert of water.

They had escaped Cragg without further incident. The Menas and its gnome army would have figured out its prey had made a beeline for Haddock, a village on the northwestern shore of the mammoth lake.

The weather had turned bitterly cold and she was thankful for the green cloak, which she kept wrapped tightly around her body. She was also thankful of the heat that her horse generated, keeping her legs warm.

Black clouds were gathering ahead of them and it didn't look like rain—it looked like a downpour was in the making.

It started to rain before they reached Haddock. The ground had turned muddy and the horses had to slug their way through the slop. The beaches were too rocky to walk on so they had to stay in the trees just past the beaches.

The land started to clear and they found places where woodcutters had logged parts of the forest and they could see in the distance a dark and dismal town. A wooden wall made out of black spruce wood surrounded the village and at regular intervals were towers.

As they approached a muddy road took shape and they noticed more peculiar things. Along the side of the road were wooden pegs with a skulls sitting on top. Merrit had stopped and examined one of the skulls, it was human, however when examined the one next to it, it was a Muskag.

"Very odd," he murmured.

There didn't appear to be any people around when they approached the front gate. It was closed and locked. They could hear nothing coming from inside.

Merrit dismounted and rattled the gate. "Hey!" he shouted, "Anyone home?"

They waited a moment.

"Who's there?" a gruff voice asked from the other side.

"We are travelers seeking a place to stay," Merrit offered.

"That isn't what I asked," the voice replied sternly. "Tell me who you are, or leave!"

Jared faced Torrent, "Not a very friendly welcome, is it?"

Torrent shook her head.

"Look," Merrit reasoned. "My name is Merrit Divine, and I seek lodging in your village."

There was silence from the other side of the gate. A moment later they could hear the sound of a wooden beam being moved and the gate creaked open. Standing there was a man dressed in a dirty tunic, a black shield and a rusted sword in his hand. His face was tired; his salt and pepper hair uncombed and he didn't have very many teeth left.

"We don't welcome its kind," the man sneered pointing at Torrent.

Merrit ignored the comment and strode into the town. The village was dreary. All the buildings look uncared for; very few people walked the streets and those that did kept their heads down and hustled as quickly as they could. The town center, which Torrent told them later, used to be beautiful and green, now it was a muddy pit with a stockade for criminals and a gallows.

"Can you direct us to the nearest Inn?" Merrit asked.

The dirty guard motioned up the street to a dilapidated building. The four marched down the street, holding their horses, ignoring the gazes that followed them.

The Inn was named *The Lion's Liar*.

"I think they misspelled Liar—shouldn't it be Lair?" asked Avery. Merrit shrugged.

The place smelled of hard alcohol and vomit, as they entered. Avery pinched her nose shut. The place was in shambles, like a brawl had broken out earlier and no one had cleaned it up. Chairs lay broken in piles, tables were turned over, and shattered glass dotted the floor. A bar was located at the back of the room and a tired looking man stood behind it rinsing dirty glasses in a bucket of water, drying them and then placing them on shelves.

He looked up at the intruders. "What do you want?" he asked. His voice sounded tired.

Merrit reached the counter and sat down on one of the only bar stools. "My name is Merrit Divine. I am searching for the man that used to call this giant daughter."

The bartender stared at Torrent for a moment, a sparkle of recognition twinkled in his eye. "Sorry, he's dead. And if you want to stay alive, you should leave now."

"How?" asked Torrent. Her eyes glistened with a few tears.

"I don't know, the same way you got here I guess!" he spit.

"No, how did papa die?"

The man's face dropped. His voice turned to a whisper. "His eldest son!" the man said. "He killed him. Sentenced him to death as a conspirator against the Queen."

"You're not talking about Quagmire?" Merrit's gaze narrowed.

The man nodded. "Haddock had a pretty good thing going with her. She left us alone as long as we fed her with fish. Her papa brought trouble by allowing the giant to live here—when he was told to get rid of her, his sons captured her and handed her over to the Muskags and they sentenced him to death—that is when they built the gallows."

"Why are we in danger now?" Jared asked.

The man's voice lowered again. "They control the town council. If anyone plots against them, that person disappears or is sentenced to death."

"But Quagmire is dead," said Avery.

"True, but they are still loyal to her."

Merrit's face hardened. "Nevertheless, we need to speak to them. We have to find out where Torrent was found as a baby."

The bartender smiled, he was missing two front teeth. "I can tell you that."

"Really," asked Avery, "where?"

"I owned this bar even back then, and I remember one night your ol' papa showed up saying that the current had taken him to the other side of the lake; to the Roc Mountains. His boat had a hole in it and in order to repair the damage he went into the forest. It was in that forest on the side of the Roc Mountains that he found you," the man said. "He knew right away that you were a giant, but he couldn't leave ya there, so he brought you home and raised you as his own."

"So we have to get to the Roc Mountains," said Avery quickly. "Can we make it before tonight?"

"Aye doubt it," the man replied. "The best way to get there is across the lake. I can sell you a boat, if you want it?"

"We don't have a lot of money," Merrit replied. "How about a trade. I have three horses out front, you can have them, in exchange for a boat."

The bartender mulled it over. Avery wanted to say no, she had grown fond of Gôntlit. "It's a deal," the man said. He reached under the counter and brought out a small tin. Opening it up Avery saw some dried seaweed. "You should be taking this with you," he said, snapping the tin shut. "The Mers are getting restless and have capsized several fishing vessels the last while. If you don't have the weed, you'll drown."

"I don't think I could put that into my mouth, not now," Avery said. She remembered the feeling of having seaweed completely covering her.

"It'll be better than drownin'."

"Fine, we'll take it." Merrit grabbed the tin. "Where do we find the boat?"

"Follow me. I'll take you to the dock."

As they exited the building the weather was in an all out downpour. Water ran down the road like a river. Standing on the opposite side of the street was a mob of people; it looked like the entire population of the town had gathered in the one place.

Standing center and in front of the rest was a man wearing black slacks, a black silk shirt buttoned up to his neck, a top hat, and he had a full black beard and black hair shaved almost to the scalp. In his hand he held a cane.

He strode into the street. As he moved two other men followed with wooden umbrellas opened, keeping the rain off the leader's head, even though they were getting completely soaked.

"We don't allow giants in this town!" he yelled. His voice sounded like a foghorn, a bit whiney, but loud.

"We are leaving!" Merrit replied.

Jared kept his fingers close to the hilt of the Nightshade. Avery motioned Lumpy behind her.

"It'll be too late for that! Who are you? My man at the gate said you are Merrit Divine."

"He spoke right," Merrit replied.

The leader turned to face the crowd. "Look here people, we have the baby King that thinks he can rule this land better than her Majesty Queen Quagmire."

"That is treason," Torrent yelled.

"Ah, little sis. I thought that the Muskags would have killed you by now. That, after all, was the plan."

"You killed papa," she said.

"He was getting in the way," the leader replied.

Merrit stepped onto the street; his hand was holding the hilt of his sword, even though he had not drawn it yet. "You know my name, but what is yours?"

"Lufnis, if you please. At least that is what I call myself these days." His voice darkened as his gaze came to rest on the horses. "I see that you brought us some meat, instead of bloody fish."

"No!" shouted Avery.

"And a little lady for company," he added with a cold puckering of his lips.

The mob took a step forward until Merrit, Jared and Avery drew their swords. It stopped them for a moment. Merrit kept his eyes on Lufnis; but motioned to the bartender. "You can take the horses, but you must leave this village now. I see that the devil has taken it." The bartender nodded and grabbed the three horses reins.

"The boat is at the dock, just at the end of this street. It bares the same name as my Inn." The bartender mounted Merrit's horse. "I thank thee Haddock, but now it is time to leave!" He gave the mount a kick and the animals darted up the street and through the open gate.

"That was rather foolish," Lufnis said. "You just let your only means of escape—escape! You can't really believe that we will allow you to get to the dock."

In defiance the companions started to back down the street towards the dock.

Lufnis laughed, "You can't take all of us!"

Merrit smiled and shook his head. "Nope, but we will take as many of you as we can. Who do you think will die first?"

Lufnis motioned his goons holding the umbrellas to attack. The two men dropped the covers and drew swords. The weapons looked rusted and old.

"I think you are making a mistake," Merrit warned the two men that approached.

"They are just children!" Lufnis roared. "Take them!"

The two men attacked. Merrit met the man on the right with a block. Avery was able to step in front of Jared and Lumpy. With her weapon drawn she parried and jabbed at the man attacking her. It felt good to be fighting with her sword again. The battle was just like she remembered them at home, the exhilaration of battle, the smell of sweat and the clang of steal. Suddenly she was aware that this was no mock battle. This man was trying to kill her. She had never fought another human before, intent on killing, besides Queen Quagmire.

The man attacked with added fervor when he saw that she was hesitating. She block again and again. More people were moving forward, but Jared was keeping them at bay with the Nightshade. It would probably only work for a short while longer.

Torrent picked up Lumpy and made a run for the dock. Avery remembered the Sinking Stingray, a maneuver that Earo had taught her. Faking to the left she sunk onto one knee, the attacker's blade whizzed harmlessly above her head. She stood up behind her assailant and brought the hilt of her weapon down on the back of the man's skull. He crumpled to the ground unconscious.

Merrit disarmed his opponent and they all started running for the dock. They could hear the roar of the mob as it gained frenzy. Lufnis was whipping them up with words, telling the people not to let the infidels escape.

They stormed onto the dock. Torrent had chucked Lumpy into the bottom of the boat called *The Lion's Liar* and was untying the moors. The crowd rushed on the dock behind them. They piled into the twelve-foot banana boat and Torrent took the oars and started rowing them out into the lake. Lying at the bottom of the boat was a mast and sail. They found the riggings that would host the mast.

Lufnis was on the dock. Suddenly his face started to change and contort and he looked like an evil gargoyle with fish-like eyes and he let out a scream. Everyone inside the boat, besides Torrent, covered his or her ears. The sound was high-pitched and eerie. He screamed again like a demon from the darkest parts of hell.

When he stopped it was silent for a moment; suddenly something solid smacked into the side of the boat.

"What was that?" asked Jared looking over the side.

Avery glanced over the side as well and saw a shadow swim under the boat. "There is something down there!" she warned.

They felt another thud on the side of the boat and the whole structure shuddered.

"Gather around," Merrit said opening the tin. "We are going to be capsized in a moment by the Merpeople. Have the seaweed ready!"

The boat was hit again knocking the tin from Merrit's grasp. The contents spilled onto the floor. The bottom of the boat was damp, but they managed to grab bits of the seaweed between their fingers, while the mermaids and mermen continued to career into the side of the floating vessel.

"What happens after we capsize?" Avery asked suddenly.

Merrit rested his hand on her shoulder. "Once we are in the water, as long as we stay under water they will not attack us. Do not surface, unless your seaweed runs out and you need air. They will pull you under and kill you."

"Do I swallow it?" asked Jared sniffing the seaweed.

"Just chew on it, the rest will happen on its own."

They heard the sound of wood splintering and taking a hold of their weapons; all five of them placed the seaweed into their mouths and started chewing. Immediately Avery felt like she could not breathe. She saw that the others were having the same sensation as her. Merrit motioned for them to all jump in the water.

The mermaids and mermen slammed one more time into the side of the boat and water started rushing in. Avery dove into the water. She closed her eyes and held her breath. She felt the urge to swim to the surface so that she could get more air. But she had to remind herself that the water was air.

She had watched people drown on movies and it did not look like a comforting experience. Opening her eyes, she found herself face to face with a mermaid. She could tell it was a mermaid because of the womanly figure. But the creature was nothing like she imagined. She remembered Ariel from *Disney's The Little Mermaid.* This creature looked more fish than person. Her mouth had sharp teeth and thin lips. Her eyes were beady and along the back of her spine ran fins, like a sea monster. She had a tail like a fish's, but arms with webbed fingers. Scales also covered the mermaid's entire body. The creature was sniffing her. When she seemed satisfied Avery wasn't a threat, the mermaid darted away like a small trout from a large sturgeon.

Avery needed air; she wanted to climb to the surface. Finally she gave in and opened her mouth. Water flowed into her lungs, but instead of drowning her, she felt better and she started to breathe the water. It felt much heavier than air, but she could breathe.

After the initial panic had subsided, she found the others floating under the water. Torrent was smiling and petting fish as they swam by. The merpeople had disappeared suddenly. Lumpy darted through the water like a salmon and Merrit and Jared floated near each other laughing, which only caused a few bubbles to surface. She could hear the faint sound of their laughter, but it sounded like a hundred miles away.

Swimming over to them she spoke. Bubbles shot out of her mouth and the sound reminded her of when she and her cousin had tried to share a secret under water at the local swimming pool. It was possible to make sound, you just had to shout, and it sounded very bubbly. This time, the volume of water coming out of their mouths deadened the sound—it felt weird to have water flowing over her voice box.

"What do we do now?" she shouted. She found that she had to speak as open-mouthed as possible to articulate what she wanted to say.

Merrit pointed in the direction they had been sailing and he screamed back, "We head for the mountains!"

"I could use the staff!" she said.

Merrit shook his head. "The seaweed will give us the strength of a fish. You'll be surprised at how fast we can actually travel this way! Remember to return to the surface when you feel the seaweed running out!"

"How will we be able to tell!" Jared yelled and shrugged his shoulders to try and show meaning.

"You will know. You'll be able to start feeling the water in your lungs. At the first moment, you'll know, and then return to the surface. You will have to breathe out all the water you can, as you head to the surface."

All of them followed Merrit, who seemed to be following a fish. Suddenly they felt a current surround them. Avery's eyes widened as she realized she didn't have to swim anymore. The undertow was pulling them along and very quickly.

Merrit motioned to her and said, "At this rate, we should be on the other shore before nightfall."

CHAPTER FOURTEEN

It is not only fine feathers that make fine birds.

--Aesop, The Jay and the Peacock [c. 580 B.C.]

Avery rolled closer to the fire. They had crawled up to land several hours earlier like fish at the dawn of evolution. Even though she believed in the Creator she couldn't help but feel the simile was appropriate.

Exhausted from the trip across the lake, under water, Merrit and Jared had barely managed to get a fire going before they all collapsed into a deep sleep.

They must have lost the Menas and gnome squadron that had followed them from Bogmarsh—they would have had no means of getting around the lake.

It was nearing dawn when she got up and stoked the fire so that the flames reached as high as she was tall. Pulling out several slices of jerky she gnawed on the meat waiting for the others to awaken. Her gaze shifted across the lake. She could barely make out the village of Haddock; it was nothing more than a dot on the horizon. She hoped that Lufnis thought they were dead; yet she was sure that Merrit would not tolerate the open rebellion, once matters were settled in Bogmarsh he would probably send the army to Haddock next.

Fog was rolling in off the lake and the cool air seeped into her nostrils—it reminded her of Vancouver in the winter. The cold wind would whip up the coast bringing with it the smell of ice and snow.

Here, however, the faint smell of pine trees was also mixed in. The fog cleared and she could see the sole island of Sagacity Lake. It appeared much larger now, since it was closer to the east side of the lake. The island was large and a dense forest covered it with tall trees, in her mind she knew that tall cedar trees grew there, much like the ones that grew on Vancouver Island—trees so large they were wider than a car.

Closing her eyes she waited for the others. Her enjoyment of nature was interrupted by the sound of wings. Large wings. She remembered when Merrit was the Dragon Incubus and her heart fluttered in momentary fear. The wing beats were closer together, and powerful.

Opening her eyes she saw a large bird flying towards her. It looked much like the eagle that Jared and the others had created to help her fight the Dragon. However, this one was totally brown and its beak was much smaller.

She started as the bird landed in front of her. It stood as tall a she was, and twice a long. Instantly she was intrigued as she noticed that the bird wore a silver medallion around its neck. What animals wore jewelry?

"Are, *caw*, you the ones who sank?" the bird asked. Its voice sounded like a bird's voice, but human too.

Avery was startled, "You can talk?"

"*Caw*, course I can," the bird replied. "Are you the ones who sank?"

"Ah, yes, that was us."

"I have some news, for you."

Avery couldn't believe her eyes, she turned and looked back at the others who were still sleeping, they would never believe her. "Um, just let me get the others, first," she said hesitantly.

"Whatever," the bird replied.

"Guys!" Avery yelled.

Merrit and Jared rolled over and opened their eyes. It took Lumpy and Torrent a moment longer to fully wake up.

"This bird here says that it has news for us."

"Saint Petrels, *caw*," the bird said.

"Sorry?"

"That's my name."

"Oh," replied Avery. The others stumbled over to stand next to Avery. "What news do you have?" she asked.

"I fear that you are being followed by a nasty enemy indeed," Saint Petrels replied. "I observed a flock of Agitates flying this way and they were carrying a Menas and several gnomes."

"Agitates?" Jared murmured. "Boy, if only I never had to see one of them again,"

"*Caw*, they are very dangerous and the Menas is worse."

"We know it," sighed Merrit. "What should we do? I don't think that we can fight all of them at the same time."

"The answer lies in the skies," Saint Petrels said. "Several of my brothers will be arriving soon and we will take you to Saint Ferruginous—he is our, *caw*, leader."

As if it were a command several other birds soared across the lake and landed next to Saint Petrels.

"These are my brothers."

They were a mix of different birds. One was a robin, the other a dove, and the third was an eagle, much like Saint Petrels. The only things they had in common were their size and they all wore a silver medallion. The medallion was round and had three birds on it; at the top sat a dove, to the left a Pelican and on the right, what Avery thought looked like a Canadian goose.

"Saint Stellers Sea can carry your giant," and Saint Petrels nodded at the other eagle. "He is the strongest of us all. You can ride with me, the others can ride with my other brothers."

Avery assumed that Saint Petrels was speaking to her and so she climbed up onto his back. The bird's feathers were soft and smooth and as his wings spread apart and they soared into the air, she could feel the powerful muscles under her legs.

"Where are we going?" she asked Saint Petrels.

"To the island. It is our home!"

"Where did you see the Agitates?" she asked hugging the neck of the massive bird.

"The Menas and the gnomes have harnessed the evil birds up near the plains. I saw them from a distance—they have been following you since Cragg."

"You seem to know a lot."

"The Creator made birds special. We have a view of the world that not many have. We see what many try to hide; we go where many fear to go; we are closer, physically, to the Aver'd One than any other."

"You serve the Creator?" Avery asked.

"For certain. Aver'd One be praised!" Saint Petrels murmured with awe in his voice.

They flew for only a few moments when they landed in the forest on the island. The island was much larger than Avery had first surmised.

The birds' kingdom, or Sanctuary, was located in nests of the tall cedar trees. Each nest was unique to the type of bird that lived in it. Somewhere higher off the ground, others lower, she even noticed that some of the nests were made on the ground, dug out, large burrows.

Saint Petrels and the other brothers flew to one of the largest trees in the Sanctuary. They landed on a branch, which they could all stand on; it was wider than a sidewalk, before a large hole in the tree. This tree was not a cedar, it was oak, and a refreshing smell emanated in the air.

"This is the home of Saint Ferruginous, he is an owl."

The bird motioned them forward and everyone entered the dark hole. Inside it was lighter, a hole in the ceiling allowed light to enter. Sitting on a nest at the back of the hole was an owl. Even though he was still as tall as the children, Avery could tell that he wasn't like a massive Great Horned Owl; he was of a smaller species, a burrowing owl. He had long legs and bright yellow eyes. Avery noticed that he also wore a medallion similar to the others.

His eerie gaze rested on them. Avery noticed Jared visibly swallow when he saw several bones in the corner. Saint Ferruginous saw the gaze. "*Whoo*, never fear, we do not feed on the Aver'd chosen." His voice was not deep like Avery was expecting it to be. She imagined the owl from *Winnie the pooh*.

"Why are we here?" Merrit asked stepping forward.

Saint Ferruginous tilted his head sharply and jerked it back and forth rapidly. "The Creator, may the Aver'd be praised, has shown us—we are to aid you in your quest, *whoo*."

"We are searching for my homeland," Torrent offered. She was constantly smoothing her clothing, like she would in the presence of someone great. "I was raised an orphan and now I get to go home."

Saint Ferruginous tilted his head again. "There is more to your quest than this?"

"Yes," said Avery. "We are searching for the Seerer Mirror. It will help us vanquish the darkness that is covering the land."

"I have seen this, *whoo*, darkness. It grows stronger with each passing day. But I warn you, *whoo,* sometimes what you seek, isn't what you need, even if it aids you."

"Huh?" Jared said.

"As you seek the Truth, it will all be brought to light." Saint Petrels hopped over to where they were standing. "My bravest birds will fly you to the Giant Kingdom. It is in the remotest parts of the Southern Mountain Range. I fear that you already have salt on your tail—"

Jared interrupted, "Sorry, uh, salt?"

"My apologies, my bird analogies do not make sense to you. Salt on one's tail is an incredible inconvenience. You have an inconvenience on your tail. The Menas will not stop until you have perished. But I warn you again, not all Menas are what they seem to be, to you. As the Guide Book says, "Some men are Menas, all Menas are killers, But not all men are Menas, despite their appearance.""

"This guy loves to speak in riddles, doesn't he?" stated Jared. "So when do we leave?"

"Immediately."

Avery paused, as they got ready to leave. "I've been meaning to ask—what does the medallion stand for?"

"Ask Saint Petrels on your journey. He will answer your questions, *whoo*."

They had all crawled back onto their birds and were flying south, over Sagacity Lake. The view was much more staggering than from the ground. They could almost see the plains in the distance, and the endless forest stretched up to the walls of Bogmarsh. On her left she could see mountains and more forests. It reminded her of home. British Columbia was a vast wilderness, and even though she had only been as far as *Cypress Mountain*, she always felt amazed by the wilderness. *Stanley Park*, though often seen as a hazard to young girls, was a place she liked to go and visit.

She returned her attention to Saint Petrels, the bird carrying her. "Saint Ferruginous told me to ask you about the medallion; what does it mean?"

"*Caw*, it stands for the pillars of our faith. It is the triune of faith. At the top there is the picture of the dove. The dove traditionally has represented peace, and oneness. That is why it stands for profession. Each day, as I see my medallion I am reminded to aver my faith. It recites like this: I aver that there is no god but the Creator, maker of Heaven and Earth and so shall the Creator be called the Aver'd One."

"You recite that everyday?" asked Avery. She wondered how many times she had prayed since her last encounter with the Dragon Incubus. She hadn't even bothered once she had returned home. This bird was so much more diligent in his faith. She had believed in Jwen, and when Jwen told her to be like the Creator, she had completely forgotten about it. "What about the other two birds on the medallion?" she asked a little shamefaced.

"The pelican stands for Petition. According to the rules of our faith we are to pray five times a day. It does not matter where we are; it becomes our place of prayer. We pray at sunrise and sunset, high noon and breakfast and dinner."

"Those last two seem a little out of place," she remarked.

"*Caw*, it is to remind us that the Aver'd One is the provider of all things, even the insignificance of the food we eat. All is provided by the Aver'd One."

Avery felt a sense of calm. It must be nice to trust that everything is in the hands of the Creator. Faith would make life so much simpler if she could just release all the worries of day-to-day life to the Creator and trust that all her needs, even the insignificant ones would be looked after. But that was impossible in the world she lived in. It was too busy, too much to be accomplished, and too many expectations and responsibilities. Such a carefree life could only be for the birds. She felt guilty the moment she thought it.

"Finally there is the goose."

Avery heard the tone of reverence. Funny, she had never thought of geese being all that revered. They squawked and honked, were all in all rather chaotic.

"What does the goose mean?" she asked.

"The goose has always represented largesse."

"Huh?"

"Charity. We are required to be charitable to our brothers and sisters and to those that the Creator has chosen. As Saint Ferruginous said, humans have a special place in the Creator's heart and so we help them as our brothers and sisters."

"Is that why you are helping us now?"

"For sure," he replied. "It says in the Guide Book that by doing so we are storing up treasures in heaven. Our acts of charity will not go unnoticed by the Aver'd One."

"Don't you ever not do what you are supposed to do?"

"For sure," Saint Petrels answered. "However, I can only hope that my charity will be more than my misdeeds."

Something suddenly didn't sound quite right. There had to be a better way. No one can be good all the time. She didn't know how to respond, everything else Petrels said made complete sense. She wished deep down that she could be more like him.

The attack came suddenly and without warning.

The group of companions had flown into some low-lying clouds when a screech of an Agitate sounded through the fog. There was a loud thump and then the clouds parted. She saw Merrit falling towards the ground, the bird he had been riding, Saint Fantail, a majestic looking pigeon, was crumpled next to an Agitate, also starting a rapid descent.

Riding the Agitate was the Menas. It glared over at Avery.

CHAPTER FIFTEEN

The horns of Elfland faintly blowing.

--Alfred, Lord Tennyson, The Princess
[song, The Splendor Falls] St. 2 [1847]

"Welcome to Lumino-City," said the elf.

Ruth stared open-mouthed at the scene that played out before her. The horizon was decorated with brilliant red, orange and yellow light that stretched like glowing fingers across the horizon. She could see no sun or moon, just the majestic sunset colors.

"I have never seen colors so beautiful before," Ruth uttered in awe. "Is it always like this?"

"Yes," the wood elf replied. "Lumino-City is different from your world. We do not have a sun to govern the day nor a moon to govern the night. The Luminescence, our sun, circles the horizon all hours of the day."

"When do you sleep?" asked Ferris. "If it is never night, how do you sleep?"

The elf smiled, "We are immortal beings, we don't need sleep in the traditional sense. We nap when we need to and remain awake as long as we need."

Ruth felt warm as she looked up towards the Lumino-City. It was a three-tiered city, where each tier was built increasingly smaller, until at the top she could see a beautiful white palace. When the red light of Luminescence, as the elf had called, struck the side of the city it lit up so brilliantly that it seemed afire. As she watched she could see elves working in the fields surrounding the city, several soldiers wearing gold plated armor, and many others walking in and out of the city. Her gaze returned to the elf that had saved them.

"How did you know that we needed help?" she asked suddenly.

The elf's gaze lowered. "I am an outcast. I have been banished—even entering this far into Lumino-City I may be punished severely."

"What did you do?" asked Andora.

"Do?" she replied. "Nothing. I have and will always remain the Queen's most loyal servant. I have served for generations in the Queen's rooms as her attendant and confidant. That is until Trammel."

"Who is Trammel? Last year he arrived from a distant elven kingdom and the Queen fell desperately in love with him. Then she started to change—her beauty started to fall away and she developed a distasteful disposition. Trammel said that he found me going through the Queen's personal things and had me banished."

"Were you going through her things?" asked Ferris.

"Of course," she replied nonchalantly. "I am confident that she is under a curse, and the only way to keep a curse up for that long is to have it hidden in some object that she uses regularly."

"So you were trying to find out what was enchanting your Queen," stated Ferris.

"Yes."

Ruth held out her hand, "My name is Ruth," she said. "What is yours?"

The elf took Ruth's hand and held it tightly, not like a handshake, but like they were friends going for a walk. "My name is Pyper. When I was banished from Lumino-City I thought I would be a restless wanderer for the rest of eternity. But now, I have returned and Trammel will have me sent to Oblivian. But I am pleased to have met you first," she said.

"Well then, we should leave, go back to the Taboo Forest. At least there you will have a chance to escape," said Andora, also introducing herself.

"It is too late. They already know that we are here. Soldiers will be arriving soon to take us to see the Queen."

They started walking towards Lumino-City. As they approached Ruth saw a number of soldiers exiting the main gate, marching towards them. Many of the elves working in the fields looked up from their plows, hoes and seeding to watch as the warriors surrounded the group.

The leader was the most handsome being that Ruth had ever seen. The elf stood as tall as a man, he had wavy black hair and piercing silver-white eyes, cobalt, and when his gaze rested on her she felt completely weak in the knees. He was muscular and wore a beautiful green shirt woven from the finest silk; cotton pants hugged his muscular thighs. His belt was black with a rapier sheathed at his side. His fingers looked soft and well groomed, but strong.

The elf glared at Pyper. "You were banished!" he said. His voice was strong and exuded authority. Ruth could see that it almost brought Rat to his knees.

Pyper glared back and did not show any weakness. "Trammel, I appeal to the Queen," she stated bluntly.

"She already banished you!"

"I have brought travelers that required our help."

"We don't welcome strangers here."

"We welcomed you when you needed it," Pyper replied.

Trammel considered it for a moment. "Because you have returned Pyper, you will be sentenced to Oblivian before the end of the week. You can appeal to the Queen all you wish, but we shall see how far that gets you!" He motioned to his warriors, "Bring them to her Majesty!"

Pyper walked with her head held high. Ruth followed with less enthusiasm, as did Ferris and Andora. It now appeared that being saved by the elf Pyper was a blessing in disguise as trouble. Yet, maybe the Queen would be able to give them some assistance in finding the Gnomedom.

The city opened up to them as they entered the main gate. There was only one road, which was lined with houses, shops and stables. The streets were bustling with elves and few paid attention to the travelers as they wound their way up to the second tier.

The second tier of the city looked out over the bottom layer and they could see much further. It appeared that a smaller city was built a thousand yards to the north of Lumino-City. Pyper informed them that many of the common people lived in that city, called Raystream. The street was not as busy on the second tier, and the houses looked much nicer. It was the nobles' section of town and most of the bustle consisted of servants scurrying hither and dither to the bidding of their mistresses and masters. They had to squeeze to the side of the road when a noble elf riding a Llama passed by them. The Llama spit just missing Rat's head.

Finally they arrived at the gate leading to the top tier, the palace. More guards stood at attention at the gate with spears and swords. Their golden armor glowed in the Luminescence. They parted immediately for Trammel.

On the third tier Ruth could see for miles around the city. The land stretched out like a gigantic globe. She could see the curvature of the world and the horizon dipped like a frown. The palace was white marble and stood ten stories high. The white marble glistened in the Luminescence like a flaming torch with glass windows. A beautiful garden surrounded the entire structure and they would have to pass through it to reach the inner courtyards of the palace. It was the largest building that Ruth had ever seen.

Guards stood at attention in many places. Nobles dressed in the finest clothing walked arm in arm. The women had long flowing gowns, blond, black and red hair with green leaves as berets and crowns. The men had clothing similar to Trammel's, however; some of them wore distinguished robes with jewels for buttons and gold trim at the hems.

The oddest thing that Ruth noticed was that no one seemed to be older than seventeen. There were no children and no old people. She recalled their march through the lower levels of the city and could not recall seeing any children.

She hurried up to Pyper's side. "Where are the children?" she asked.

Pyper whispered, "We do not have any children."

"Then how do you reproduce and how do elves come to be?"

"We have always been. The Creator made us, the embodiment of life. As long as elves live, so does the world."

"Afflatus?" quizzed Ruth.

Pyper shook her head, "All worlds, the magical, the palpable and the hidden."

"What happens when an elf dies?"

"We do not die either. We are sent to Oblivian. Elves are spirit and soul of the world—when we are sent to Oblivian, what we are is absorbed into creation."

"Silence," Trammel ordered.

Ruth fell silent.

They marched through the forest surrounding the palace, birds of numerous variety sat in the trees, singing politely. The ground was not dirty or disheveled, rather, trimmed grass and moss created a cushioned carpet. Large mushrooms grew around trees and in the sunshine, a few ferns dotted the landscape and Ruth almost forgot that she was standing on top of a city. A few other elves were quietly walking through the forest. She noticed that most did not walk alone; they always appeared in the company of at least one other elf.

The forest thinned and in front of her was the palace. It was even larger standing in front of its main entrance. It might not be as tall as the skyscrapers back home in Vancouver, but, the height and breadth of the palace was utterly breathtaking. Marble stairs led up a steep rise to large oak doors. There were no guards here, just a few elves sitting on marble benches with embroidered cushions. They all spoke in hushed tones, to the left sat three minstrels playing three different sized harps.

Massive oak doors opened as if invisible hands pushed them and the children stepped into the palace. Once again Ruth was amazed. She had expected it to be the first darkness of the land—everything else appeared so brilliant. But she was mistaken. The walls were still white marble, but they glowed. It was like the walls allowed light from outside to penetrate through. There was not a single shadow in the building; no darkened corners and even the living did not cast a shadow.

Trammel led them to the throne room. Sitting on a flat black marble table was the Queen. Many attendants, pillows, and blankets surrounded her. Immediately Ruth felt that something was amiss. Every other elf she had come across was beautiful, a creature that put the most beautiful model in her world to shame. But the Queen was ugly!

Her face was larger than normal with a nose like a dwarf's nose, lips that looked like they had been injected with too much botox. Her chin was disheveled and sunken into her fat face. She looked fat with rolls of skin on her arms and legs. Her hair was thin and bald spots dotted the top of her head.

In her hand was a golden mirror and the Queen's gaze was locked onto her features. She would raise a fat hand and stroke her thin hair.

"My lady," said Trammel bowing low.

"Hamper Trammel, my love," the Queen replied. Her voice sounded like a hoarse cough. "Why did you leave my side?" Ruth was startled as she had the briefest of moments to look into the mirror; the Queen's reflection was without blemish.

"I had business with these intruders, my lady." He glared back at Pyper and the children. "As you can see, my lady, Pyper has returned, even after you banished her."

The Queen's eyes shone for the briefest of moments and then the dark coal gaze returned. "Pyper, why did you return?"

Ruth stepped forward. "Your Majesty," she started, "if I may?"

"You may."

"Pyper saved us from a Menas and gnomes that were attacking us in the Taboo Forest. She would not have returned except to save us. She is a hero."

"Ha!" sneered Trammel. "Pyper is a thief and mischief-maker. Her banishment has brought order to the kingdom. And look, she returns with outsiders. We have not had humans in our land for a millennium."

Pyper piped up. "We were not created to set ourselves apart from the land. We are the life of the world. If we hide ourselves—we will die. There is a darkness coming! A darkness that will vanquish the world, unless we are willing to be involved in the affairs of mortals."

"Enough!" yelled Trammel. "We don't need any more evidence against you. My lady," he turned back to the Queen, "her very presence is disobedience to your dominion. You must have her sent into Oblivian."

The Queen raised a hand and every one fell silent. "Pyper, do you have any last words before I pass judgment?"

"Mistress Mikado, my Queen, I have ever been faithful to you. Do not be deceived by this darkness that clouds your soul."

The Queen's eyes lit again for a microsecond, then faded with a cough from Trammel. "Pyper, you are sentenced to Oblivian at the turning of the day. In two hours time the Luminescence will return to starting and you will be executed," the Queen decreed.

Trammel's eyes lit up. Pyper's sank.

"What do we do with these humans?" Trammel asked.

"Send them on their way."

Ruth's heart leapt, if they were sent back to the Taboo Forest right away the Menas and gnome warriors would capture them.

Pyper realized her fear at the same time. "My lady," she said. "I request that the humans be my Soothe-Solace."

The Queen was taken aback. "You would choose humans to spend the last of your days with?"

"I do."

"Very well, we will send the humans away after the execution of Pyper into Oblivian."

A chorus of voices arose to the left of the Queen, "As it is said, so it is written!" Ruth glanced to the Queen's left and noticed five other elves with parchment and quills writing down everything that took place in the hall.

Pyper and the students were led to a room in another part of the palace. There were wooden benches covered with cushions. An altar stood at the head of the room right below a window that looked out over the forest surrounding the palace.

Pyper walked immediately over to the altar. "We have two hours. You are free to wander in the garden, but I request that you return an hour before my execution. You will know because a bell will chime three times. It is calling the Senate to attend the execution. In my last hour you will be my Soothe-Solace."

"Do you want us to stay now?" asked Ruth.

"No, I need an hour to attend to my spirit in prayer."

They left the room and headed for the entrance to the garden. Ferris was walking with Andora, his face was downcast and he reached out and took hold of Andora's hand. Ruth felt the coolness of jealousy sweep over her.

As they reached the garden Ruth darted away from the other two. She didn't want to watch them holding hands and talking. Rat had become a rat again—he had only cared for her because Andora wasn't around. The other two didn't even notice her leave them.

Running as fast as she could, Ruth darted between trees, over the cushioned grass and moss until she felt her lungs burning. She came to a stop in front of a fountain. The water was clear and shooting ten feet into the air casting droplets of water all around. The red light of Luminescence glowed through it, fragmenting into beautiful rainbows.

Ruth sat down on the rim of the pool surrounding the fountain. The droplets were creating ripples in the water. She reached down and stirred her image that reflected back to her. The ripples contorted her face. Was she really so ugly that Ferris didn't want to go out with her? Did he see her like they saw the Queen, ugly? Ruth looked at her image again. She was beautiful—maybe not like the elven people, but she was pretty. Or did she see herself like the Queen did in her magic mirror—beautiful when really the opposite was true?

Ruth stopped. The mirror. There was something about it. Pyper had said that Queen Mikado was under a curse and that an object had to be the source of the enchantment. Could it be the mirror? And why would another elf want to put the Queen under an enchantment? She had to answer the first question first. But how could she get the mirror?

Standing up from the pool she decided to find Ferris and Andora.

She started running back the way she had came. It took her fifteen minutes to find the two of them. They were sitting on a marble bench surrounded by ferns. She watched as Ferris held onto Andora's hand. They had obviously been talking. The green monster of jealousy reared its head again. She wanted to rush in and stop what she was watching, but she could not tear her eyes away. Suddenly Rat started leaning in, she watched as his lips puckered to kiss Andora. Closing her eyes she ran away.

Ruth ran back to Pyper's room. She knew that Pyper was not yet ready for her, but if the mirror was the source of the enchantment, maybe they would be able to stop the execution.

She skidded to a halt when she heard voices around the corner of the hall. It was Trammel and he was speaking with someone whose voice she did not recognize.

"Will we continue with the plan," the voice said.

Trammel answered. "Everything will happen after the Turning of the Day. Once that nosey elf Pyper is gone, we will have no one to stop us. The Queen's blood will feed the darkness."

"Shh!" the voice said. "I just felt something." Ruth pressed her self against the wall. "It must have been nothing," the elf replied after a moment.

"Until the Turning," Trammel said softly.

Ruth heard footsteps descending down the hall. Rounding the corner she saw the backs of Trammel and another elf disappear around the distant corner. A rebellion? But what elf would want to kill another elf? She had to find Pyper and soon. There was only just over an hour left until Pyper was sent to Oblivian.

Ruth burst through Pyper's door. The blond haired elf glanced up from her place at the altar.

"Why have you interrupted? If I don't complete this I will forever be in torment."

Ruth was breathless. "I just heard Trammel conspiring to kill the Queen. He said something about killing her after you were gone."

"What?"

"He said that the Queen's blood would feed the darkness."

Pyper's face darkened. "I knew there was something evil about him." She glanced at Ruth who looked confused. "He is a vampire. Elves are the source of life; vampires are the source of death. They also look beautiful in certain forms, and it is impossible to tell they are vampires until they change. Before they feast on life, their features contort into the demon spawn they were bred to be."

"Vampires?" Ruth's eyebrows raised. "They really exist?"

"Since the Fall of Creation, evil and good have both existed—life and death—light and darkness. We must stop this."

"How?" asked Ruth.

"We need to find the curse that keeps the Queen enchanted. As long as Trammel has her in sway, the elves will obey their Queen."

CHAPTER SIXTEEN

Theirs was the giant race, before the flood.

--John Dryden, Epistle to Congreve [1693]

Avery watched in horror as Merrit plummeted towards the ground. The Menas, riding the Agitate circled to attack Avery. Jared positioned himself and his bird, Saint Falcon between them. In his hand was the Nightshade. The Menas had a black sword drawn as well. The two birds collided and they started falling, both birds clawing and biting at each other as Jared and Menas swapped sword strikes. The birds parted and Jared reached out to hang onto Saint Falcon's head feathers. Then they collided again, it was a battle of dart and attack, pull away and attack again.

Avery took her eyes off the battle that ensued and saw Merrit rapidly disappearing—they had been flying high indeed. Saint Petrels suddenly cocked his wings and started diving towards Merrit. Falling next to them was Saint Fantail, but Petrels ignored his brother and continued to dive towards Merrit.

Three Agitates seeing Torrent and her bird gave chase and she disappeared into the clouds, followed by Agitates and gnomes.

Avery could see the ground rapidly approaching, but the small speck that had been Merrit was getting larger as well. Gulping in air, they dove until they were even with Merrit. The King had a look of absolute terror in his eyes. His arms were reaching out like he was trying to stop himself, but had nothing to grab onto.

Avery held out her hand and tried to shout to the king, but the wind was rushing by so quickly her words were lost, even to her own ears. The ground was only a few hundred meters away and if she didn't act quickly they all were going to die.

She wrapped her legs around the thick neck of Petrels and stood up as far as she could. Merrit was flailing still, but he had seen Avery now and was trying to reach out to her. Their fingers just barely touched. She risked another glance to the ground—this was the final moment or else they would die. She stretched as far as she could and her hand clasped Merrit's. She just had time to pull the boy to herself when Petrels pulled up and they skimmed the surface of the earth. Behind them they heard a loud, *wuff*, as Saint Fantail hit the ground.

Saint Petrels dropped the two off on the side of a tall hill; his bird gaze looking back into the clouds. A dozen Agitate's soared down through the foggy haze, carrying gnomes. Jared and his bird, Saint Falcon were still engaged in combat with the Menas.

"You stay here," Petrels ordered. "I'm going to help my brothers." Without another word Petrels took flight. Several of the Agitate's carrying the gnomes took off in pursuit. The others landed and started to circle Merrit and Avery.

Avery drew her sword. Merrit had lost his weapon in his fall. Andora tossed him the Staff of Terminus, it wasn't much of a weapon, but it would be better than nothing. The gnomes dismounted with weapons drawn, they all had a distant look in their eyes, like they were in a trance.

Pouncing on Avery and Merrit, the gnomes tried to stab and jab—however the small creatures did not have the muscle power or ability to fight two grown people. Merrit swiped with the staff and three gnomes went flying.

Avery didn't want to kill the small creatures because it was like fighting a child. In her fencing club young children were often registered and the older fighters were not allowed to spar with the children because of safety issues.

The gnomes had no clue how to fight and so Avery continued to block their jabs. She was taking on three gnomes herself when Merrit appeared and started knocking them on their heads. The Agitates, having stayed out of the battle at first started to circle. Their screams of hate pierced them to their eardrums.

"Here," said Merrit. He tossed Avery a clump of moss. "Stick this in your ears—the Agitates' scream won't affect you then!"

Avery did as he had instructed her and plugged up her ears. She found that she could concentrate again. Dancing with her sword she descended upon the birds. The evil creatures screamed at her again and again, but when they realized their screams fell harmlessly away they backed off and took flight.

A moment later Avery stared at half a dozen gnomes lying unconscious at her feet, Merrit rubbing his wrists from where Avery had grabbed him and saved him from his fall, and the land was very quiet. Merrit motioned for her to remove the moss from her ears.

"That was rather exciting," the king said breathlessly. "I don't think I ever want to experience that again."

"Nor I," echoed Avery.

Jared and Saint Falcon landed next to them, as did Saint Petrels. Torrent landed last and dismounted.

"They just gave up," said the giant. "We were being chased all over the blue heaven when suddenly it was like they were called away."

"Same here," stated Jared. "That Menas howled and I think that called off the attack. As soon as he realized that the attack had failed."

"Why are they after us?" Avery asked.

Merrit shrugged. "I've been trying to figure out what the gnomes are up to. But aligning themselves with Menas and Agitates is an evil thing to do."

"I don't think that they had much choice in the matter."

"What do you mean?"

Avery reached down and picked up one of the unconscious gnomes. "Look at his eyes," she said.

They pulled the eyelids back and found that the gnome's eyes had returned to normal.

"They look fine to me," said Jared.

"Let's tie these little buggers up and when they wake up, maybe we can get a straight answer out of one of them." Merrit pulled a bit of rope from the pack still slung across his shoulder.

They started a fire and propped the six unconscious gnomes against a nearby tree. The birds decided to go hunting and eat, leaving Jared, Avery, Torrent and Merrit to sit around the fire and wait.

Merrit sat close to Avery. "I wanted to thank you for saving me today," he said. His eyelashes lowered and a pink tinge glowed on his cheeks. He reached out and brushed a piece of hair from Avery's ears. "You really are an amazing girl."

"Please!" said Jared loudly. "There are other people around here."

Avery glared over at Jared; he had been acting more bitterly. It was like the old Jared was starting to come back.

"You jealous or something," she sneered back.

"Shut up!" he yelled. "I would never be jealous of him. He thinks you are such a great person—well I know you better. You are a stuck up little..." he trailed off. Without finishing he stormed away from the fire.

"What's his problem?" Merrit asked.

Avery shrugged. "He just isn't used to another guy being better at something than him."

Torrent frowned, "He was fighting the Menas. That was very brave."

"I guess," replied Avery, "but he is such an adrenaline junkie. He wanted to come back here to Afflatus because he wanted to fight and that is it."

Torrent frowned again and then stood to follow Jared. He had gone a short distance into the forest.

Avery sat stiffly next to Merrit. She always hated it when she fought with Jared. But he was turning into a jerk again. Back in Vancouver he was willing to steal from his foster parents in order to keep his brother happy. Jared had had a lighter, which meant he was probably getting into drugs like his brother too.

Feeling tense and stressed out she let a tear fall down her face. Merrit reached out and put his arm around her shoulders. She allowed herself to fall into his grasp. The king was handsome and strong. She glanced up at Merrit's face. Imagine a King paying attention to her; it made her feel in some way special.

"Don't worry about your friend," Merrit said. "I'm sure that he will be all right. I mean its not like you guys were dating or anything."

"No," replied Avery. "Its not like he and I are dating."

One of the gnomes let out a soft moan, his eyes fluttered twice and then he opened them fully and stared around. His eyes widened and his mouth opened and closed a fish out of water.

"Look," said Avery sitting up.

The gnome heard her speak and glanced in her direction. "Er, em, excuse me," he coughed. "Where am I?" His tone sounded pinched.

"Who are you is a better question?" demanded Merrit. The two humans approached the tied up gnome. "And why were you attacking us?"

"Hmm, what?"

"Who are you?"

"My name is Boogey Chews. I am a Blunder lord of the gnomes."

"Do I dare ask? It seems like all gnomes are one kind of lord or another!" She remembered how when she had first met Bigwig, he had said he was Overlord of the gnomes.

"So Boogey Chews, why were you and your mates here attacking us?"

"We weren't attacking you," the gnome was put out. "The last thing I remember was sitting down to a nice little meal when suddenly that lady appeared."

"What lady?" Merrit and Avery were confused. Avery remembered Merrit saying that Governor Swale was probably behind the dark wall.

"She was a clear lady."

"Huh?"

"You could see right through her. She kind of looked like my Gnomey Granny Sniffles. But I knew it wasn't her because she left to the wild nothingness."

"Do you understand a thing that he is saying?" asked Avery.

Merrit hesitated, "I think so. Gnomes believe that when you die you go to the wild nothingness—sounds a bit like hell to me because in theory all the gnomes in wild nothingness get to sing and dance all day long."

"It's heaven," Boogey Chews added.

"What about the Menas? Why are the gnomes helping the Menas attack Bogmarsh?"

"What is a Menas?" the gnome asked.

Avery tried to describe it. "Well, it looks a bit like a man and wolf put together, but it can't be a werewolf because they only come out during the full moon."

"Nope, never seen one of those," Boogey Chews stated. "Now, can you untie me? I think I want to return home now."

"Where is your home?"

"In Gnomedom. I have a nice little tree house, all my own."

Merrit returned to the fire without untying the gnome. "It is obvious that he doesn't know anything.

"He could be really good at hiding information," Avery offered. But she wasn't willing to resort to torture to get the gnome to speak. Besides she didn't know what would be considered torture for a gnome. "I think that we should just let them go."

The other gnomes started to come too and they had the same startled look in their eyes that Boogey Chews had had. They started to converse with each other in wild chatter and Boogey Chews tried to explain what he knew. They squirmed and chomped, trying to get out of their bonds.

"Just let them go," sighed Merrit.

Avery took out her sword and suddenly all the gnomes started crying. They sounded like little babies. "Shut up!" she said. "I'm going to free you." But they were crying so loudly they didn't hear her. She cut the ropes that bound the little creatures and as soon as they all realized they were free they darted off into the darkness. Boogey Chews was trying to lead them, but another of the gnomes said he was the Younger lord and that all the others should follow him. It was rather confusing and their discussion disappeared into the darkness.

A moment later Jared and Torrent came running back to the clearing around the fire.

"Where are the gnomes?" Jared demanded looking at the loose ropes.

"We let them go," Avery replied, sitting down at the fire.

"What did you do that for?" he said staring hard from Avery to Merrit. "They were our only clue to what is going on around here."

Merrit sighed loudly. "We questioned them and they had nothing to answer."

"Look!" Jared said sternly. "You may be King here in Afflatus, but you are not King of me. You should not have made that decision without consulting all of us."

Merrit stood up with a scowl on his face. "Well this is Afflatus and as long as you are here I will make decisions that affect you whether you like them or not. If you don't like it, go home!"

Jared stepped up until he was a nose away from the King's face, "I do what I like and you'd best remember that!"

"And I'll take your arrogant head down a notch if you don't get out of my face, now!"

"Bring it on!" Jared shoved Merrit and the young King fell to the ground.

Standing up quickly he approached Jared with his fists clenched. Avery stepped in and placed a restraining hand on both of the boys. "We can't fight among one another," she said. "We have a quest and we need to finish it."

Merrit backed down. "I will do what you wish Avery."

Jared smacked her hand off of his chest and stomped back to the far side of the fire.

Torrent had stayed out of the exchange and sat down. "When are we going to leave again?" she asked when she felt sufficient cool down time had passed.

Merrit looked up to the sky, "I guess as soon as the birds return."

"Good guess!" said Jared sarcastically. Merrit narrowed his gaze at him.

They flew late into the evening. Avery was just beginning to doze on the back of Saint Petrels when she saw mountains, higher than any she had ever seen before rising up ahead of them. The peaks were covered in snow and great canyons with avalanche crevices reaching out like claws from a demon's hand.

"Just over there is the Land of the Giants," Petrels said. His head turned to the left.

He swooped and the others in their company did the same.

The land of the giants was a huge plateau at the base of two peaks. It was covered with snow and Avery could see a town of large stone huts. They had chimneys with smoke rising out of them. One hut, larger than the rest, stood at the very base of the taller of the two peaks.

"That is the Head Giant's home," Petrels offered. "You will need to speak to him before you can traverse in the giants' land.

There were no roads to walk on, and when they landed and dismounted they sunk into the snow, all except Torrent; it wasn't too deep for her.

Avery turned back to Saint Petrels. "Thank you so much for all your help," she said.

"It was for our charity. Now we must return to where Saint Fantail fell. It is important that we give the proper rituals for his crossing into the after life. He gave his life in sacrifice for the Aver'd One, that means a great reward is waiting for him. We must make sure that he receives it."

"Farewell," waved Avery.

They stood watching the birds disappear into the darkness of the night.

"Odd bunch," mocked Jared.

"I respect them," Avery said back. She was quiet for a moment. "Their faith seemed so real to them. I only wish we could be as devote, it seems to give peace to their lives."

Merrit tried to take several steps forward, but the snow was up to his waist. Jared also tried to move, but had even more difficulty because Lumpy was clutching to his neck.

"We're never going to make it to that hut," grumbled Jared.

Torrent took a couple of steps. It was a slugging for her as well, but she could manage. "I can't carry all of you," she said. "But I'll try to make a path for you to follow."

Moving slowly, they entered the giants' village. In the town the snow was more trampled down and they found it easier to move. They did not see any other giants around; instead, Jared was amazed to see a herd of blue buffalo, bigger than a house in his world, walking through the village.

"This place is rather deserted," stated Merrit. "I hope that the Head Giant is home. He might be able to help us find the Seerer Mirror."

They reached the large stone hut at the base of the mountain peak. There was a thick wooden door and the smell of wood smoke greeted them. Torrent reached up and knocked on the door.

Movement could be heard inside and then the door stood open. Torrent was stunned. Avery was awed, and Merrit and Lumpy stood with mouths open.

Jared's gaze darted from Torrent to the other giant and he blurted out. "Twins!"

CHAPTER SEVENTEEN

~

The face is the mirror of the mind, and eyes without speaking confess the secrets of the heart.

--Saint Jerome, Letter 54

"The mirror," said Ruth. "I think it is the mirror."

"That would make sense," Pyper said quietly. "We don't have much time. Where are your friends?"

"Making out probably," Ruth said snidely. She quickly clamped her hand over her mouth. "What are we going to do?"

"We have to get into the throne room and talk to the Queen. In order to break the enchantment, she is going to have to smash the mirror."

"Can't we just take the mirror and destroy it?"

Pyper shook her head. "Most curses can only be overcome by the person that is cursed. The power of a curse is only powerful because a person believes it. Mistress Mikado has to believe that she is under a curse in order to then break the mirror and destroy the enchantment."

"So how do we get her Majesty to believe that she is under a curse?"

"I don't know. Come on, at least let's go and try to talk to her. I hope that Trammel is not around, his breath-taking beauty seems to be part of the enchantment."

They exited the room. The halls of the palace were empty as elf and human walked towards the throne room. The Queen often spent her whole day there because she had gained so much weight. Ruth asked how it was possible that no one else commented on the Queen's change in appearance and Pyper replied that elves serve their Queen faithfully and any change is accepted as part of the Creator's great plan.

They came upon the door leading into the throne room and the pair stopped. A guard was stationed at the door. He wore a grim face.

"No one may enter," he stated. "The Queen is napping."

"It is important that I speak with her," Pyper replied stoutly. "She needs to hear this information!"

"I don't think so," the guard replied.

Ruth immediately recognized the voice and fear crept into her heart. She took a hold of Pyper's cloak and pulled her back.

She whispered into the elf's ear, "He is the one I heard plotting with Trammel," she said.

Pyper glanced back at the guard. "But that is one of her Majesty's elite warriors. This is far worse than I expected it to be." Glancing around they started to leave the main hall.

"There is a back entrance to the throne room, but it will also be guarded. With a surprise attack we might be able to sneak in."

They strolled around the corner and down the hall towards a small wooden door. There was no one standing in front of it so they entered and closed the door behind them. The room was like the back stage of a rock concert. Boxes, curtains, and other miscellaneous items were scattered haphazardly on the floor.

Directly in front of them was another small wooden door. Pyper quickly told Ruth that it led into a short corridor that opened to the left of the queen's throne. The Senate and Scribes would often use this door as their entrance into the throne room.

The two skirted past the riggings and into the corridor. At the end was a guard. He was watching them as they approached. Pyper pulled a dagger from her boot and suddenly attacked the guard. She was able to disarm him quickly and she placed the edge of her dagger at his throat.

"What are you doing?" the elf sputtered at Pyper. "This is treason! Do you think that her Majesty will go lightly on you because you threatened one of her guards?"

"I don't expect so," she responded.

She led the guard into the throne room with Ruth close behind. As they entered, the Queen gave out a cry of shock and the main doors burst open with the elite warrior darting in with weapon drawn.

The elf that Pyper had disarmed yelled, "Kill her, even if it means killing me!"

The elite guard approached.

"No!" yelled Ruth. Everyone froze. She had never felt such power in her voice before, and even now she didn't know where her authority came from.

The main doors opened again and Andora and Ferris stepped into the room. They were chatting idly, minding their own business and had decided to find Ruth and Pyper.

"Wait," Ruth said again.

The Queen held the mirror tightly in her hand. "No one orders me around in my throne room," she said. "Someone bring Trammel!"

Everyone waited in apprehension until the doors opened a third time and Trammel strode into the chamber. At once Ruth felt her heart flutter and she felt her knees start to weaken. She had been resolved to tell the Queen that Trammel was behind a plot to kill her; but suddenly everything she had heard didn't seem so correct.

"What is going on?" Trammel asked in his strong voice. He eyed Pyper. "You are sentenced to Oblivian—how do you plan and settling your spirit before you depart—you will be sentenced to torment if you don't!"

"I'm not worried about that," Pyper replied defiantly. "You have the Queen under an enchantment!"

Trammel laughed. The sound echoed in the room and it was catching. The Scribes to the Queen's left started to giggle as well, even though they were not sure why they did so. "I have the Queen under an enchantment. You are afraid to go to Oblivian and that is what you have come up with. Do you hear how utterly ridiculous you sound?"

Ruth suddenly felt her own strength returning as she watched Pyper stand up to the vampire. "It's true!" she said. "I heard you!"

"Really? And what exactly did you hear?"

"I heard you say the Queen's blood would feed the darkness!"

Trammel's gaze shifted instantly to the Queen. She was staring in her mirror. "My lady," he said, "these are all insane conjectures. You must send them out and have all of them executed immediately!"

The Queen continued to stare into the mirror, "Have them executed immediately," she echoed.

Ruth glared at the magical object that the Queen held in her hand. Instantly she knew what she had to do. Rushing forward Ruth reached out and took a hold of the mirror, ripping it from the Queen's hand. It happened so quickly that no one had time to react.

Ruth landed on her side next to the throne. She stood up holding the mirror—in a single thrust she smashed it against the throne; but just as Pyper had predicted it did not break.

"You think that is going to stop me," said Trammel. "Give her Majesty her mirror back."

There was such power in the elf's voice that every fiber of Ruth's being wanted to oblige. She lowered her arm. She felt a bulge in her pocket; she had forgotten about it, her blush and make-up mirror were in her pocket. She had to make the Queen see that she was under a spell. Reaching into her pocket Ruth pulled out the tiny mirror. Flipping the container open she saw herself, quickly she turned the mirror to face the Queen.

Silence erupted as the Queen reached out and took Ruth's make-up mirror from her. Ruth was still holding the enchanted mirror when suddenly she felt muscular arms wrap around her shoulders. Looking up she saw that Trammel had her firmly in his grasp—he was breathing lustfully into her ear.

The Queen dropped the mirror and looked down at Ruth. "What is going on?" she asked. "Why am I so ugly?"

Pyper piped up. "My lady, Trammel has had you under an enchantment. Even though you are in your right mind right now, you have to smash the enchanted mirror that Ruth holds."

Trammel tightened his grip. "That is never going to happen!"

Ruth felt that it was going to be the end. Trammel's face suddenly transformed into a hideous demon. His teeth sharpened and he lowered his mouth to Ruth's neck. Ironic, she thought, her first kiss was going to be from a vampire. She glanced over to where Ferris had been standing, and she could not see him. He obviously was so over her that he had left her in peril.

"Give me the mirror," Trammel ordered. She clung to it.

She felt the fangs of the demon pierce the first layer of her skin. Suddenly there was a scream and Ruth was yanked free from the demon's grip. Turning around she saw that Ferris had tackled the demon and was now wrestling with the vampire on the floor. Ruth immediately tossed the mirror to the Queen.

"Don't look at the glass," Pyper yelled as the Queen caught the flying object. "Smash it, smash it quickly!"

The Queen brought the glass mirror down on the black marble throne and the object smashed. Pieces of glass shattered and flew in every direction; even the handle started to fall apart and disintegrated in her grasp. Suddenly, with the enchantment broken the queen started to change. Her face narrowed, her eyes turned into a deep-sea blue color, her blond hair grew back, long and luscious. Her fingers and figure narrowed and after a moment a beautiful, young elf Queen was sitting on the throne—her entire form returned to its normal self.

The Queen looked at her fingers and felt her skin. The other elves in the chamber gave a cheer as they saw their Queen restored.

"Trammel!" the Queen's voice rose.

Everyone looked to where Ferris and Trammel had been fighting; all they saw was Ferris lying on the floor with a touch of blood on his temple. Trammel had smacked the boy's head against the floor and he was out cold.

Ruth rushed over to Ferris and knelt down beside him. She could feel the healing sensation begin in her hands as she caressed Rat's temple. The blood disappeared and reappeared on Ruth's temple for just a moment and then it disappeared.

Ferris woke up and looked into Ruth's eyes. "I couldn't bear seeing you in trouble," he said. "Were we able to break the enchantment?"

"Yes," Ruth replied still caressing his temple.

"I'm in love with you Ruth," Ferris said suddenly.

She stopped. "What?"

"I am in love with you."

"But I saw you and Andora kissing outside in the garden!"

"No, we didn't. She told me that she only saw me as a friend and that we could never be anything other than that."

Ruth stood up. "So what! I'm the contingency; the second place; the one you want if you can't have her?"

"No," he stuttered. "I mean..." he trailed off.

"You are a miserable, little, er, Rat!" Ruth said. She was mad and could feel the sting of his rejections surfacing to her face.

"I'm sorry!" he tried to say.

Ruth turned to the Queen.

The Queen smiled deeply at Ruth, her lips sparkled with silvery speckles. "I am grateful for what you have done for me. Is there anything I can do for you?"

Ruth glanced over to Pyper who had released the guard she had disarmed. "It would mean a lot to me if you would revoke the execution of Pyper. She is completely loyal to you, my lady."

The Queen smiled again, "Of course and I do hope that Pyper will again join me in service."

Pyper bowed low to her Queen.

"Also," Ruth added. "We are searching for Gnomedom. We were sent on a quest to find out what happened to the gnomes—at this very moment they are attacking Bogmarsh and we need to know why."

"It would be my pleasure to assist you," Mistress Mikado said. "I will have Pyper take you to the city Raystream, there you will find a portal that opens near the Gnome Tree houses."

"Thank you," Ruth said and she bowed to the Queen.

Pyper led them out of the city. There was no great fan fair, or military escort. The Queen had turned her attention to what had happened since the enchantment. Trammel and his henchman had disappeared. Pyper didn't know where vampires went—but it was dark in Afflatus so they may have escaped there. She said that since there was no sun in Lumino-City, the vampires were able to abide there in hiding.

Raystream was a quaint city, most of the people were common and few paid any attention to them. Pyper led them to a tree in the center of the town. A beautiful garden surrounded the tree. It was true what people said about the elves, they love nature.

Pyper pressed her fingers against the tree and again it started to tear like ripping paper. The dimensions were being pulled apart. Ruth could see the darkness of the Taboo Forest on the other side.

"Pyper," she said taking the elf's hand. "Thank you for saving us!"

Pyper leaned in and gave Ruth a kiss on the cheek. "It is I who should thank you."

"There is a darkness that is covering the land of Afflatus," Ruth stated. "Do you think that it is the same darkness that Trammel said the Queen's blood was going to feed?"

"I don't know," Pyper replied. "The darkness has always represented death. Vampires want to destroy all life—they are demons intent on destruction."

"So I guess the best way they could accomplish that, was by destroying the elves, the source of life."

"Yes, and I am glad that you were able to stop them here."

"Where is here?" Ferris asked. He was sullen since the rebuke back in the palace. "Are we in a different world?"

"No, you are still in Afflatus. Lumino-City is like the heart of Afflatus. There are many elven communities in many different dimensions—your world also has a heart—if you went there you would find the elves."

Pyper was silent for a moment and everyone stared across the tear into Afflatus; the daunting task still a head of them rested heavy on their shoulders.

"It is time for you to go," Pyper said. She reached into her pocket and pulled out a silver ring. "This is my ring— whenever you need aid, it will help."

"Thank you," Ruth said again. They held hands for another moment and then Ruth stepped into the land of Afflatus again. Andora and Ferris followed.

Ahead of her she could see Gnomedom.

CHAPTER EIGHTEEN

Body and spirit are twins: God only knows which is which.

--Algernon Charles Swinburne, The Higher Pantheism in a Nutshell [1880]

"Twins," echoed Avery.

The large giant standing in the doorway growled. "Humans!" He noticed Torrent beside them and there was a brief moment of recognition, but it was immediately replaced with anger. "What do you want here?"

"May we come in?" asked Avery. "It is quite cold out here and as you can see we didn't really come prepared for winter weather." She wrapped her cloak tighter around her body, feeling very self-conscious about her chest.

The giant grunted but let them enter.

The hut was two rooms. The room they entered contained a large rocking chair, a counter with a bucket of water and sink (obviously they did not have indoor plumbing), a kitchen table and two chairs. There was a fire raging in the hearth and the logs looked to be the size of a person.

The young people and the gnome immediately went to the fire and stood next to it warming their hands and feet. Torrent on the other hand approached the giant.

"What's your name?" she asked.

The man giant tried to ignore her and he lumbered to the rocking chair and sat down.

Torrent repeated her question; she moved to stand directly in his vision. The giant finally replied. His voice sounded loud and large to the young people, but Torrent didn't seem to mind. "My name is Deafen R'or," he said. "I am the Overseer of these Colonies."

"Is there anything that you would like to say to me?" Torrent asked hesitantly.

"Why would I?" he grumbled.

Torrent glanced back to the children. She noticed that Lumpy had left his place next to the others and was exploring the hut. He had disappeared into the adjoining bedroom, out of sight.

"Well," she continued. "You have to admit that there is a striking resemblance to the two of us," she said.

"Nothing but a coincidence," he replied. "I don't know you from a tree in the forest!"

Torrent was hurt, but backed away to where the others were warming by the fire.

Avery spoke up. "We were told that we could find a magical item called the Seerer Mirror here in the Land of Giants. Would you be able to assist us in our quest?" she asked.

Deafen R'or grumbled again, "Don't know nothing about no Seerer Mirror. Now if that is all and you are warm, I'd like you to leave!"

In the other room they could hear Lumpy start to whistle. It was cheery tune, and one that he often sang when he felt in a good mood.

It was Jared's turn to grumble, "Sounds like something is making him happy!"

"Get out of there!" Deafen Roared. The sound shook the house and the young people had to cover their ears until their drums stopped vibrating. "You have no business in my house!"

Torrent frown at the mean giant, "Don't you have any hospitality?"

"Not to humans and gnomes, I don't."

Lumpy exited the adjoining room. In his hand he carried a painting, his pockets also looked full of other knickknacks he had managed to get his hands on. In other circumstances Avery would have made him put it back, but at the moment she wasn't feeling so inclined towards this giant.

Torrent took the picture from Lumpy and looked at it. It was a family of giants, a mother, a father, an adolescent boy and a baby. The baby wasn't wearing any clothing except a large diaper with a safety pin stuck in the front. The adolescent boy was obviously Deafen R'or.

"Who's the baby?" asked Avery glancing around. "I don't see anyone else here!"

"This is my home," the giant replied. "She can be wherever she wants."

Avery admired the picture one more time; she noticed that there was a birthmark that looked like a half moon on the baby's thigh.

213

Lumpy pressed up beside her, also keen on the picture. "I've seen that before," he said pointing at the mark Avery was looking at.

"You have?" she asked.

"Yes," he replied and he nodded at Torrent. "When me and the Overlord found Torrent in the mountains, we didn't realize she was a giant and when she stood up we accidently looked up her dress. I feel horrible about it now." He didn't look like he felt horrible about it and Torrent blushed.

"Give me that painting," Deafen yelled. "That is none of your business!" He reached out to take a hold of it, but Torrent stopped him and grabbed the picture.

"Wait," she said and she examined the painting. "I do have a birthmark exactly like that. This is me and you are my brother!" she said excitedly.

"I don't have a clue what you are talking about," Deafen said again. "Now it is time for all of you to leave and I don't care if you all freeze to death out there!"

He ushered them to the door and a moment later they found themselves standing in the cold. A northern wind rushed past them and Avery felt goose bumps start on her arms and legs. If they didn't find somewhere to hideout for the night, they were going to freeze to death.

Torrent was still holding the painting when the door opened a crack and Deafen's hand reached out and plucked it from her grasp.

"What do we do now?" asked Torrent. "I'm sure that was a picture of my family. And that evil man was my brother. I wonder where my parents are?"

Huddling close together they had to decide what to do. A moment later a voice called out to them, another giant. "Child! Child, you'd best come in out of the cold."

C.R. Endacott

Avery glanced around and saw a door to a hut nearby opened a crack and an inviting light creased the frame. They immediately entered, welcoming the invitation.

The giant that had invited them in was much shorter than giants are concerned. The average giant stands ten to fifteen feet tall. This lady was about eight feet tall, her back was hunched over slightly and she looked very old. Avery quickly introduced everyone and they made their way over to the fire to warm anew.

The lady introduced herself as Peaking Molehill. Even though she seemed intrigued as to the humans, she could not take her eyes off of Torrent.

"Would you like a glass of tea?" she asked. Her voice was much softer than Deafen's and Torrent's.

"I would love one," Avery replied and the others nodded their heads.

Peaking placed a black kettle on a hook inside the fire and sat down. "You can't mind ol' Deafen," she said. "He is the Overseer of the Colonies now. He has been for some time."

"How can such a grump be elected the Overseer?" asked Avery. "Most times it is better to get on the good side of the people you want to govern."

"We don't elect our Overseer, at least not any more," Peaking replied.

"What happened?"

"Fifteen years ago Deafen's parents were the Overseers, they governed fairly and honestly. However, disaster struck their family that year. They had a baby girl born to them, a year to the day of her birth the child went missing. At first they thought that a giant dingo had taken their child, but no remains were ever found.

215

"Things changed after that. Deafen became much meaner and he would start tormenting other children of the colonies. People thought that it was because his parents stopped caring about him, all they wanted to do was grieve the death of their baby.

"Ten years ago, five years after their baby disappeared, Hillary, the mother got ill. One day she was fine and the next she was dying. She passed away within a week. No one ever knew what sickness overcame her. Some think it was the grief.

"Finally, six years ago, Ponderosa, the father started to get ill as well. It seemed to be the same affliction that his wife had died from. He lasted almost a month before he died. Deafen than took over control of the Colonies and immediately passed a law that stated he would govern until his death and then his son would take over for him. That is how things have been ever since."

"Why doesn't someone just fight him on the issue?" asked Merrit. "If you don't like the ruler, revolt."

"Giants are firmly attached to their law. Without law, there is no order. Because the law states what it states, giants do not want to attack it for fear of being ousted by their own Colony."

"There must be something that you can do?" added Avery.

"There might be a way," Peaking said and again her gaze strayed to Torrent.

Avery looked the same way and noticed that Torrent was crying softly. "And Torrent is probably the missing daughter," she concluded.

Peaking nodded her head. "Without a doubt. Her and her brother have always looked a lot alike, and both of them bear a striking resemblance to their mother."

"Torrent could replace Deafen as the leader and then return the Colonies back into a democracy," Avery said.

Torrent looked fearful, she still saw herself as a young giant. "I couldn't do that. He is much more powerful than I."

"It would not come down to a fight," Peaking said. "If we can show Deafen to be a murderer, the Council would have no choice but to sentence him, and then, since they want to follow the law, would have to appoint you, Ponderosa's daughter, Overseer of the Colonies."

"How can we go about proving that Deafen did as you say?" asked Avery.

Peaking sighed and rocked in her chair. "I'm sure that when you were just a baby Torrent, Deafen sent you down river. I am sure that he hoped you would drown or that some other wild animal would find you and eat you. I am also sure that he poisoned his parents. It seems odd that no one has ever suffered from the same disease that killed your parents."

"And you are sure that I am the daughter of Hillary and Ponderosa?"

"I couldn't be more sure."

Avery thought for a moment and suddenly an idea came to her. They were seeking the Seerer Mirror. The Jester had said that it would shine through falsehood and expose lies. "I have an idea," she said. The others looked at her. "Peaking, we are here looking for a magical item called the Seerer Mirror. It is used to break darkness—it will help us expose the lies of Deafen."

"I have never heard of the Seerer Mirror," she said.

"We were told that it was in the Land of Giants. Is there some place where giants have relics stored?"

"The museum in the South Colony carries many types of relics, what you are looking for might be there. I must say however, that I have never seen anything there that resembles a mirror."

"It's as good of place as any to begin looking," Merrit added. He threw his cloak on over his shoulders.

"Where are you going?" Jared eyed the young king.

"To the museum."

"What, you going to break in?"

"No, it just seems like we are so close, and if we go and get this done, the sooner I can get back to my Kingdom."

"I don't know why you came in the first place, if you are so worried about your Kingdom."

Peaking stood from her rocking chair and took the kettle, which was steaming, from the hook by the fire. She poured cups of tea for everyone. The mugs felt huge in Avery's hand, but she enjoyed the hot beverage as it warmed her tummy.

Avery finished her tea and curled up in front of the fire. Peaking brought her and the others several blankets and said that even though there were no extra beds, they could just make themselves comfortable where they were able. In the morning she would take them to the South Colony.

The next morning the crew set out for South Colony. Avery was amazed to see that Peaking owned a blue buffalo. The beast stood larger than an elephant and everyone except the two giants were able to ride it. This made the traveling much easier since they, being the shorter members of the team, didn't have to slug through the waist deep snow.

Avery admired the scenery as they rode during the daylight hours. The snow was packed nicely making it almost like a road. There were few other giant travelers on the road. At one point early in the morning Avery had seen a dozen men wearing plaid shirts, brown wool pants and two bladed axes for cutting down trees heading down the side of the mountain. Peaking said that most giants are lumberjacks and they use their buffaloes for hauling the felled trees out of the bush. Avery vaguely remembered myths from her childhood about a giant woodcutter and she wondered if that giant had somehow lost his way in Afflatus and stumbled into her world; thus creating the legend.

The South Colony was even smaller than the Central Colony where Peaking lived. It consisted of twelve huts, all made out of stone and logs. There was perpetual smoke wafting out the chimneys and the smell of burning wood gave a homely feel to the valley. Central to the colony was a building made purely out of lumber; a large sign was posted above the door, which read: Trading Post.

"That is where we're heading," stated Peaking. She had been mostly silent during the trip. It was tough slugging for her because she was slightly shorter than Torrent was.

Inside the Trading Post is smelled like dust and fur. It was a wooden room; a barrel stove was burning in the right corner. Next to the stove were a pile of woodcutter axes, nearby a hundred plaid colored shirts hung on wooden hangers, they were all red and white. Next to the shirts were brown wool pants; various sizes were the only distinguishing characteristic. In the women section were dozen of dresses, slacks, cotton shirts, heavy wool cloak and pantyhose, at least the women could wear a variety of clothing.

A friendly giant was standing behind a counter next to the food supplies. He was tall, heavy set, even for a giant, with a belly that partly covered the table when he leaned over to look at the children.

The counter was as high as Jared was tall and Avery had to stand on her tiptoes just to look over it.

"What 'ave we got 'ere?" the jolly old man said. His hair was graying and his fingers looked like extra large sausages.

Peaking introduced them. "They are looking for a magical object somewhere in the Land of Giants," she offered.

"Magical object, eh? Can't recall any of those around 'ere." He scratched his head and a flake of dandruff as big as Avery's fingernail floated to the counter top.

"I thought they could check the museum, you know, just to see."

"No 'arm in trying, I suppose," the jolly giant replied.

He stepped from around the counter and Avery had to guess that he was about fourteen feet tall. More than twice as tall as a tall man in her world. He led them to a door she hadn't noticed upon entering; the door had a rusted doorknob and when the giant turned it, it squeaked.

The room on the other side was darker and had only several candles in stands. The jolly giant lit one of the candles with matches from his pocket and light flooded into that one corner of the room. He proceeded to light the others and soon it was bright enough to see everything.

"Look away," he said, "I'll just be in the Trading Post."

After the giant was gone Avery turned to Merrit. "How are we supposed to know what we are looking for?"

"I don't know. You're the Truth Seer, shouldn't you be able to do this?"

Jared stepped over, "Just go around touching everything, it might stand out!" he offered.

Peaking and Torrent decided to leave the Museum and admire the clothing in the Trading Post. Torrent had never seen so many clothes that would fit her before. Lumpy on the other hand was excitedly exploring every nook and cranny in the place and his pockets were starting to bulge as more and more knickknacks found their way into his pockets. Finally Jared took control of the gnome, made him empty his pockets and then held tightly to the gnome's hand; still with one free arm and when Jared wasn't looking, Lumpy managed to pilfer numerous things. Since they were giantish things, his pants started to sag from the weight.

Avery had been going around the room touching objects. She touched several mirrors; a couple of axes, even a buffalo halter, but nothing stood out.

"It has to be easier than this," she muttered.

Once she had walked into every corner of the Museum, she returned to where the others had gathered. She shook her head, nothing had stood out. There was nothing here that could be considered a magic object.

As they left the Museum back into the Trading Post the jolly giant shopkeeper was waiting for them. "Find what you were looking for?" he asked.

Avery frowned. "No," she said.

"I was thinking about what you had said about a magical object," he started. "I don't know if this will help, but there is a legend around these parts—it could be what you're looking for."

"What is it?"

The jolly giant came back around the counter and sat down by the barrel stove. "The Legends tells of Iniquitous the Sinful. Maybe a thousand years ago, could have been more, there lived a family; they had been cursed by the Bright One, the maker of all things. The giants had been blessed and given a beautiful forest to live in. The trees stood as high as the heavens, water flowed through streams to rivers, into oceans, and there was so much food, more food than they could ever hope to eat. In the center of the forest the Bright One planted the Beholden. No one knows what the Beholden was, but the Bright One told the giants that they were not to look at the Beholden. They could go anywhere in the forest they wanted and use whatever they wanted in the forest, but they must stay away from the Beholden.

"The family grew and they had two sons. The eldest was named Iniquitous the other named Decent. Iniquitous was searching the forest for entertainment one afternoon with his brother, and he decided that he was going to look at the Beholden. Decent tried to prevent his brother from doing this evil thing. They got into a fighting match, as brothers often do, and Iniquitous grabbed a stone and smashed his brothers head, killing him. Iniquitous dragged the body with him to the center of the forest where he found the Beholden.

"As I mentioned, no one knows what the Beholden is, but when Decent's body touched the Beholden, legend says he was transformed into a magical object that exposes the guilt of ones actions. Iniquitous was so overcome by his guilt that he ran away taking with him the magical object that used to be his brother—some say that he took it to remind himself of his guilt.

"The Bright One was so upset that he sentenced the giants to toil the earth as woodcutters until the end of time. They all settled in the mountains, near forests that reminded them of the Great Forest they used to live in. But Iniquitous settled in the mountains; in these mountains, and on cold winter nights the Beholden object shines forth, it casts green and blue lights on the sky and you can hear the cries of Iniquitous on the wind."

Jared stood from his place on the floor. "Fascinating tale and all, but how does that help us?"

"It think that the Beholden object is the Seerer Mirror. It is an object that exposes a person's deception and evil," Avery said. It made sense to her. But how could they find the place were Iniquitous had hidden the object. It had to be in the mountains somewhere.

The jolly giant continued as if he had read Avery's mind. "The lights on the sky have been called the Southern Lights, but they always arise over the tallest peak in these mountains. If I were to look for Iniquitous, that is where I would start."

"Thank you," Avery said. "You have been very helpful."

"I had forgotten all about the legend of Iniquitous the Sinful," said Peaking as they trudged back outside into the cold. "But you have to admit there are some interesting parallels to what you are looking for."

Avery nodded her head. "Tomorrow we go mountain climbing!"

"Wait," said Peaking as she rushed inside the Trading Post.

The others waited for her patiently, peaking into the window to see what the dwarfed giant was doing. A moment later she returned and in her hands were three sets of giant children's snowshoes. "These might help," she said.

CHAPTER NINETEEN

~

Away, away, from men and towns, To wild wood and the downs.

--Percy Shelley, To Jane: The Invitation [1822]

Gnomedom was exactly as the elves had described it, tree houses. Upon leaving the Lumino-City, Ruth, Andora and Ferris had found the Gnome village and spent the night on some leaves near its base.

As daylight came Ruth was able to get a better idea of what they were up against. The tree houses were all twenty feet high, built in large branches and looked like places young children would play in. The homes were connected with an integral network of rope-bridges and ladders. Ferris had placed his foot on one rung and it immediately gave out under his weight.

The trees were mostly oak and cedar and the smell of the forest was lovely. But there was no one around. The village was completely deserted, not even animals had decided to call the abandoned village home.

They split up and started exploring. Ruth headed to a large structure that was located near the ground level of the forest. It looked large enough for humans to enter. As she got closer she could see that it was a square building that hung from a tree branch by a thick steel chain. Reaching out she pushed the structure and it started to swing.

The door was burst open like a bomb had gone off and it hung by rusted hinges. The only window of the structure was barred with thick wood that was part of the building's skeleton.

Ruth found it was low enough to the ground for her to climb into the one room cage. A single bed sat in the corner; the mattress was a mix of leaves, ferns, and branches. Examining it closer she found that it was long enough for a grown human to sleep on. Her fingers brushed the outline in the leaves of a human form. Whoever, or whatever had been kept prisoner here, had been for a long time.

There was also a small chair and writing desk in the opposite corner of the room. The wood looked old and worn, she strode over to the desk and sat down in the chair. The legs creaked as her weight sank onto the seat, but it did not collapse.

She was stunned to find several pieces of parchment.

"Hey guys!" she shouted to Ferris and Andora. "I think I found something."

The two other young people arrived a moment later and soon they were all crowded into the cage. The chain holding the cage squeaked above them, from the added pressure. Ruth picked up the top parchment and started reading.

This is the last will and testament of Gerald Lee Prig.

"Hey, this is Mr. Prig's writing. That means this must have been his cell."

"But where is he?" asked Ferris. "This place is utterly deserted; a regular ghost town."

"Read some more," said Andora leaning against the desk. The movement caused the cage to swing again.

Ruth continued reading.

I do not know where I am or how I got here. But these little buggers are gnomes and they have forced me to marry their queen. They are like a bunch of children, at first I thought marriage would mean making children, but in the case of gnomes, it is all a status thing. Needless to say, I am perpetually locked up in this cage!

I am writing this will because I am fearful of my life. Gnomes have started to disappear from the village. I have watched from my prison window— there is a sense of panic. One night I caught sight of the creature that is taking them—it looks like a wolf that walks on hind feet. If it should come for me, I know it will kill me.

The page ended there and Ruth went to the next page. It didn't appear to be sequential; because this page was part of a diary entry.

Day 52

I was allowed to go for a walk today. They took me past a cemetery for gnomes. It was the oddest thing because they don't use headstones like we use headstones. If a gnome dies they cut down a tree to leave a stump and then they bury the gnome under that stump and write an elegy on top.

This part of the forest was clear, like a logging company had come by and clear-cut it. Despite having a chain around my neck I was able to see some of the elegies. More than a dozen of them said, "killed by a werewolf." I thought that odd because the creature I saw resembled a werewolf, but I distinctly recall that it was not a full moon. That was most intriguing.

Ruth turned to the next page. Again it looked like some time had passed.

Day 79

I am alone. I have not been fed for over a week. All the gnomes have left—they have deserted me. This is the last parchment I have so I fear no one will be able to find me and save me.

It is late at night and I hear many things happening around my cage. There is sniffing and growling, but I am too afraid to peer out and see what is happening. Wait there is something opening the lock—

The page ended there. Ruth searched for more parchments, for all the missing sections, but there was nothing around. "I guess that's all we get," she said.

Ferris took a hold of the pages and skimmed through them again. "I knew that we should have brought him back the first time. Something terrible has happened to him and it is all our fault."

"How were we supposed to know that something would kill him, or capture him, or do whatever!" Ruth said. Every time Ferris spoke to her she could still feel the anger at him mounting. For the most part she tried to ignore him.

Suddenly the cage started swinging and Ruth could feel a sickening feeling start in her stomach. "Stop shaking the cage," she said to the others.

"I didn't move," Andora replied and looked over at Ferris.

"Neither did I," he said looking up from the paper.

Chills swept up her spine as Ruth quietly walked over to the door and looked out. There wasn't anyone or anything in sight.

"It must have been the wind," she gulped. But she couldn't feel any breeze.

"Let's get out of here," said Ferris hastily folding the papers and putting them in his pocket. "This place is creepy, all the silence and you never know if the creature, the werewolf, or Menas, is out there or not."

They stepped out of the cage. Their movement caused it to swing more violently as they jumped clear.

Ruth stood up and was brushing dirt from the knees of her pants when she heard a rustle in the bushes to her left. Without using abrupt movement she glanced in that direction and saw two small eyes staring at her through the foliage.

Through the corners of her mouth she directed the others to look in that direction.

"Let's get him," Ferris said quietly.

In a sudden attack Rat darted for the small creature in the bushes. They heard a loud squeal; much like a baby pig trying to escape the slaughterhouse and a small gnome, smaller than Bigwig and Lumpy, dart out of the trees and through the Gnome village.

"Wait!" yelled Ruth.

"No! You want to eat me!" the gnome shouted back and kept running.

The gnome was not the brightest, as most gnomes are not, and he started to run around in circles, rotating from large to small, in what he thought were evasive tactics. Which did thwart the young people for a moment because they started chasing him in circles. They would reach out and try to grab the gnome but each time he would slip through their fingers.

Ruth finally had the bright idea to let the other two chase the gnome. She moved to cut him off and the tactic seemed tricky to the gnome because on one of his rounds of the circle he suddenly found himself face to face with one of his pursuers and he skidded to a halt, dirt and leaves bunching up at his feet. He turned to run and found the other two right on his heels, so he did what any intelligent gnome would do. He dropped to the ground, belly up and pretended to stop breathing, like he was dead.

Ruth chuckled at the gnome. He was playing dead, but if she waited five seconds his chest would move up and down, and he kept opening his eyes to see if the enemy had left him alone. Each time he saw them staring at him he would clench his eyes tightly closed and pretend to stop breathing.

"We know you're not dead," Ruth said.

"But I look dead," he said and then instantly clamped his mouth shut.

"See you just spoke," Ferris added snidely. "You're not dead."

The gnome shook his head.

"Look, we're not going to hurt you," Ruth said softly. "We are your friends."

The gnome opened one of his eyes and eyeballed the big people. "Why did you try to attack me then?"

Ruth smacked Ferris on the arm. "Because Dufus here doesn't know how to be polite!"

The gnome sat up. "Well, what is wrong with Dufus?"

"That is a good question, a very good question," Ruth replied and laughed.

"My name is Ferris, not Dufus," Rat said, his tone sounded hurt.

The gnome crawled up into Ruth's lap and she held him tightly. "Where has your tribe gone?" she asked him.

The gnome's face contorted into a look of terror, his mouth started quivering and his eyes moistened up and his eyebrows danced up and down. "They were taken. They were taken to the north into the Dark Taboo Forest. The darkness covers everything there."

"He has to be speaking about the dark wall," said Andora. "Why are the gnomes attacking the humans?" she asked.

"I don't know," the small voice replied. "Evil darkness spirit comes and takes Grims family away. They go away and leave Grims alone."

"What about the human that was kept here?" Ferris asked.

He looked up with large brown eyes from Ruth's lap. "What does Dufus want to know about the mean man?"

"I'm not Dufus. And yes, what happened to the mean man?"

Ruth chuckled again. "He looks like a Dufus to me." The gnome nodded.

Grims' eyes widened again and his lip started quivering again. "The mean man was taken by the Evil darkness spirit, but not like Grims' family. The Evil darkness spirit took over the mean man's body and made him meaner."

"This isn't good," Andora stated. "We still have to find out what happened here."

"I think that it is pretty obvious," Ferris replied.

A twig snapping in the forest behind them startled them all. Grims jumped up from his snuggled place in Ruth's arms and darted in the opposite direction. The three young people stood and faced the sound.

A moment later Baron Cache exited the woods. He was still wearing his dark cloak, but his hair looked messed up and he had a look of ire on his face. "Where have you been?" he demanded stomping over to the young people. "I have been searching this cursed forest since last night trying to find you little buggers," he cursed and spit out a twig that was caught in his beard. "How did you disappear and get away from the Menas and gnomes?" He stopped directly in front of Ruth.

"It is a really long story," she said.

"I don't think I want to hear it anyway," he growled. "Now, what have you found out? I just want to get this over with. Here we are in Gnomedom—pitiful little hole—and there isn't anything around."

"We think that the gnomes were taken by the Menases to the Northern Taboo Forest."

"We knew that much already," he sneered. "What else?"

"Our principal may have been turned into one of the Menas," Ferris added. "We still don't know who is behind the dark wall or the disappearance of the gnomes."

"Shame," muttered Cache sheathing his weapon. "I thought you might have figured more out by now."

"What?" Ruth was confused.

A grunt sounded behind them and the three young people turned abruptly. Standing behind them was a platoon of Muskags.

"What are they doing here?" Ferris' eyes were wide in horror.

The first Muskag with blue tattoos decorating his arm to his elbow spoke. "Don't you recognize me kid!" his voice gruff, but familiar,

Ferris' face fell.

"Who is he?" Ruth asked quietly. She looked over at Andora's face and she also recognized this creature.

"He is the tracker that brought me to Bogmarsh from the river," Ferris replied.

The Muskag added. "And the one that you sliced up in the Cook House. I just about died!" He motioned to the other Muskags. "Take them to Hokum and with any luck we will be eating human tonight." The other Muskags roared in approval.

Ruth glared over at Cache. "Aren't you going to help us?" she cried.

Cache sneered. "I don't think so. I have to get back to Bogmarsh and open the gates. With the King gone, the Dark Army will be able to sweep the city."

"You traitor!" Rat cursed as they were shackled. He started fighting, squirming, pinching and clawing. Finally one of the Muskags slugged Rat over the back of the head and he sunk to the ground.

Ruth barely had time to give a cry of shock when she felt something hit her on the head. A brief bright light flashed through her brain and then everything went dark.

CHAPTER TWENTY

Great things are done when men and mountains meet;

--William Blake, Poems from Blake's Notebook.

Great Things Are Done [c.1807-09]

The tallest mountain in the Land of Giants was called Cryptic Peak. Jared was immediately skeptical of their ability to climb it, considering the name of the mountain. But he agreed to come along nevertheless.

They set out at first light after Peaking had made them a delicious breakfast. She had mentioned that she was too old to be making the trip with them, but wished them good fortune. Jared had been selected by vote, to be the one that carried Lumpy on his back and they had created a makeshift rucksack that the gnome fit into. Jared only agreed to carry the extra weight, if Lumpy got rid of his extra weight—and all of them made the gnome empty his pockets. They found everything from left over food, a stuffed rat, which smelled funny, frying pans (no one knew why he needed two), paperweights that had been in the Giant Museum, a diary from Deafen's hut (it didn't say anything incriminating) and several pairs of shoes, human shoes not gnome.

The snowshoes were a blessing, but Avery found it was difficult to walk in them, and it took her awhile to get the rhythm of it.

The mountain was steep, snow would blow down from the top and cut through the thin layers of clothing they had. Peaking had also provided warmer cloaks, but Avery found the wind still went right through the wool.

As they hiked higher they came to a large ridge, on one side of them was a drop off straight down, and to the other a cliff stretching a hundred feet high. As Avery looked up she could see some snow overhanging the cliff above them and she feared that any sudden noise would create an avalanche that would blow them over the drop off.

Avery moved to the drop off and looked out over the Valley of Giants. They were very high now and she could see all of Central Colony. In the distance was also the smoke from Southern Colony. She wondered how many giant colonies there were.

Jared shuffled up beside her. "Pretty ain't it?"

"Mmm," she said.

Suddenly Jared shouted, "Hello!" The valley echoed back, *Hello, hello!*

The cracking of snow sounded above them and Avery looked up. Quickly pulling Jared to the cliff they placed their backs against the stone. Merrit and Torrent followed suit.

"Are you stupid?" she whispered at Jared. "Any kind of noise could set off an avalanche up here!"

"Just having a little fun," he said a hurt tone in his voice.

"Well this is serious, don't treat everything like a joke!"

"Just trying to lighten a dark situation; stop being such a know-it-all stuck up snob!"

"Errgh!" she stomped away from him. She would have yelled but she was afraid that her voice would also set off the avalanche.

At noon they stopped for a brief lunch of cold bread and cold tea. Peaking had provided them with some sliced ham, and it added flavor to the already dull meal.

Staring up she saw how much mountain they had left to climb. Everyone was feeling tired and cranky. Merrit had stopped interacting with everyone, Torrent sat with her head in her hands, and it appeared she was trying to get some sleep. When they stopped Jared had unceremoniously dumped Lumpy to the ground, not even bothering to free the gnome from the rucksack, and Lump was so tired he just walked around with the rucksack on, it looked like a brown diaper.

The air was getting thinner and Avery could feel a headache starting at the back of her temples. If they didn't find the cave soon, she would have a splitting headache in a couple of hours.

The snow was crunchy this high up on the mountain and the wind blew with unceasing anger. It cut into their faces and hands, the only skin that was exposed on their bodies. They had decided against a fire during lunch, but now everyone was regretting that decision.

Finally Avery stood, "Best get moving. If it gets dark while we are up on the mountain, we could be in great danger."

Everyone stood and brushed the snow from their clothing.

They were about to continue when Avery felt a different chill along her spine. At first she chalked it up as being the weather. But the more she dwelled on it, the more she felt that they were being followed. She looked behind them but could see nothing through the snow and clouds below them.

"What?" Merrit asked.

"I don't know," she replied.

"Someone following us?"

"Maybe. Come on, let's go."

They hiked through the rest of the afternoon. The sun was beginning to set behind the mountains and the orange orb was stunning and Avery had to stop and just admire the beauty. Her breath was evident in the even air and she could feel the hair on her head start to harden. They had been walking the whole day and were close to the summit of the mountain. She had hoped that they would be able to find the cave, so that they would have somewhere to sleep for the night. It would be very cold to sleep just out in the open.

In eighth grade, the class always took a trip to the mountains and spent a survival weekend in a snow camp, however she hadn't done that yet.

The sun set quickly and they were alone in the darkness. "Where are we going to spend the night?" asked Torrent. "It will be dangerous to continue hiking in the dark—could take wrong step and fall off a cliff."

"We need to find shelter," Merrit agreed.

Avery glanced up the mountain ridge. "We have to be near the summit. This ridge will take us to the top. The cave is to be around here somewhere."

"We can look for it in the morning," stated Jared, he sounded exhausted.

Suddenly from a short distance below the ridge they heard a howling wolf. "What was that?" asked Avery.

"It was either a wolf, or one of those Menases!" cried Merrit. His gaze darted to the ridge. "We are very exposed here. We won't be able to fight them."

Lumpy wasn't paying attention to the howling sound. He was pointing up the slope. He tried to speak but snot had dripped out of his nose and frozen over his mouth. The snotcicles had made two streams down both sides of his lips and he looked like a frozen samurai warrior.

Avery looked to where Lumpy was pointing and her heart cheered. A green light was bursting through the snow not more than a dozen paces in front of them. Jogging to the point she started to dig into the snow. A loud *crack* sounded and she could feel the snow start to give, then she was falling through the crevice. She gave a startled scream, but dropped five feet through the snow to rock below.

Jared rushed over to the crevice where she had fallen and looked down, "You okay!" he hollered.

"Fine," she replied.

Green and blue light was shinning out of the cave entrance in front of her; she had found it, the source of the light.

"You guys need to get down here," she shouted. She could feel that it was much warmer. She could hear the sound of water trickling inside the mountain.

It took the others a moment to reach her side.

The green and blue light cast eerie shadows on the ice wall, but it provided enough of a glow to help them see. They exited the smooth ice cavern walls into the rock cave in the side of the mountain.

The rock cavern caused their footsteps to echo off the walls and floor. A small stream of water only a couple of inches deep flowed past their feet. Avery took a sip of the water and found it was pure and refreshing. The walls of the cave were completely smooth, like a worker had intentionally made it so. The deeper they walked, the wider the cave became.

"I think we found it," said Avery. She glanced back at the others, Merrit was staring at her, and there was a twinkle and smile in his lips.

Merrit brushed up beside Avery. "You are the most beautiful girl I have ever met," he said. His voice had changed from its normal tone to one of awe and peace.

"Huh?" she blushed. She stepped back and stared hard at the young king.

"But I'm afraid I cannot marry you!" he confessed. He reached out with one hand and held her shoulder softly to console her.

"Who's talking about marriage?" she was startled. Boys were by far the weirdest creatures in creation.

Merrit continued unabated. "You see, I am a King and Kings have to marry princesses. You are not one of those! I need to think about what is best for my Kingdom."

"That was a little blunt and—mean!" she said flabbergasted. Not that she really wanted to get married and stay in Afflatus anyway. She had just been thinking it was fun to flirt with the handsome king.

"It really is a shame, because you are beautiful!" continued Merrit.

"Stop talking like that," she said, her eyes wide in wonder. "What's gotten into you?"

Jared brushed up to her other side. They were now all standing side-by-side in the greenish-blue light. "He's right you know," said Jared. He reached out and took hold of her other shoulder. "You are very pretty!"

"What is wrong with you guys?" her eyes darted from one boy to the other.

"Avery I have loved you for a long time," Jared confessed.

"Is that a tear in your eyes?" she shouted. "Are you crying?"

"It is only because I am so aware of how much I love you! I don't understand this feeling I have in the pit of my stomach. I don't understand how you have the ability to make me feel so much! I love you!" he practically shouted.

"Stop talking like that!" she said. She pulled herself free from both of the boys. But inside she felt herself beaming.

Jared continued. "You can be very judgmental, you have no idea what it is like for me. CJ is my brother, he is the only family I have and so I will do what he wants so that he will still accept me."

"And you make me so angry," Avery felt herself saying suddenly. She didn't know by what power she was confessing this! "You have so much potential but instead you try to get yourself kicked out of every foster home you are placed in. I think that you are using drugs, you have a lighter, and that brother of yours is no good. I care so much about what happens to you; but you continually shut me out of your life."

"I am not using drugs," Jared retorted.

"How can I believe you?"

Torrent ignored everyone else's conversation and chimed in. "I think I am going to stay with the giants. They need me and I need them. Once we get rid of Deafen, I will return the land to a democracy."

Jared's head had lowered, "Is that the reason you were flirting with King Merrit and not me, because you are ashamed of me? I lost that fencing match to Olly, you think I do drugs, and I steal to gain my brother's affection; is that why you don't like me anymore?"

"Jared, I have always liked you. I care deeply for you. That is why I was so upset, I want the very best for you!"

Lumpy was hugging Jared's neck, "I love you!" he said. The gnome's eyes were closed and he was purring with his chin next to Jared's hairline.

They entered a large cavern and sitting on a stone boulder was a golden shield. The green and blue light was being cast from it. As they stepped out of the light all of them suddenly remembered the things they had been saying to one another. Jared turned beat red and did not look at Avery in the eye. Avery too suddenly felt very sheepish.

Merrit's eyes widened in shock. "I think I know what this mirror does," he said. "As long as you are in the light, it makes you speak the truth."

Avery went over to Jared, "I'm sorry I was so judgmental, you're right, I don't know what it is like to be you. But we are friends and I love you too!"

Jared's gaze lifted and a smile crossed his lips. Without another word he reached out and gave Avery a hug. His strong arms wrapped around her shoulders and she wanted to melt in his grasp. He really was an amazing guy. He had saved them from the Seaweed Monster, he had fought the Menas in the sky and he cared for her. It made her feel pretty good.

"So is this the thing we are searching for?" he asked releasing Avery.

"I think so," she replied.

Avery stepped over to the boulder and reached out to touch the shield. Suddenly the light stopped and they were plunged into darkness. It was pitch-blackness and they could not even see their own fingers in front of their eyes.

A growl sounded from the front of the cavern, it was echoed to by two more different deep-throated growls.

"Did you break it?" asked Merrit quickly. "We need some light. We can't fight those demons if we are blind!"

Avery grabbed the shield with both hands, but nothing happened. Closing her eyes she concentrated on the shield. What was the trick to making it work? Her fingers grazed the edges of the shield, it was smooth; she felt the front and bottom, but still nothing. Grazing her fingers along the back of the shield she felt to straps for holding an arm in place. She reached her arm through the leather and grasped the shield tightly. Suddenly light flooded into the room again.

All eyes turned to the entrance, three Menas were standing there with their hairy bodies, and wolf-like jaws, claws as long as short sword, and muscle. The muscle sinewed around their chests to their arms and legs.

The middle Menas had a bald spot on the top of his head, and his fangs looked longer and more deadly than a vampire's. He shook his head like a dog riding fleas and then in hunched over movements starting circling around the outer edge of the cavern. The beasts were snarling in rage and the smell of wet dog permeated the room.

Avery faced the leader of the Menas, the one with the bald spot. Drawing her sword she waited for the attack. The others would have to fend for themselves. They did have the beasts outnumbered.

Closing her eyes she saw the deeds of the beasts, they had killed many people including a farmer in southern Afflatus, a worker from the Ruins, as well as many others. She opened her eyes and saw the evil that they represented. The creature attacked her and she held up the shield to block. The greenish blue light hit the demon full force and even though it did not physically stop the strike, Avery saw. While in the light from the Seerer Mirror she could see the Truth about the Menas. This Menas was Mr. Prig. She saw her old principal, his bowling ball head, his hairy arms and chest, he was naked under the cloak of magic and so she did not look further down.

"Mr. Prig?" she said.

The Menas stopped on all fours. His attack thwarted. In the light from the Seerer Mirror, the shield, he could see himself for what he was and for what he had become. He gave an incredibly mournful howl and then darted from the cavern. Avery could hear the cry of shame disappearing down the halls. The moment he had left the shield's light he had returned to the form of a Menas again.

If Mr. Prig was a Menas, did that mean that the Menases were humans, cloaked in Deceptive magic too?

Avery turned the shield onto the other Menas. Their features did not change so much, but Avery recognized them immediately. They were werebeasts, creatures that had served the Swamppond in the Eternal Bog, during Quagmire's reign. The creatures were not phased by the recognition that they were evil.

Avery saw the truth. They had turned Mr. Prig into the Menas; it was another form of the werebeasts. They hunted like wolves, but their natural selves had tusks and boarish features. The Menas, and werewolves and werebeasts were of the same breed. But that meant that they still had to fight these Menas.

Suddenly the light in the cave grew brighter, and it wasn't from the shield. A glow started in an upper corner and started to spread. Then a moment later standing on top of the boulder was the ghost of a massive giant. This giant was over twenty feet tall; his arms and legs massive, he wore a fur coat, and shackles held his arms and feet in place. The Menas cowered, as did the others.

The ghost spoke. "I am Iniquitous the Sinful. For my crimes I have been sentenced to eternal pain and torment, to wander the world a restless spirit."

Avery admired the giant's face. He was sad and remorseful.

The giant turned his attention to the Menases, "Your time is up!" He pointed both of his fingers at the Menas and the two creatures started whimpering. Tails dropped between their hind legs and they curled up into balls, tighter and tighter until bones started cracking and they lay still.

The giant when he had finished turned his attention to Avery, who was still holding the shield.

"That is my brother. I killed him in my anger. In my sorrow I pass him to you. You have great need for this shield, may it expose the lies and guilt and restore the world to peace."

"Will you still have to wander, restless?" Avery asked.

"Yes, it is my fate. The Bright One shows mercy to whom He shows mercy."

Suddenly, as if the words were magic the shackles opened and fell to the ground. The sound of clanking metal greeted their ears. Iniquitous stared at his hands and feet.

"I am free?" he asked. "I am free!" he said realizing. "No longer shall I be called Iniquitous the Sinful, but my new name is Shrift the Redeemed."

Slowly the ghost faded from the room.

"Can we get out of here now?" asked Jared.

Avery nodded and started to remove her arm from the shield—the light went dark again, so she quickly replaced her arm. They needed the light to get out of there.

"Wait, let's use the Staff of Terminus!" she said. "We can return to Peaking's hut that way."

Merrit handed the staff to Avery.

CHAPTER TWENTY-ONE

~

The brain may devise laws for the blood, but a hot temper leaps o're a cold degree.

--William Shakespeare, The Merchant of Venice [Act 1, ii, 51]

The companions had flown down the side of the mountain like a meteorite. The staff created a light force around them. It took only a matter of moments to land on the porch of Peaking's hut.

She opened the door having heard the sonic bomb of their arrival and let them in. Her gaze immediately rested on the shield. Avery was no longer wearing it on her arm and had it tied onto her back.

"Is that the item you were searching for?" she asked.

Avery nodded her head. She briefly recounted their adventure and Peaking was very pleased that none of them had been hurt. She approached Torrent and rested her arm on the giants shoulder. "Are you ready to confront Deafen?" she asked.

Torrent nodded her head but Avery noticed a small shiver coarse through the giantess. She was afraid that her people would not accept her for who she was. Avery could understand the fear—she never felt like she really belonged with the people in her school either. It had to be harder, never having experienced how other giants lived; Torrent was probably terrified.

But, as far as Torrent was concerned being with her own people was the most rewarding feeling she had ever had. She had never before felt like she belonged anywhere, but here the tables and chairs were set for her height, the portions of food more for her size. People could look her in the eye and she didn't feel like she had to slouch all the time.

The shiver was brief and she nodded briskly. "I'm ready," she replied. Defeating her brother who had tried to kill her would be her first order of business.

Peaking sat down in her giantsized rocking chair and crossed her legs. The others gathered around her. Peaking smiled, "Good, tomorrow morning I have called a Gathering. The Council has agreed to meet at the Hedge at first light. I have said it is to discuss the arrival of Torrent. I want the giants to approve and accept that Torrent is the daughter of Ponderosa and Hillary."

"How will they accept that?" asked Torrent.

"Everything is run by rule of law. If we can get a majority vote to say that you are the daughter of Ponderosa, they will automatically accept it—even those that may have voted against you," Peaking explained. "We will have to be aware of Deafen, he will think that something is up. We will have to be on our toes with him. He will try to convince the Council that you are not his sister."

"But we have this to help," added Avery holding up the Seerer Mirror.

"I hope that it works like you say," Peaking said. She rose from her chair and started to walk towards her bedroom. "Get some sleep. I will wake you early so be can be at the Gathering on time. Good night."

It was getting late. They all said good night to each other and set up makeshift beds by the fire again and soon all of them curled and fell asleep.

Morning arrived and the sun was just starting to cast its long golden hairs out over the land. The clouds that had surrounded the hostile mountain, Cryptic Peak, had dissipated. The sun even felt warmer on their shoulders as the motley crew made their way to the Hedge.

The Hedge was a circular hedge of rocks that stood twenty feet high. Entering them was like entering Stone Hedge, there was no ceiling, but the hedge of rock was solid and prevented any wind from blowing through. Situated at the center of the Hedge was a roaring fire and as the crew approached they noticed twenty other giants sitting on stone benches around the outer edges. Deafen made twenty-one. He wore a beaver hat with a foxtail sticking out the back. The foxes and beavers in the Land of Giants must also have been giants to have made that hat.

One of the elders motioned Peaking and the others to a bench next to Deafen. Since they were to be guests at the Gathering, they were given seats of honor.

It was Deafen's job to bring the meeting to order. He stood and smacked his fist in his hand—every one ceased their speaking.

"This Gathering has been called by Peaking Molehill. She claims to have found the missing daughter of Ponderosa and Hillary, my parents. I have seen this supposed sister of mine, but I leave it to the Council to decide," he sat back down. "Discussion to begin."

Peaking stood from her place next to Deafen and addressed the Council. She motioned to Torrent to rise and she obliged. "This is Torrent," Peaking started. "She came to me two nights past and immediately I saw the resemblance, she is the spitting image of Hillary and as you can see with your own eyes, she looks a lot like our leader Deafen R'or."

There were nods of approval.

Deafen stood. "Just because she looks like me, it doesn't mean that she is my missing sister. There needs to be more proof than this."

Torrent recalled that they should have returned to Deafen's home and taken the portrait of her as a baby. They could have shown the birthmark. Torrent's face sunk at this realization. Their evidence seemed rather flimsy at the moment.

Peaking cleared her throat. According to the rule of law she was permitted to complete her opening statement without interruption. Deafen sat down and scowled when several of the older council members shook their heads.

Peaking continued. "As I was saying. More evidence suggests that we have never seen Torrent before. How many giants willingly disappear and come back years later? She has not lived among us. I dare any chief to say she has been staying in their village," she waited for effect; none responded. "Since she is a stranger, but still a giant there must be another explanation as to who she is. I put to you that she is Ponderosa's daughter, and she was kidnapped as a baby or sent away and has finally returned to us—that is the only logical conclusion." She sat down to allow discussion to commence.

Another Council member stood. He was an older gentleman. He wore the typical giant clothes; a red and white plaid shirt and brown wool pants. However, he also wore spectacles and he pushed them up his nose as he examined Torrent.

"My name is Doctor Forte Overhill. I was the one that helped the dear departed Hillary give birth to her daughter and I was the one that counseled the couple after the child disappeared. I happen to be in the knowledge that Ponderosa and Hillary's child had a birthmark."

Deafen's face darkened.

Doctor Forte Overhill continued. "It is the shape of a moon on her inner thigh. If this giant, whom you claim is their daughter, must have this same birthmark." He turned and faced Torrent like he was expecting her to drop her slacks and show everyone.

Torrent cleared her throat. "I do have the birthmark, but I am embarrassed to undress in front of all of you."

"Ah ha," said Deafen. "If you cannot prove that you have the birthmark, we cannot agree that you are who you say."

Peaking intervened, "I have seen the mark and I attest to its origin."

"Of course you would," stated Deafen in a loud voice. You are the one who wants her to be proven their daughter."

Torrent began to shuffle nervously until another female giant stood up. She wore a blue dress and white apron, under which she wore tanned slacks and loggers boots. Her voice was gruff. "There'll be no need to make the wee lass undress before all ye dirty men!" she said. "Have her show me the mark out back and I'll tell ye all what is there or not!"

"I agree to this," replied Doctor Forte. "I trust Misses Hide Duster!"

Torrent nodded her head and a moment later was walking out of the ring with Misses Hide Duster. They were gone for only a moment before returning, a smile was on Torrent's face.

Misses Hide Duster remained standing. "She has the mark!" she announced.

Deafen stood up with a roar. "It still isn't good enough."

"You doubting my word!" Misses shouted.

"Enough!" yelled Doctor Forte. "I say we call this to a vote. Anyone who believes Misses Hide Duster raise a hand and say 'Aye'." Fifteen hands went up and a chorus of 'ayes' was heard. "Passed. Torrent is indeed Torrent R'or, daughter of Ponderosa and Hillary."

"So be it!" another giant added. "Now can we get some breakfast!"

Peaking stood. "I have one more order of business."

Deafen was growling, but because the Gathering had been called, all orders of business had to be addressed. "Very well, what is it?"

Peaking turned and faced Deafen. "I want to charge Deafen R'or with the abduction and attempted murder of his sister, Torrent R'or."

"Are you insane!" Deafen roared. "I see the plot here, you are intent on disposing my authority; that is treason. I shall see you put to the Sleep."

"I also want to add to those charges. Deafen R'or needs to be charged with the willful murder of both his parents, Ponderosa and Hillary."

Deafen was roaring his outrage. Finally Doctor Forte stood and announced silence. "Peaking, you must have proof of these charges—they are very grievous indeed. What evidence do you have to offer?"

There was a murmuring around the circle. It was going to be difficult to prove. Avery shifted uncomfortably. She had seen the mirror work, but she hoped they could solve this problem without the help of magic.

Peaking cleared her throat and continued. "First and foremost, Torrent disappeared as a child and as all of you will recall he was not sympathetic to her disappearance, he said that a coyote probably did it and even had his parents believing that possibility. Second, he has always been a selfish boy and with the birth of their daughter, Ponderosa and Hillary stopped paying undivided attention to him—he got jealous and got rid of the competition. So you see he has every motive for getting rid of her. Her very presence says that someone sent her down river; a coyote did not eat her. It is him or my name isn't Peaking Molehill!"

"Purely conjecture!" Deafen stood from his place at the head of the Council. "These are nothing but terribly erroneous charges. Since the Council has ruled that Torrent truly is my sister I welcome her back. It will be so nice to have a family again after mine died from an illness."

Avery heard another giant mumble under his breath, but no one else seemed to catch it. He said, "Poppycock and twaddle."

Peaking retorted. "That was no illness, it was poison, how come no one else has ever died from this disease?"

Deafen snarled at her, "Lucky you haven't caught it! Yet!"

"Is that a threat?" she asked.

Merrit finally could not contain himself any longer he stood up. "My name is Merrit Divine and I am King of Afflatus," he announced. "I want it to go on record that this giant, Deafen R'or treated me and my friends unkindly. He knew about the birthmark on Torrent and he kicked us out of his house, refusing his own sister refuge. He is a liar and as such has demonstrated the aptitude to do what is necessary to get what he wants!"

Deafen responded snidely. "The King of Afflatus has no power here! I sent them out because they are thieves!"

Avery knew what she had to do. She took out the Seerer Mirror and placed it on her arm. Immediately the greenish light burst forth. It surrounded her first and then became like a flashlight cutting through the darkness. She pointed the greenish blue light in Deafen's direction.

As the light hit him his mouth started moving, but it appeared outside of his control and he quickly added, "But I got the painting back and it really also belongs to my sister Torrent." His voice had changed to a softer tone. He seemed startled that he had spoken such words and he clapped his hand over his mouth and muffled his speech.

Doctor Forte faced Avery; there was concern in his face. "What is that object?" he asked. "We do not trust magic!"

"This is the Seerer Mirror. It is a magical object; but you need not fear it, for it is part of your tradition and legends. This is the Beholden that Iniquitous the Sinful took after murdering his brother. It shows the truth!"

"I don't believe it!" another giant shouted and a chorus agreed.

A riot was going to break out. Some of the giants were curious where Avery had got the magical item, whereas others demanded she hand it over to the museum. It was very intimidating to be surrounded by half a dozen giants. Suddenly she started shining the light around the circle and various confessions started to sound. Giant after giant admitted to misdeeds he or she had done, each clamping their hands over their mouths the moment the words were out. Avery returned the light to Deafen.

That move brought a halt to all the commotion. Doctor Forte's face was red from embarrassment. "I for one," he coughed, "agree with what the human girl says. Ask the questions that need answering!"

Peaking faced Deafen with a stern glare. "Did you abduct your sister and send her away from the Colonies?"

A look of horror crossed Deafen's face, and he nodded. "I was so upset that this little baby was getting so much more attention than me. I remembered how my parents would cuddle me, kiss me to sleep, hug me, and tell me how great I was and then she came along and ruined everything. I bound her up and dropped her in the river—she was supposed to die!"

Peaking continued unrelenting. "And did you poison your parents?"

Again Deafen wanted to not respond, but the light of truth was forcing his will. "I killed them! I killed them both! They couldn't get over the loss of that stupid baby girl. All they did was mourn her and every time I saw them, they made me feel guilty. I killed them to make them shut up!"

Doctor Forte stood again from his place on the bench. "I think we should have a vote. All in favor of revoking Deafen R'or's status as leader raise a hand." There was an overwhelming response. "All in favor of sending Deafen to the Sleep, raise a hand!" Again the response was overwhelming, one hundred percent in support for both motions.

"Wait!" stated Torrent. "He is still my brother! Please don't send him to the Sleep, whatever that is, but it doesn't sound good."

"He will sleep beneath the mountains for the rest of time. If we do not send him to the Sleep, he may try to poison you!"

"I do not fear my brother! I motion that Deafen be allowed to live, however, he may never harm another being, not even the smallest flea and he must swear to it!"

Avery stepped up. "I think that I can make sure he doesn't lie."

Avery approached Deafen with the Seerer Mirror tightly gripped in her hand. She had him place his right hand on the shield's surface and she asked. "Deafen R'or, do you swear on this object of truth that you will never cause harm to another person again and that you will only use your strength and power for good deeds and you will always listen and do what your sister Torrent tells you to do?"

Avery could see that Deafen felt something coursing through his body. He saw how his misdeeds and his murder had hurt others and the guilt of his actions became overwhelming, he started to weep. Falling to the ground, with his hand still firmly pressed against the shields surface he swore to abide by those conditions.

When he had finished Avery withdrew the Seerer Mirror and returned to her seat. The shield was called the Seerer Mirror because when used the person looking into it saw the reflection of their evil self—any one that had any remorse and guilt would succumb to the power of the mirror.

"Torrent, since the law has been passed that only a relative of Deafen can govern, would you be willing to accept the job?" asked Doctor Forte.

"I would," Torrent responded. "But I am young and haven't lived in the Land of Giants for a long time. I will need the help of the whole Council and would humbly ask their support in all decisions."

"Agreed," a chorus of voices stated.

"Now," said Doctor Forte. "We need to discuss you given us back our sacred object."

Torrent cleared her throat. "I understand that this magical item is an important part of giant history and legend. However, I am equally aware that it is the only thing that can save the world of Afflatus from the evil overtaking it. I ask that the council let the humans take the Beholden, and use it to vanquish the evil. When they are done," she glanced at Avery and Merrit, "will you return it to us?"

Merrit bowed deeply and replied. "I swear on my entire kingdom that you shall have the mirror back when we have finished using it."

"That's good enough for me," said Torrent. "Any others want to repeal?"

The circle was silent. There were a few looks of disgust, but it was true what Peaking had told them. The giants followed law, and since Torrent was now in charge, they sided with her.

"It is settled," and Torrent slammed her fist into her hand as she had watched Deafen do, to call the meeting to order.

The meeting was adjourned and the giants all filed away, many offering their congratulations to Torrent. Deafen stayed as a lump on the ground weeping for a long time after the meeting was dismissed—he would never forget the guilt of his sins.

When Torrent had finished speaking with many of the other Council members she returned to Avery, Jared, Merrit and Lumpy by the benches.

"Well, I guess this is going to be good-bye," she said sadly taking hold of Lumpy and giving him a big hug. The gnome started balling and she had to put him down. Lumpy flung his arms around Jared's neck and sobbed.

"I guess so," Avery smiled half-heartedly. I know that Bigwig will regret not getting to say bye."

"I'll miss him too. He was a good tribe leader. But this is where I belong."

"I know," added Merrit.

They spent only a few more minutes saying their good-byes when Peaking arrived to show Torrent to her new home. The young people waved to her as she disappeared into the Colony.

Avery held the Staff of Terminus in her hand. "I guess we can use this to get back to Bogmarsh," she stated.

"Finally," sighed Merrit.

Bigwig stood on the walls of Bogmarsh. He suddenly felt a deep sadness overcome his soul and he started to cry. He didn't know why, but he couldn't help but feel something had changed.

Wiping his eyes, he sighed. He had peeled every potato in the city and a mound of potatoes now covered the kitchen floor and the chef had finally got tired of tripping over them and sent Bigwig to the wall to act as sentry. It had been difficult to find a place to stand where he could see, but now that he was there, he wanted to turn tail and run. The wall of darkness was pressed up against the walls of the city. People were sticking their hands into it, watching their fingers disappear. It had been fun before; but the ominous sense that the darkness now gave him was unsettling.

Thus, Bigwig, having already experienced that turned and walked off the wall in search of more potatoes to peel. He was entering the street when he saw Baron Cache running towards the front gate. Odd, wasn't he supposed to be with Ruth, Rat and Andora? He let the thought leave his mind and he followed Cache towards the gate, maybe there would be more potatoes there.

Cache reached the gate. All the guards had disappeared and Bigwig noticed how quiet everything was. Something was going to happen. Cache removed the main beam holding the gate shut and slowly opened the only thing standing between Bogmarsh and the hordes of gnomes on the other side.

"Hey, Baron!" Bigwig shouted. "What are you doing that for?"

The Baron didn't respond because he was running back up the street. The Baron grabbed a hold of Bigwig as he ran by. "Shut up you little twerp," he said clamping his hand over Bigwig's mouth.

Behind them a surge of bodies started filing through the open gate—the gnome army had penetrated the city's defenses.

Bigwig did not like to have his mouth covered with another person's dirty hand, so he opened wide and bit the soft skin on Cache's hand, right between the thumb and the index finger. The Baron cursed and cuffed the gnome so firmly Bigwig was knocked unconscious.

CHAPTER TWENTY-TWO

Her rash hand in evil hour

--John Milton, Paradise Lost

Book IX, l 780 [1667]

Avery stared in wonder at Bogmarsh as the Staff of Terminus brought them closer to the city. It looked like an anthill, completely surrounded by the dark wall and gnomes were crawling over everything and everyone.

The staff brought them to a halt in front of the King's Mansion. Gnomes and men, women and even children were engaged in hand-to-hand combat. There were thousands upon thousands of them scurrying everywhere. The humans were killing few of them, because no one could really find it in their hearts to kill such a small creature. But the gnome army was trying to kill them.

Upon landing, Lumpy immediately disappeared to find Bigwig.

Merrit grabbed a hold of Avery and Jared and pulled them into the mansion. They raced up the stairs to the meeting chamber. Upon entering they found Baron Cache sitting looking at some paper work. When the king entered he glanced up startled.

"Your majesty," he said, quickly standing and bowing.

Merrit was ecstatic, "What are you doing in here? There is a battle for Bogmarsh being fought out there!"

"Thank you, your majesty, but in an effort to keep some semblance of order I have been trying to work out a better defense strategy. The gates were opened by someone and now we have a major gnome problem, as you may have noticed!"

"We did notice!" Jared shouted.

"Did you get the magical object?" Cache asked suddenly.

"Yes," Avery replied. "And I think it is time to go and use it."

"Good," the Baron said. "Your majesty, you should stay with me, while they go into the darkness and try to get rid of—whatever they need to do!"

"I like that idea," muttered Jared. "How come we are the ones that have to fight the bad guys all the time?"

Avery slugged him playfully on the arm. "Come on, I thought you wanted to come back for some adventuring. What is Afflatus without our lives being in mortal peril?"

"Right, let's go!" he championed.

"You guys be careful. The Baron and I will work out some strategy. If you see Earo, let him know that we have returned," the king said taking a seat next to Cache.

They nodded and parted ways. Avery took out the shield and Jared drew the Nightshade—they were going into battle again—but this time they didn't even know who the enemy was. She didn't even stop to consider it odd that Baron Cache was there and Ferris and Ruth were not.

Ruth sat up and rubbed her head, it stung intensely and felt tender to the touch.

"Finally!" a whiney voice said behind her. "I thought that you would never wake up and now that you are awake you can start thinking of a way to get me out of here because I don't want to be here and I don't even know where here is and for some reason all of the guys deserted me to these little people and these hairy people and these other guys that are really mean and..."

"Take a breath Holly," Ruth interrupted. She turned and saw the blond haired bully from Jeerson. She did not look well. The girl's hair was a ratted mess, her makeup and mascara had run down her face from crying so much and fingernails and skin were filthy. "It seems that you have seen better days," she remarked.

"Ha, ha! Now, where am I? And don't tell me you don't know. I know that you know and I know that you are going to tell me or else I'm going to..."

"Shut up!" said Ruth. She saw Rat lying next to Andora, they were both unconscious still. She approached and placed her hand on both of them—a moment later she felt the throbbing sensation of their pain, but they were completely healed and they opened their eyes.

The first thing that Ferris noted was Holly. "Great they have brought us to hell!"

"What are you saying?" the blond girl asked, her voice high-pitched.

"That if you are here, it must be hell."

Andora had stood and moved to the edge of their cell. It was a wooden jail, much like the one that Mr. Prig had been held in back in the Gnome Forest. "Hey, you should come look at this," she pointed out the window.

"I know hey!" said Holly in excited tones. "It's like the whole world died, or something."

Ruth was confused and approached the window to look out. The world did look like it was dead. Everything was rotting and a dull brown and black color. The world had turned into a shadow.

"I think that we are inside the dark wall," she said.

There was a lot of movement outside the cell. Muskags were patrolling different areas of their vision. Several tents had been set up and two Muskag guards stood by a larger tent nearby.

"We have to find a way out of here before that tracker Muskag decides we would make a better lunch than prisoners," Ferris said.

"There is no way out," Holly sobbed. "I tried absolutely everything. I even flirted with that—ugh—green looking person."

Rat looked to where she was pointing and he saw a Muskag. He started laughing. "I bet he was thrilled with you flirting with him. He probably only looked at you like dinner!"

Holly was horrified. "Boys usually do what I tell them."

"Don't think of them as boys," Ferris muttered. "They are more like demons."

Holly gulped and backed away from the window.

Ruth continued to watch the activity outside; suddenly she was startled. "Look who it is!" she said. "Trammel is here!"

"What?" Ferris asked moving next to Ruth.

"Trammel, the vampire. He is here! He has to have something to do with this darkness!"

"I'm going to kill that guy!" cried Ferris unconsciously rubbing his head where the vampire had struck him.

A hairy wolf creature, with a baldhead, suddenly ran into the camp, it was howling a mournful sound, like it had lost the most precious thing to it. This howling caused a lot of ruckus and a moment later the flaps to the large tent flew open and Governor Swale exited. He was wearing a long dark robe and his hair had turned completely white. His fingers looked singed and his face looked worn, but there was no mistaking the man, according to Andora, it was her uncle.

Swale approached the Menas and gave it a solid cuff on the cheek and fell to the ground and stayed there whimpering. "Some great warrior you are!" Swale cursed at the Menas. "You can't even take care of a couple of children." Swale spit and left the beast lying on the ground. The Menas curled into a fetal position and refused to move—it was like it had died.

The Governor glanced at the prison and noticed the children watching him from their cage and he ordered the Muskags to bring them over.

The Muskag, opened the door and grabbed a hold of Ruth. Putting his razor sharp dagger to her throat he ordered the others to go and stand in front of the Governor, or else Ruth would have her throat sliced open. There was no point in resisting as the Muskags forced the children onto their knees.

Swale eyed each of them intensely. "Andora, why am I not surprised to see you here? And my little Rat—it has been a long time. I was rather disappointed in your performance. You were supposed to be just like me!"

"I'm nothing like you!" Ferris retorted. He glared at the man that freed him from the Muskag prison in Bogmarsh on his first trip to Afflatus.

Trammel approached and stood next to Swale. He once again looked like the handsome elf that Ruth and the others had defeated in Lumino-City. He licked his lips as he glared at the children. "These brats managed to lift the curse on the elven queen. I would have had those sickeningly perfect elves begging for their lives. The Queen's blood would have fed the darkness!"

"You have caused a lot of problems," Swale said to the young people. "It would have been much easier to defeat Afflatus, if the heart of it, Lumino-City, was also destroyed. But that's okay, because once I am finished with Afflatus, I will move on to the Southern Lands, and ultimately the entire world of Terik. You may have slowed the inevitable, but I will win this and destroy all that the Creator loves."

Swale rested his blackened hand on the vampires shoulder—the vampire pulled away in contempt; it was obvious to Ruth that this vampire still did not like to be aligned with humans, even wicked ones.

"Let me turn one of them," Trammel asked. Ruth thought she saw some saliva drip from the corner of his lips.

Holly unconsciously pushed Rat forward. Startled, Ferris pushed back.

"All in good time," Swale reassured the vampire.

Ferris, puffed out his chest and stepped in front of Holly, Andora and Ruth. He kept his head high and Ruth had to give him some points for his courage. "We aren't afraid of you, Swale!" Rat said. "Haven't you figured it out yet? Evil will never ultimately win this war—and you want to know why?"

"Of course," Swale responded. "I am curious with what your puny human brain can come up with."

"You were defeated a long time ago when the Creator kicked you and your kind down to this earth. You want to hurt the Creator! How pathetic to base your entire existence on revenge. It must get tiring being defeated all the time."

"I am never defeated!" Swale roared. "Why do you think I keep coming back in different forms. And you have no idea how much this hurts the Creator. Someday I will dispose of him and become the new god. I will create as I see fit, and it will not be good and perfect, like the Creator wants—it will be evil and cloaked utterly in deception."

Rat turned to Ruth. "I don't think that is Governor Swale speaking any more. That man there is completely possessed by Depravity himself."

Andora moved up. "Uncle. What happened to your hand?" Andora asked, she didn't really care, because she also knew that this man was no longer her uncle.

"This?" he replied staring down at the blackened hand. "This I received as a reward for my faithfulness."

"A deformed hand is your reward," Ruth was incredulous. "Doesn't seem so great."

"Ah, yes but it is a reward, in exchange for my hand I have received power. After the fall of Quagmire," he glared at Ruth and Ferris, "I escaped to the Taboo Forest. The mysteries of that forest are many. The curse that held Merrit in the form of the Dragon Incubus also escaped to this forest. There we both found each other and through a bonding became one. You think that you were able to defeat Depravity; that the spirit of Depravity was in the Lavaryn Squall. You couldn't have been more mistaken. You cannot defeat Depravity—he is a spirit and flesh cannot defeat spirit—You can only defeat the physical form that the spirit decides to take."

"So you are the new demon?" asked Ruth.

"Hardly the new one!" he scoffed. "I am the improved one. Hokum gave me power unimaginable. I could control small solar systems—and after I have the land of Afflatus under my control and that baby King is dead, I will have the Divine Inspiration as well and I will be a god!"

"So that is what this is about!" demanded Ruth. "Why do people always think that by aligning themselves with some dark power they will become gods. There can only be one God. That is the definition of God—all powerful. If you are not all powerful, you are not, nor ever will be, a god! Don't you get it, even if there is no God—nothing else can then be a god either."

"It doesn't matter, little philosopher. I will have power greater than you can imagine. I will have the ability to destroy worlds—"

"But will you have the ability to create them?"

"Who would want to?" he sneered. "I will have all of the Creator's work bowing before me. What greater power is there?"

"Truth!" a voice called from behind them. Ruth immediately recognized the sound of Avery's voice. "The Truth is more powerful than your Deceptive magic, anytime."

"Ah, I see that the crusader has returned and what is that on your arm? Do you think that the Seerer Mirror will have any power against me?"

"We'll have to give it a try!" Avery retorted. She was confident that it would and she wouldn't allow any doubt to creep into her heart. Darkness' greatest power was doubt. When evil makes good doubt itself, the battle is already lost.

The Muskags kept weapons pointed at Ruth, Ferris, Holly and Andora. Ruth gave a silent cheer as she heard Avery speak. Her friend looked like a Zena warrior priestess. She had absolute faith that Avery would get them out of this situation.

Governor Swale turned to face the new enemy. His Menas was still curled in a fetal position at his feet; giving the wolf creature a swift kick he ordered it to attack Avery. Muskag warriors also approached. Their green skin looked dead in the shadow of the dark world; but their red eyes glowed with evil intent.

"You take the warriors, I've got him!" Avery said to Jared.

Jared's eyes glared black in the darkness of the world. The Nightshade shone darker than the death around it and the darkness was echoed in Jared's eyes. Olly would have crapped his pants had he had to face the evil Muskag warriors. Jared allowed a sinister smile to crease his lips—he was ready to fight the battle of his life. He had fought with the courage of an eagle against Incubus the first time he was in Afflatus.

"As you wish!" he responded, clenching his teeth. He approached the Muskags. He held the Nightshade ready as he stared down his enemy. The six evil creatures with their dread-lock hair and long fingers and slimy skin hunched over and proceeded with their attack like animals hulking for a kill. They all carried dark blades that reflected the red lights of their eyes. In a swift motion Jared twirled the Nightshade above his head and attacked the closest beast. Another jabbed from behind and Jared turned to meet the attacker. He danced like a man gone wild. His blade moved so quickly that it whirred, blocking each jab and slice that searched for a weakness to penetrate the moving warrior.

Avery crouched low with the Seerer Mirror pointed at the Menas. Whenever the wolf approached the light, he would return to his natural form as Mr. Prig and the beast would give howl of rage and dodge out of the light. It started to circle Avery to stay out of the light, and Avery had to turn with the beast—however, she did not want to leave her back exposed to Governor Swale who was laughing like a mad man.

"Mr. Prig," she called. "Don't you remember who you are?"

The Menas shook its mane and moved in closer. "I am no longer Mr. Prig," its voice was husky and low and barely resembled a growl. "That human creature died when I was born."

Avery however could sense the truth. This man was still a man inside. He was lost in the Deceptive magic that penetrated deeper into his soul, deeper than anything ever had before. There was hope that he would remember if she could help him recall his life back in the real world.

"You are a teacher and principal!" she pleaded with him. "You only came to this world because of us. But you are a man and one that is looked up to by many other teachers back home. Don't you want to go home?"

Swale laughed at Avery, "There is nothing that will bring him back to sanity!" he crowed.

"We'll see!" she shouted, lunging at the Menas. At the same moment the creature dove for her and they caught each other in mid air. Time and space slowed down and it looked like she was in the *The Matrix*. The Menas' claws scratching at her body in slow motion and she was able to dodge in the air and the flat of her sword smacked the beast's hairy hand. The beast reacted and swung a reverse blow at her catching her just below the chest.

Falling to the ground Avery could feel the wind knocked out of her. The beast seeing an opportunity struck. Just in the nick of time Avery brought the shield up and jaws and claws scraped alongside the Seerer Mirror and Mr. Prig in the form of the demon gave a scream of agony. Pressing her advantage Avery stood and the Menas backed away; suddenly it tripped over a fallen log and he fell to his back. Avery pushed the Seerer Mirror into the chest of the Menas. It started to howl and squirm, but she held the shield in place. She could see the visions as they flooded into Mr. Prig's head.

There was as scene of him writing a Naughty Card to her. He was yelling at another student. She saw him follow Jared into the girl's washroom where she and Ruth had first thrown the *vaporatium* powder.

Mr. Prig was squirming more and more, and his physical being was rapidly changing from wolf to human and back to wolf again. He rolled and tried to escape the human visions that reminded him of who he was—he saw every sin he had ever committed, he saw how he had killed the farmer and his wife, he was the one that devoured the worker at the rock quay, here in Afflatus. He had tried to kill Avery and Jared—he saw everything and he was cut to the heart. His form started to stay longer and longer in the form of a man and Avery could see tears rolling down his cheeks. His lips were quivering and snot ran out of his nose like a river. Suddenly he started coughing and choking; he gave a final scream and suddenly a bright flash erupted from the Seerer Mirror and Mr. Prig stopped moving. He lay calm on the ground—everyone immediately turned his or her eyes away because he was naked, hairy, but still naked.

Avery stood up breathing heavily. It had been an intense struggle. Jared was finishing off the last Muskag that had attacked him and the pair moved towards their friends who were still being held prisoner.

"Don't you see," Avery said facing the Governor again. "It doesn't matter what darkness tries to hide. The light will always break through the darkness. When the Creator made the world, it was made so that the day defeats the night, every morning!"

"That may be true," Swale responded, "but darkness always returns and it is powerful enough to keep light away!"

"Not really," she replied. "The moon and stars still break through the darkness. Even at the darkest time of night we can still see. No matter what darkness a person goes through in their life, they still have the ability to see through it. This reminds me of something—we are all given Choice; it is the greatest magic, if it can even be called magic. Even you Swale have a Choice and that is what the Mirror shows you. It will show you all the wrong Choice that you made and that is what will cut you down because we always feel bad when we make the wrong Choice, it is over time that we are able to push down our conscious and continue making the wrong Choice. But all humans were created good, even you and so somewhere inside of you the Mirror will start to set you free!"

Swale's grin had turned into a look of fear. "There is no way that you can use that on me. I have the spirit of Hokum in me." His gaze returned to the ground and he started chanting, "*Aufero meus animus quod repleo mihi universus!*"

The Governor's back started to arch and pain crossed over his face. Trammel backed away from Swale, his face in terror. The Governor's skin started to rip from his body and black skin, and claws broke through his fingertips and at his neck. As the demon arched up to his full height, it stood a staggering twelve feet tall. It had the mouth of a crocodile and the skin of a sea serpent. Its feet were like dinosaur claws and jaws that could snap a car in two. The demon gave a roar throwing its arms wide, sinewed muscle ripped on his arm and the beast flexed, hunching over so that its fangs and claws were on the same level as Avery. Why did she have to fight the demons all the time? She wondered briefly.

Trammel fell backwards over a stump in his attempt to escape the demon that was storming around. Ruth saw the vampire and she nodded to Ferris and Andora, she didn't bother with Holly because the girl was screaming ecstatically.

Jared also seeing the vampire fleeing descended upon the Muskags that held his friends prisoner. "Hey Slimeballs!" he shouted at the red-eyed beasts. "Want to dance?"

Abandoning their posts they attacked Jared. The teen was ready for them. The Nightshade was like an extension of his arm as he dodged and dove, jabbed and parried. He met the leader of the beasts, the tracker, he faked an upper cut which the beast stepped back to dodge, in mid motion Jared switched his stroke and sliced through the neck of the Muskag, and his head dropped to the ground. The Muskags tried every strategy to take Jared down, but the boy moved like a madman, with the speed and agility of a hummingbird, his Nightshade caught enemies, disarming and slaying them like a knife through butter.

Ruth grabbed a hold of Ferris. She was focused on Trammel flying towards them, trying to escape into the darkness. "Don't let that vampire escape!" she screamed.

Ferris and Andora jumped onto Trammel. Had they taken a moment to think about what they were trying to do, they may have hesitated; but there was no hesitation. As they collided, the three fell to the ground. They rolled over and over on the dirty ground crushing dying plants that crumbled into dust. The demon's face changed form and fangs slid through his clenched jaws. His skin turned deathly pale white and his eyes turned hollow and vacant. What had once looked healthy and alive suddenly appeared skeletal.

"You cannot defeat me, I am immortal!" he squealed as he battled Andora and Ferris. He knocked the two young people back with a swipe of his hand. He moved faster than lightning, but the two teens refused to give up. Andora managed to catch his deadly hand on a return strike, but he turned and in a flying kicked connected with her chest knocking the wind out of her lungs.

At one point Ferris grabbed the demon's arms and tried to force them behind his back, but the vampire head butted him, sending the boy flying backwards. Andora grabbed a hold of the arms in turn and the beast tried to kick her in the head again. Ferris quickly recovered from the head butt and jumped back on the demon's back and gave a tight squeeze around his neck. This caused Trammel to roar in anger. His teeth were snapping and he looked like a wild zombie.

Ruth watched the battle in horror. She had to help somehow. Running back to the cage that had imprisoned them she looked for a weapon; with a hard kick she snapped off a board, it fell to the ground a pointed stick. She knew the stories about vampires and how to kill them; a wooden stake through the heart was their best bet.

Andora and Ferris were still struggling to get the animal under control when Ruth approached. She had the wooden stake ready as she looked for a place to strike. There was fear in Trammel's eyes as she closed in. With a fatal thrust she found her opening and struck the heart of the vampire. In a flash of powder, he turned to ash and disappeared. Ferris and Andora fell to the ground! They were stunned and looked around for their enemy, thinking that he had managed to disappear. Then they saw Ruth holding the wooden stake and they realized what had transpired.

Avery had eyes only for the demon that hunted her. Behind her she heard that Holly had stopped screaming and had fainted.

Keeping the mirror lowered on the demon, she waited for it. It was not like the Lavaryn Squall. This demon looked strong and dark magic surrounded the creature; despair fell off it like a cloak.

"You must be Hokum," she said snidely. "Funny, I was expecting something a little more scary." She had to choke back her fear. Jwen had taught her so long ago that as long as she was in the care of the Creator, everything happened for a purpose. Hokum was evil, but everything that happened only made her stronger in her faith. She uttered a quick prayer for help.

The beast spoke and it sounded like thunder. "You have no idea the power I possess!"

Suddenly Avery felt a peace come over her. "All you demons sound alike," she commented. "You claim to have this great power, and that you are going to kill me and yadda, yadda, yadda!" It never failed, it seemed that all darkness had was boasting and pride and in reality they had nothing to boast or be prideful about. At the heart of evil, it was nothing more than an insecure spirit that didn't want to be nothing—but really that is all it was: nothing.

The demon stepped towards her and its massive claws struck. Blocking with the shield, Avery was stunned by the force behind the blow. Maybe she was wrong; there was something substantial to this creature; the Lavaryn Squall, when it had transformed, wasn't even that strong.

The beast struck again and Avery dodged to the side. There had to be some way to defeat the demon. With her sword drawn, Avery attacked. She skirted under the demon's arms and her blade found the belly of the beast. With a jab she pushed with all her might against the evil skin. It didn't pierce even the most outer scale, instead her weapon shattered.

There had to be a magic that would defeat this animal. The shield did nothing as the greenish blue light cascaded off the demon skin.

She had to move quickly as Hokum brought his foot down on the ground she had been standing on. How did the Truth play into this? There had to be a component of Truth that needed to be exposed—why the Seerer Mirror didn't show her she didn't know.

Finally it dawned on her. Blind faith! Jwen had taught her so long ago to just trust the Creator and trust the Truth; as long as she saw in the spirit world, not the physical one, she would see the truth. The only way to defeat this demon was to see it; really see it. She knew that that meant really seeing herself.

The demon thrust his claws at her and she went sailing across the clearing. She fell against Swale's tent and the structure fell down around her. In the tangled mess she had to see herself.

Taking the mirror off her arm, she turned the front side of the Seerer Mirror so that she was looking into it. Clutching the sides with both arms she peered into the mirror.

The greenish blue light hit her eyes full force and she saw herself for who she really was. She didn't see all the sins that she had ever committed, she didn't see how cruel she had been to others, she didn't see every lie she had ever spoken. Instead she saw herself through the eyes of the Creator.

It stunned her to see that she looked like a demon. Selfishness oozed off of her like slime, pride and vanity covered her like warts and boils, immoral thoughts floated around her head like a black cloud, and anger flashed from her eyes like bolts of lightning. She looked like a demon from the darkest parts of hell.

That is how the Creator saw her! So ugly! So disgusting!

"I'm sorry," she started weeping. "Jwen told me to be like you and I have failed. I am no more pure than that demon that walks out there!"

Despair started sinking in her heart. She watched her evil reflection as a white light appeared beside her—it looked like the hand of Jwen. The white light brushed lightly across her face and the warts and boils disappeared, the bolts of lightning stopped flashing. The hand covered every part of her body, and everywhere that it went, the darkness was wiped away. With each wipe of the hand, Avery noticed that it got a little bit darker and a little bit dirtier. Until finally she was completely clean. There wasn't an ounce of evil left on her. Then she heard the sound of Jwen's voice.

"You are made clean when you repent! But remember a price must always be paid—the Creator has taken your darkness from you, and placed the pain inside himself. The Creator is good and what does light and darkness have in common? The Creator takes it away and make everything new again—but it cost the Aver'd One everything!"

"Jwen, Jwen!" Avery called. "Thank you!"

"Be at peace!"

"How do I fight this demon?"

"Look at it again, and you will see!"

Avery stood from her place, dropping the Seerer Mirror in the folds of the collapsed tent. The demon was approaching her—but it didn't look the same. It looked like water, a moving mud puddle. Her gaze rested on the demon, but she could no longer hear its thunderous voice, it now sounded like a trickle of water. It was clear what she had to do.

Avery gazed around her, the world seemed different, color was starting to reappear, life was returning to the darkness and it started everywhere that she stepped. But things seemed different to her too, when she looked at her friends she didn't see them as they were, but as what they could be, she was blind to everything that decayed and saw only that which was life; it was the most beautiful sensation she had ever had.

The puddle approached her and she didn't have to dodge any blows, she was looking at the creature purely from the realm of the spirit, it could not deceive her any longer. The beast struck at her but the demon's arm flowed around her like a waterfall is split by a rock.

To her left she saw a crystal blue pond. She went and stood on the opposite side of the water. The puddle, not realizing the water in its way, slid right into the water and disappeared, suddenly all the darkness that surrounded it was sucked into the pond as well—there was a bit of turmoil in the water and then it was clear.

CHAPTER TWENTY-THREE

Any eye is an evil eye
That looks in on to
a mood apart

--Robert Frost, A Mood Apart [1947]

Ruth rushed over to Avery who was kneeling by a crystal blue pond. Jared was sheathing his sword, he had slain the Muskags. All the rest had disappeared. The dark wall that had been taking over the land had been sucked into the pond along with the demon.

Ruth had watched as the twelve-foot creature stepped into the water and it instantly melted—being sucked under and like a tornado disappearing the dark wall was sucked in after the demon.

She reached Avery's side and grasped her friends hand, "Are you alright?" she asked.

Avery looked up at her and Ruth inhaled sharply.

"Avery," she said. "Your eyes, they are like Jwen's, completely white! Can you see?"

Avery smiled, "I am fine Ruth and I can still see—it's just different. I see things as they were supposed to be seen by the Creator. I see the goodness of everything created and Deception has no power over me because I also see it as it is supposed to be."

"How long will it last?"

"I don't know, maybe forever!"

"But that would be terrible," Ruth was shocked.

"No, no it wouldn't. Because I am seeing the world for the first time what it was created to be. I am seeing a new earth and a new heaven. It is like everything has been made brand new."

"What do I look like to you?"

"You are so beautiful Ruth. Your beauty glows like the hottest sun, or the most poignant star."

Ruth closed her eyes as Avery spoke and imagined what it must be like.

Ferris stormed over and interrupted the conversation. "Where is King Merrit?" he asked.

Jared responded. "He is with Baron Cache!"

"Cache is a traitor. He was in league with Governor Swale the whole time!"

"That means the Merrit is in danger!" shouted Andora. "Come on, we have to go and save the king!"

Avery stood and walked over to the pool, "One moment," she said. Reaching down she placed her hand into the water. "It is as I feared," she said. "The demon Hokum is familiar to us. I was able to sentence it back to its pond."

"What do you mean?" asked Jared.

"You and I have one more mission," she said. "Ruth, take Ferris and Andora back to Bogmarsh and warn Earo that Merrit may be in danger." Ruth nodded. Avery turned to Jared, "You and I have to visit the Swamppond in her swamp."

Ruth watched as Avery walked over to where Mr. Prig was lying on the ground. He had not moved from his fetal position, tears of grief were still pouring down his cheeks.

"Andora?" Avery asked. "Do you still have the *vaporatium* powder and a cloak for him to wear?" Andora nodded her head. "Sprinkle some over this man and that blond girl, Holly, over there." Holly was still, having fainted during the fight, and had not regained consciousness yet. "Now go rescue the king!"

Ruth, Ferris and Andora stormed through the forest back to the walls of Bogmarsh. As they arrived they saw a very entertaining sight. Thousands of gnomes were walking around like they were lost. Some of them were sitting and tanning themselves on the sidewalks, other walked aimlessly from person to person and they were occasionally kicked aside—they grunted at the mistreatment, but moved on. The battle had completely stopped and the soldiers of the king's army were shocked at the sudden change in the gnomes.

They found Earo; he was standing by the main gate. His sword was dry, he had not killed a single gnome, but the handle end had spots of blood, from him smacking so many of the small creatures over the head. Despite hating gnomes, he couldn't kill them.

"Earo!" Ruth said as the three ran up to him. "Avery defeated Swale, he was behind everything—actually the demon Hokum was behind everything."

"Enough of this!" Andora yelled. "The king is in trouble."

"What!" Earo demanded. "The battle has stopped!"

"It was Baron Cache who opened the gate!" said Ferris. "He has betrayed you!"

"That weasel!" Earo swore. "Come on, I think I know where they are!"

They bolted, running fast. Earo quickly took the lead; his sword was drawn and ready to defend his King. They reached the King's mansion and found the place strangely quiet. No gnomes wandered the halls, and all the rooms were empty.

"I know where he took the King," Earo stated.

They ran to the backyard and found a massive hedge maze. "At the center of this maze is the altar where all the kings of Afflatus have been crowned. It used to be located in the Castle Ruins to the north, but Merrit had it brought here."

"Do you know your way through?" Ferris asked.

Earo flicked blond hair out of his eyes, "Of course."

The cedar hedges smelled nicely, but the company did not have time to sniff the air. They darted through the maze following Earo's lead until they came to the center garden. They found the three-sided altar where Merrit had placed it. The King was tied and gagged and his neck was resting on the stone. Baron Cache was standing over the body of the king with his sword drawn.

"Stop!" ordered Earo. He ran up to the walkway that went through the pond to the altar. The others stayed further back.

Cache stopped in mid stroke. He could have finished off the young man right there, but he held.

"Don't do this!" Earo said. "Just put the weapon down!"

"This boy ruined everything!" Cache cried. "When he was that Dragon Incubus, he killed my people, destroyed our fields, and burned our homes and barns. Some one has to pay for that injustice. He returns and wants us to trust him as some benevolent ruler!"

"You opened the gates, many innocent people," and he added, "and gnomes, suffered needlessly here too!"

"It doesn't compare!" Cache swore. "I am going to kill this king and all that he stands for! He is evil!"

"He is not evil, he is good!" said Earo. "And if you kill him you will have to kill me to because you are not going to leave this garden alive! You know that if you start the strike that will kill the king, I will have time to kill you immediately after."

Ruth, Ferris and Andora stood in the exit from the garden into the maze.

"So be it," Cache snarled. "I'll kill you first! He's not going anywhere."

The two men clashed blades. The walkway through the pond was only as wide as a sidewalk back home. The two men were both accomplished swordsmen and as they jabbed and dodged each other, they slowly probed for weaknesses. Every so often there would be a flurry of blades clanging together and then it would slow as they backed and reassessed each other. They didn't have any shields and so each man had to block with his sword and recover in time to cast a strike.

Cache attacked again, his blade whirling above his head, it would seem to have left an opening near his chest, but as Earo jabbed to stab the Baron in the chest, Cache's blade fell quickly knocking the sword out of Earo's hand. It was a rookie's mistake and Earo cursed himself.

The Baron slid his sword's blade next to Earo's neck. "It seems a change of fortune here, commander!"

"I willingly sacrifice myself for my king," Earo said bravely.

"Sad misfortune," Cache responded, "because you aren't sacrificing yourself for your king—you are just going first!"

Cache grasped his sword with both hands and got ready to plunge his sword through Earo's heart.

"No!" screamed Ruth and she started rushing forward. Ferris was one step ahead of her.

Suddenly every one stopped as the sword dropped out of Baron Cache's hand. It clattered to the brick ground. He staggered to the side and everyone saw Bigwig standing, soaking wet, with a sharp dirk dagger in his hand—there was some blood on the end.

Bigwig wagged his finger at Cache, "You are a very bad man! You try to kill my king; you try to kill my commander Earo! And absolutely worst of all, you locked Bigwig in a broom closet!" He placed his hands to his waist as Baron Cache fell to the ground.

Earo cheered. He pulled the small gnome off his feet and gave him a big hug.

Lumpy appeared a few steps behind Bigwig, also soaking wet. He also had twigs and branches in his clothing; the gnomes had literally walked through the maze (not the pathway) to find the center.

Lumpy was dancing like a fool. "I found the Overlord of the gnomes and I set him free!" He was proud, but he immediately stopped dancing when his stomach growled and he dug into his pocket and took out an apple and started munching on it. Ferris was amazed at what that gnome carried around.

Bigwig took his dirk and cut the ropes that bound King Merrit. Merrit also gave the small guy a hug and it was a very proud moment for Bigwig. "Anything you want I will give you!" Merrit said to the little guy.

Bigwig puffed up his chest. "I would like to be knighted!" he said.

Merrit's face fell for the briefest of moments; he then he smirked. "Alright then, Earo your sword!"

Earo handed the king his sword.

"Kneel Bigwig," Merrit demanded. Taking the tip of the sword he touched both of Bigwig's shoulders and said, "I knight thee Sir Bigwig, master potato peeler of Bogmarsh, Overlord of the gnomes and honorary protector of the King!"

Bigwig's face fell. "I'm tired of being the Overlord—I want to be lord of the gnomes instead!" But then his face brightened. "Although, master potato peeler of Bogmarsh is a pretty prestigious title! Right?"

"Right Bigwig," they all assured him. To the gnome that must have seemed even better than "honorary protector of the King!"

Merrit glanced around, "Where are Jared and Avery?" he asked.

Avery led Jared through what used to be the Eternal Bog. She had to find out if the Swamppond was still trapped in her pond. The swamp had changed a lot since they had last been there. The first time Avery had been struggling from the Lavaryn Squall's poison and so she did not remember too much about the experience.

"Why are we going here?" Jared asked. He was feeling tired; after fighting a dozen Muskag warriors even the heartiest soldier would need a break!

"We don't have too much further to go and then I will answer your questions," she replied.

As they walked, she noticed that her vision was beginning to return to normal. It was vaguely disappointing to her because she really enjoyed seeing the world the same way that Jwen had. The colors were starting to darken and the world was again beginning to look the way she remembered it.

Reaching the clearing where the Swamppond had called home, they found it drastically changed. The water was no longer swampy and covered with moss and mushrooms. Tall cattail reeds decorated the waters edge and a brown deer was standing next to the pool drinking from its depths.

"What does it mean?" asked Jared.

Avery nodded, "It is as I feared. The Swamppond is a tortured spirit. Actually, she or it is the imprisoned spirit of Depravity himself. When the Creator cast the demon out of the heavens the Creator sentenced it to this pool. But Governor Swale was able to free the demon by casting a spell that allowed the demon to possess him. He didn't realize that it would actually cost him his life. Even though the man we fought had all the memories of Swale, it was no more Swale than you or I are him."

"How do you know all this?" he asked.

Avery felt her hand. "When I could still see through the eyes of the Creator, I felt the water and the Truth was given to me."

"So Depravity is gone then?"

She shook her head and dawned a grave expression. "No, one thing that Hokum said that was true, was that Depravity is a spirit and mortals cannot kill a spirit. The Swamppond, being Depravity, is a spirit and therefore cannot die; at least in the human sense of the word."

"So you just sentenced the spirit back into the pool, back in the forest."

"Unfortunately, I didn't restrain the spirit to that one pool. It will be able to surface in any pond or lake it desires."

"That's bad!" stated Jared.

"That's bad!" she agreed.

"One thing I don't understand. Who was Hokum?"

"Just like Quagmire was the physical representation of Depravity—her and all her demons—so two Swale and Hokum were one in the same. Hokum was the demon form of Depravity using Swale's body."

"So they are all the same evil?"

"Yes, anything that uses the magic of Deception, is part of that same evil and unfortunately, as long as mankind has the ability to choose between good and evil, there is going to be pain and suffering in the world."

"When will it end?"

"When the only Choice there is to make, is what good to do! When evil is completely vanquished, there will no longer be that as a Choice. How can you make the wrong one, when every choice is good?"

The two young people walked in silence for a moment back towards Bogmarsh. They needed to find the others and return home. As they walked Jared reached out and took a hold of Avery's hand. She looked over at him, her eyes had returned to their normal brilliant green and she smiled at him. He winked.

CHAPTER TWENTY-FOUR

~

Let us go then, you and I,

--T.S. Eliot, The Love Song of
J. Alfred Prufrock [1917]

The sky opened up and Avery was falling through the roof of the school. If gave way like a trampoline and she went through it and landed on the freshly waxed school floor. The sound of Ruth, Ferris and Jared falling behind her made her look up and had just enough time to roll out of the way as they fell next to her in three successive *thumps*. It was later in the afternoon and no children were at school, even the teachers had gone for the day—most the classrooms were locked up tight.

The four students rose to their feet and started for the main foyer. Suddenly a high-pitched sound caught their ears.

"Oh great!" sighed Jared. "The alarm. In a moment this place is going to be crawling with cops.

They ran to the front entrance and then stopped abruptly. Lying on the floor were Mr. Prig and Holly Fitts. Both of them had their eyes open and were staring around wildly. Holly was in hysterics and Mr. Prig had tearstains on his face. He was wearing a brown cloak wrapped tightly around his body and he looked very cold.

He stood up and approached the young people. There was a moment of realization of what had happened to him over the past year and Avery thought that for one moment he was going to start yelling at her. Instead tears started streaming down his face again and he sat down on a bench in the foyer. Avery stepped back. This man that she had hated for so long, this man that she felt had picked on her, her entire school life, was crying. He wore his remorse like the brown cloak around his body. He looked very out of place dressed in Afflatus garb.

They were interrupted by footsteps sounding in the hall. Avery could hear Miss Creant cursing as her hurried footsteps approached. "Who set the alarm? Didn't any one know that I was still in the school—" she stopped mid sentence as she rounded the corner and saw Avery, Jared, Ruth, Ferris and Holly Fitts scattered around.

"I might have known it would be you trouble makers!" she hissed. Then she spotted Mr. Prig again. "Sir!" she was shocked. "Where have you been?"

Mr. Prig stood up, he was still crying. "I am so glad to be home," he said and he gave Miss Creant a hug. She didn't know how to respond and stood there like a wet blanket.

When Mr. Prig had released her she took a hold of Avery's arm. "What did you do to him? He is stark raving mad! I'm glad that that alarm is sounding, we will get the police here and they will throw you and all your good for nothing friends into jail. I don't know where you have been keeping Mr. Prig, but obviously he escaped and you have all tried to recapture him!"

"STOP!" shouted Mr. Prig. Avery was impressed, the man could still yell. "You will do nothing to these children!"

"Oh no," swooned Miss Creant, "Stockholm syndrome has already set in!"

"I said enough!" restated Mr. Prig. "They were not the ones that had taken me. In fact, they are the ones that rescued me." His voice softened and he approached Avery, he took a hold of her hands in his. "I want to thank you," he said. "I was lost, but somehow you were able to free me. Thank you!" He smiled at all the other children. "We had best keep this between ourselves or else all of us are going to be sentenced to an asylum or at least be given significant shrink time."

Avery nodded her head in agreement.

Holly snorted. "Like I would want to repeat any of this to anyone. Everyone would think that I was a complete dork!"

"What is everyone talking about?" asked Miss Creant.

"Someday you might find out," Ferris said out of the side of his mouth. "We have a bad habit of taking our least liked people with us."

"Take them where?"

"Never mind."

The four friends walked towards Avery's house.

"Do you think we will ever be going back again?" Jared asked. He had had to leave the Nightshade in the King's Mansion, and even though he was upset to relinquish the power of the sword he gave it to Merrit to use.

The Jester had given them all a parting blessing before sending them back to their ordinary world with the *vaporatium* powder. Bigwig, having been knighted was taking his duties as nobleman of the kitchens very seriously, at least for the first half an hour until the chef had booted him out.

Andora said goodbye to Ferris. But he had realized that they were friends and that was all they would ever be—after all they lived worlds apart, literally. Besides, it was obvious that Andora had a bit of a crush on King Merrit; she was after all noble, being a niece of Governor Swale.

Earo was happily commanding the army. Merrit had sent them on a new mission to restore order to Haddock and the other flagrant parts of the Kingdom. And since he needed a noble to replace Baron Cache, Merrit appointed the lands to Earo; thus renaming him Baron Earo.

The other nobles had returned to their homes with the Menas being taken care of. Avery had warned King Merrit that Depravity would more than likely rise up again, but the next time they would know who and what they were dealing with.

"I don't know," Avery responded to Jared's question. She reached out and took his hand.

Tires squealing behind them interrupted them and Ruth gave a small shriek. She immediately felt sheepish; after all she had killed a vampire, what in their world could scare her.

CJ, Jared's brother jumped out of the car and stepped in front of the boy. "So what did you get for me?" he asked, giving Jared a shove.

Jared let go of Avery's hand and she backed away to give him space.

"Nothing," he replied.

"What? Are you letting me down, little bro? Since you didn't get me anything, maybe I'll have to take your little girlfriend here until you can find something for me to sell!"

Avery chuckled, "You could try!"

"What's that?" he sneered.

Ferris moved next to Avery. "You could try, but you would have to go through me first," he said.

"And me," added Ruth.

"I'd also have something to say about it," stated Avery, clenching her fists.

Jared grabbed his older brother by the collar. "But more importantly, you would have to get through me first. Do you remember when we were younger and you tried to fight me, big brother! Who won that one?"

CJ brushed Jared's arms from his jacket; but hesitation echoed in his features. "I'm bigger than you are now," he said.

"Yes, but are you bigger than all of us!"

CJ stepped back until his butt was touching the door to his friends red Tempo. "This isn't over!" he yelled.

"Actually, I think it is!" Jared yelled back. "I'm not doing your dirty work for you any more!" and he tossed the lighter he had been carrying in his pocket. It hit the red Tempo just as it spun off in a cloud of dust.

"I'm so proud of you," Avery said, taking his hand again. "You know, I think we are going to be alright. We have each other!" The others nodded.

Mr. Prig having let all of them out of the school had offered to stay and speak to the police. He decided that his story would be that the trials of being a principal were too much and he had gone to stay in a cabin in the mountains for a year retreat. He didn't think that anyone would miss him, and that was why he told no one. They only briefly considered the truth might be better—but even Avery had to agree, sometimes, people were better off not knowing the whole truth.